SKEIN
ISLAND

ALSO AVAILABLE FROM
ALIYA WHITELEY AND TITAN BOOKS

The Arrival of Missives
The Beauty
The Loosening Skin (June 2020)

SKEIN ISLAND

ALIYA WHITELEY

TITAN BOOKS

Skein Island
Print edition ISBN: 9781789091526
E-book edition ISBN: 9781789091533

Published by Titan Books
A division of Titan Publishing Group Ltd.
144 Southwark Street, London SE1 0UP
www.titanbooks.com

First Titan edition November 2019
1 2 3 4 5 6 7 8 9 10

A CIP catalogue record for this title is available from the British Library.

Printed and bound in the United States.

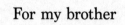
For my brother

PART ONE

CHAPTER ONE

The library is empty for the first time today. I put away the rest of the returned books as I always do at closing time: the hardbacks on the shelves, the paperbacks in the rotating stand by the window that overlooks the car park. It's blank out there, frozen under the shock of the outside light.

I think of the letter.

It arrived this morning, in a thick yellow envelope. My address was written by hand, in black pen. Above it was my maiden name. Miss Marianne Spence, like a call from the past. So I slipped a thumbnail under the flap of the envelope and ripped the past open.

The first thing I noticed was the letterhead, and then, at the very bottom, a single line written in the same hand as the address.

Each man delights in the work that suits him best.

The night is so still. I decide nobody else is coming to the library tonight, so I go into the back office and take the letter from my bag, where it hangs on the peg behind the door. I unfold it and read it through again. Am I distrustful of my memory or the typescript? Both, I suppose.

But it's the same.

I'm pleased to inform you that I have personally allocated you a place for the duration of one week (date to be arranged). This letter entitles you to free accommodation, inclusive of all meals and activities. Please contact the reception desk on the telephone number or email address provided to arrange a time for your arrival. I look forward to meeting you.

    Lady Amelia Worthington

I run my finger over the letterhead.

‐ SKEIN ISLAND ‐

I've told nobody. Not even David.

I've thought of it so often, wondered what it would be like to spend a week there: to take the classes, sleep in a bungalow, to write out the story of my life so far and leave it there for posterity. Would it change me? Would it do to me what it did to my mother?

No matter how I feel about the island, one fact is inescapable. I didn't contact Lady Amelia Worthington. Nobody has contacted Lady Amelia Worthington. She has been dead for years.

The quote on the bottom of the letter bothers me – it's a strange choice. I sit at the computer and Google it. I knew it was familiar. Homer's *Odyssey*. I read it for the first time in my late teens; it gave me a taste for sweeping tales of fate, where a man overcomes such perils, risks everything to get back to where he started. And Penelope: waiting, weaving, unravelling, with a grace that I didn't understand. Did she not feel such rage to be left behind? When it happened to me, I wasn't serene. I wanted to understand her, but I couldn't. I still don't.

I switch off the computer and go back into the library. We have a copy of the *Odyssey*: the Rieu translation, a Penguin Classic that lives on the poetry shelf. It never gets checked out. I go to it and open it at random, flicking through the pages on fast-forward. Odysseus races through his journey, spurning the nymph, escaping the Cyclops, resisting the sirens. I had hoped for my eye to fall on a line that would answer the unexpected questions – should I accept this offer? What does the dead Amelia Worthington want with me?

A soft swish and a gust of frigid air tells me the automatic doors have opened. I look around the shelf and see a man. He has a pleasant face, and brown hair that's cut very short. His cheeks are red from the cold.

'Can I help you?'

He gives me an inclusive smile, as if he knows me and I am compliant in a game we have decided to play. He's holding a knife in his right hand.

He says something that changes everything. 'Get in the back. Take off your clothes and lie down.'

CHAPTER TWO

Marianne asked to go in alone, so he waited in the car, listening to big band music on the radio.

He couldn't remember the drive. This wasn't unusual; it happened every morning, in the liquid flow of Swindon traffic. He had become attuned to the drip-feed of traffic lights leading to the factory until – standing in the cafeteria next to the tray of bacon, watching it glisten under the heat lamps – David would wake up properly for the first time each day. Everything that happened before that moment was merely a continuation of the previous night's dream, and it always worried him, that lost time. Would he react in a crash, a crisis? Could he see danger and evade it with a flick of the steering wheel, a stamp of the brakes?

He hadn't seen this coming. The look on Marianne's face as she walked through the door at ten past eight that evening was not something he had ever prepared for. Her hands were empty. Usually she put down a canvas bag, heavy with books, on the hall floor next to the coat stand. David had walked out of the kitchen and caught her naked face and hands doing none of their normal things. Her coat was still on – unbuttoned, flapping – and her cheeks were white with cold. She came to him, cupped her hands around his elbows, and said, 'We need to get to a police station, okay?' He'd felt the shock of the moment, usual rules suspended.

He realised that he was only just coming out of it, sitting alone in the din of trumpets and drums, while Marianne faced this thing alone. She was probably making a statement to a sympathetic policewoman in a small clean room, her voice being recorded as she enunciated what had been done to her in precise detail. He couldn't imagine what words she would use. She had a better vocabulary than him. He had a hard ball in the centre of his stomach that he could only describe as dread; he clenched his fists, tried to fight it off, wriggled in the seat.

The car park was half-full, and the glass sliding doors that led into the station were brightly lit. David could see a tiled floor and a standing pot plant, probably artificial. Nobody came or went.

* * *

The big band rhythm had segued into soft jazz before he saw her step out of the station and look around for their car.

He started the engine, drove to her; she got in and clipped in her seat belt, then gave him a smile and a shrug, easy and bright.

'Let's go home,' she said.

'Is it okay? What did they say?'

'They'll be on the lookout for him.'

'Is that it?' David said. He had a vision of getting out of the car, storming into the station and demanding justice, action, police cars out hunting all night. Or maybe he should take the law into his own hands and crouch in the bushes by the library, dressed in black, kitchen knife in hand – he had an idea it would make him feel better. But where was Marianne in his vision? He turned to her, took her cold little hand in his.

'Do you want to talk about it?' he said.

'What do you want to know?' She pulled her hand free.

'Anything you want to tell me.'

'I'm fine,' she said. 'Let's get going.'

He manoeuvred to the exit, and pulled out. The streets were quiet, the nine o'clock lull between tired workers on overtime and energised bunnies making for the pubs. Swindon was one roundabout after another, and he hardly had to stop at all; he turned the steering wheel in measured amounts, first to the left, then the right.

'Maybe we should get a takeaway,' said Marianne. Her voice was perfectly normal, as was the sentiment. He knew she was talking about the Chinese on Wootton Bassett high street. He wished he could look at her face.

'Can do.'

She clicked off the radio. 'I already told you it all. It was closing time, he came in, he told me to get in the back and take off my clothes.'

David heard her draw breath, and swallow.

'And I told him no,' she said. She opened the glove compartment, then shut it again, and turned up the heat control on the dashboard. He wanted to pull over and look at her face, but all he could see were her fingers: short, unvarnished nails, the ragged thumbnail on her left hand that she bit. When she was trying to concentrate on a novel she would frown and put her index finger on each line and follow the words like a child. Her fluttering hands moved around the car, touching dials and the sides of her seat.

'And he went?' David said.

'He turned around and walked out.'

'Just because you said no?' He should have stuck to silence; there was something accusatory rising inside him, and he had no idea why.

'I can remember thinking – if I go in the back, I won't come out again. That's just what I knew, and I thought about screaming, or trying to push past him to get to the door. Time was moving slowly, I mean, really slowly, and in the end I said no, in my best library voice, the one I use on the teenagers when they try to access dirty websites on the public computers. And he stared at me, and then he left.'

It occurred to David that this was his first big test as a husband. 'I don't know what to do,' he said.

'I'm fine,' said Marianne, 'I'm really fine, I'm better than... I can't explain it. All my life I've been afraid of something like this. I think, deep down, all women are afraid of some faceless man. And this guy, he came along, and I knew what he wanted, he wanted to hurt me, but he had a face. It's not at all like I pictured it. Can you understand? Do men picture it too?'

'Not in the same way,' he said, 'I don't think.'

'Maybe a man would just have fought, but for me, for women, there's this question hanging over it. Whether I'd freeze or submit to anything he wanted, and I didn't do those things. He was defeated by that. He was... surmountable, I suppose.'

'Surmountable,' David repeated. The word reassured him more than anything else Marianne had said. This was her, using a long word to describe a simple thing, a thing that a four-letter word could have covered.

'It was freeing,' she said. 'I'm glad it happened, in a way. Yes.'

'I hope they catch him before he tries it again,' David said.

She fell silent.

'You okay?'

'I keep saying I'm fine. Forget the takeaway, okay? Let's go home.'

It was just beginning to hit her, David thought: what could have happened. He wanted her to face it, to tremble, to fall towards him so that he could catch her and hold her together. They would get home, and not sleep tonight, but stay up all night talking it through, her crying, and it would be awful, but at the end of it they would be closer than before, he hoped, he wanted, closer in the way that survivors are.

He took the final roundabout into Wootton Bassett and turned into their estate. The Spar on the corner was still open, but he drove past, turned left, and parked up in their space. She got out of the car first and by the time he'd followed she was already at the front door, thrusting her key into the lock. The stiff lines of her shoulders suggested panic; he jogged to her, put his hands on her back as she threw open the door, and they stumbled into the dark house together.

'Listen, it'll be okay,' he said, but Marianne was on him, kissing his face, putting her tongue in his mouth, her hands already at the waistband of his trousers. He tried to think rationally about it for one moment, and then felt his body respond to her. She pulled off her own trousers and took the stairs two at a time to their bedroom, the coldest room in the house due to a broken radiator; but she didn't dive under the duvet as he expected. When he got into the room she was taking off her shirt, standing on the bed in her plain white knickers, the curtains open, the glow from the streetlight falling across her knees and feet.

'Right now?' he said.

'Leave the curtains.' She turned and knelt down, then took off her knickers. 'This way.'

David came up behind her and pulled her towards him, his hands on her hips. She put her head down, on the duvet, giving him a view only of her body and her brown hair, tied up. He pulled it free and splayed it out over her back.

'Now,' she said, and he did as he was told.

* * *

He woke up, much later, when he heard the front door close.

For a moment he didn't move. It took him a while to become aware of the room once more: the grey depth of very early morning, the still-open curtains that told him the streetlight was off, the suitcase missing from on top of the wardrobe, and the thin creases in the duvet beside him. He spread his arm into that empty expanse, then realised what it all meant.

Stuck to the cold blue face of the alarm clock was a Post-it note. On it, she had written, in small neat capitals:

GONE TO SKEIN ISLAND

He heard the car start; by the time he reached the street, in his boxer shorts, it was out of sight.

CHAPTER THREE

Skein Island is one of a series of women-only holiday resorts around the world. Founded in 1945, it was the first such resort ever to be opened, and until her death in 2008 it was the permanent home of the reclusive founder, Lady Amelia Worthington, heir to the Worthington fortune.

Skein Island was founded with a unique mission statement: to provide a week out of life. Any woman over the age of sixteen can apply in writing for a place, stating their reasons for wishing to attend. If a place is awarded, they are free to arrive at the resort for seven days – Saturday to Saturday, at a time of their choosing, according to availability of accommodation. The meals, the shared housing and the facilities are all free of charge. The criteria used to decide who will be offered a place are a closely guarded secret.

Facilities on the island include—

I fold the brochure and slip it back into my handbag. Lady Worthington decided back in 1945 what a woman is and who is worthy of her island, and if we want to come here we have to play by the rules that outlive her.

The room is far from full. There are seven other women; they've formed a self-conscious queue from the unoccupied reception desk to the dirty glass double doors. They have been my only company on the boat during the hour-long crossing. The pier at Allcombe had been deserted, too. A grey, slabbed stretch of closed kiosks and iron railings, icy to the touch, delineated land from sea.

I can't believe I took that boat. I stepped on board the *Sea Princess*, helped over the threshold of the pier by a lanky young man in a bobble hat and fingerless gloves who had a businesslike set to his mouth. It was that sense of the journey as the last stage in a transaction that had, in the end, persuaded me to take that final step. And already there is dislocation from what went before. This is the breaking point of my life; from now on, everything will be different.

The women have nothing in common, not obviously, anyway. I expected the island to appeal to a certain type, although I'm not sure what type that would be. But the queue gives no information except that we are a patient lot. Nobody has arrived to take down our details. Outside the glass doors, the retreat of the *Sea Princess* is visible on the choppy grey waves. It will not return until next Saturday, so there really is no rush. At least, not for those of us in the queue.

But that gives me only seven days to find out why I've received an invitation from a dead woman.

A tall woman with loose brown hair, very straight, emerges from the doorway on the other side of the reception desk. She ignores the queue until she has switched on her computer screen and arranged herself in her seat; then she looks up, and a smile appears, as if she is surprised to find somebody waiting for her attention. I watch the others being dealt with: given multicoloured paperwork, talked to, dismissed in turn. Eventually there is nobody left to be processed except myself.

I approach the desk.

'You must be Marianne Spence? You're lucky to get a place at the last minute. Usually our ladies don't just turn up at the dock.'

'It's Marianne Percival, actually. Spence is my maiden name.'

She makes a note on the computer screen. 'Well, we're having a slow week, so you've got good timing. Here's your itinerary. The compulsory activities are highlighted. There aren't many, so don't worry, there'll be plenty of time for you to do your own thing. The yellow pieces of paper are for your declaration. There's a compulsory meeting on Monday morning about how to complete it, only half an hour and there's tea and biscuits. The pink sheet is a map of the island. You can see I've put a cross in red on your shared accommodation. You're in bungalow three. There are no locks or keys on the island. It's necessary for you to place your mobile phone, laptop and communication devices in the safe keeping area, which is marked with a green cross. I'm afraid there are absolutely no exceptions to that.'

'Right,' I say. 'That's fine. I have a question, actually.'

'Okay, but the meeting on Monday should cover everything.'

'No, about why I – how I came to get a place here.'

'We really can't go into selection criteria.'

'No, but… I received a letter. From Amelia Worthington. It said it was a personal invitation.'

She purses her lips. 'We only send out standard letters of acceptance.'

'This is different. It's signed by her. Lady Worthington.'

'Do you have it with you?'

'No, I… I'm sorry.' It's still in my bag, on the back of the door to the library office. A place I couldn't bear to go. 'Is there any way to check what you sent out to me? From here?'

She taps away on the keyboard, and I wait, patiently, like a good and quiet customer. 'It says here you applied in the summer.'

'No.' It makes no sense.

'You sure?'

I attempt to suppress my irritation, but I know it's on my face, in the lines around my mouth.

'Of course. I've never applied. My mother applied, seventeen years ago. That would have been under Spence. Maybe there's been a mix-up. Do daughters get invited back?'

'No, that's not… That shouldn't make any difference. Leave it with me. I'll look into it.'

Did I think it was going to be resolved so easily? What exactly am I doing here? I dare to voice the idea that's been lurking in my head since this morning. 'Can I ask, would it be possible to see my mother's declaration? Since I'm here?'

The receptionist makes her sympathetic face. 'I'm really sorry, but we don't do that. All declarations are strictly confidential.'

'As a family member, I must have some sort of right to view it?'

She's getting frustrated with me; her eyes slide away to the door. 'No, I'm sorry, but not at all.'

I pick up my bag and papers, wearied by the polite argument, and turn away. I was expecting to find out nothing, and therefore it is no discouragement. I already have plans in place. I'm glad the mystery remains unsolved.

Over the double doors to the reception, carved into a wooden plaque in tiny letters, is a familiar quote. I approach it, and squint up at it. My eyes haven't lied to me. Homer lurks here too.

EACH MAN DELIGHTS IN THE WORK
THAT SUITS HIM BEST.

At the bottom of the plaque, four squares have been painted in a row, equidistant: red, blue, yellow and green.

* * *

Once I step off the main path I soon find myself in fields of harsh, hillocked grasses that catch at my boots. The winter sun is surprisingly strong and there are no trees, not an inch of cover in sight. Even so, the skin on my face tingles with cold.

Skein Island is half a mile across at its largest point, shaped like a lozenge, long and thin, with ragged cliffs that erode a little more every year. The buildings stand thirty metres above sea level and there is only one accessible beach, at which the boat docks for thirty minutes every Saturday. It is the definition of isolation. I know all about it. There was a book released in the seventies, black and white pictures of women with stark faces in front of small, shabby buildings; I kept it under my bed for years, then deliberately destroyed it with a pair of kitchen scissors before marrying David. To symbolise something, I suppose.

If I had a telescope, I reckon I could see Allcombe pier jutting out from the green mass of land that lies over the water. Maybe, by now, a few out-of-season holidaymakers are out, eating fish and chips, wrapped up warm against the chill of the wind over the Bristol Channel. But there is no way to tell what is happening on that far shore, except that the *Sea Princess* is about to return to it; that is the one recognisable, straight-lined shape I can spot, moving away, swaying on the waves.

I keep walking, leaving the white walls of the reception building behind. The *Sea Princess* soon falls out of sight. Now there are sheep, not white clouds of sheep, but watchful eyes in tangled stringy masses of burred wool, their shiny, crusted droppings lying all around, and the cloying, earthy smell of them filling up my nostrils. They are simply loose, free to go where they like without fences or hedges to hold them back. Something about that thought triggers the memory of the man walking into the library and saying to me, *Get in the back. Take off your clothes and lie down.*

I push it away.

Seventeen years ago my mother came here, to the island. Then, when her week was up, she had decided not to come home. I received birthday cards with a Bedfordshire postmark, but in all other ways she had gone. My father and I were consigned to her past.

And now, to suit some unknown purpose, I am here.

The lip of the island becomes visible. I stomp onwards. I walk up to the edge and stand as close to the drop as I dare. I examine the chalky angles of the cliff, the jagged points of the rocks upon which the sea flicks itself into foamy exclamations. My hatred of heights presses strongly around me, insisting that I take a step away. On holiday, skiing in La Grave, high in the toothbrush-clean mountains of the Alps, I lost my nerve at the ski lift and shuffled back to the hotel while David laughed from the slopes. But there was no embarrassment, just a mutual understanding of who we both were, why I was the weaker one. *David is good at skiing and Marianne is good at reading E. M. Forster novels in front of open fires.* I know my limitations. Except that I thought this trip was beyond me; I always stipulated that I didn't want to come here, to follow in my mother's footsteps.

I walk along the cliff edge, keeping to its undulations, watching the sun dip lower. A small blue bench comes into view up ahead. Upon it sits a woman, still and stretched out, palms down on the wood, legs long, crossed at the ankles.

I consider turning back, but then the woman moves her head in my direction, and there is something welcoming in the way she cocks it to one side. She has a square face with smallish eyes, lost in a nest of energetic crow's feet.

'Lovely sunset,' she says, when I get close enough to hear.

'Yes.'

'What number are you in? I'm in three.'

It takes me a moment to realise she's talking about the bungalows. 'Me too.'

'Takes some getting used to,' says the woman. I nod, and stand beside the bench, keeping my eyes on the sea. 'Can't take too long to settle in, though. We've only got a week. I'm Kay, by the way.'

'I'm Marianne.'

'I've already got half my declaration done in my head. As soon as I found out I had a place, I was thinking it over. You?'

I haven't considered this – the writing of my own declaration. 'I don't know. I think it might come easily to me, though. I love reading.' How smug that must sound. The breeze picks up. The sun is completing its inexorable trajectory into the sea.

'I wonder what the food will be like,' says Kay. She pats the square of bench beside her, and I perch on the end.

'I think we have to cook it ourselves.'

'Really? Crap. I live on microwave meals back home.'

'I'll cook, if you like. For us. Or anyone.'

'Can I tell you something?' says Kay. 'It's not the kind of thing I'd usually tell a stranger. I know we're meant to be getting used to the seclusion, saving up all the private stuff for the declaration.' She takes a deep breath. 'I couldn't have been a nun. This place is already too quiet for me. Have you handed in your phone yet? I did that first. I thought – if I don't do it now, I never will.'

'No, I haven't done mine yet.'

'Really? Can I check my email?' She holds up one hand; she has bitten fingernails, painted purple. 'Actually, no. Scrap that. I bet you don't get reception out here anyway.'

We sit in silence. Oddly, I'm relieved that I don't have to give her my phone. Eventually, I say, 'You wanted to tell me something?'

'Yeah. It's only that when I get back home I'm going to buy a motorbike.'

'Okay.'

'I suppose that doesn't sound like a lot to you. Let's just say there are reasons why everyone is going to have a meltdown about it.' She wriggles, and stands up. She's very thin; her combat trousers hang low on her hips. 'I'm going to go check out the bungalow. You coming?'

So I stand up too, and fall into a fast walk beside her, keeping pace, negotiating the dishevelled, uninterested sheep and their turds.

'I bet you're good at everything,' says Kay. 'You look the type.'

There is no reply that can be made to that. I think of how difficult I once found sex. David is the only man I've ever really relaxed with. It was difficult to switch off my brain, to stop worrying that I was taking too long, trying my partner's patience. But he had endless persistence. He ordered some erotic books on the internet, and a door opened for me. I could become the heroine of the book, and do and say the things that I wanted for the first time. Technically, it was pretending to be somebody else, but that had never seemed to bother David.

'I wasn't very good at school,' says Kay. 'Not great as a mother, either, if I'm honest. My three kids will tell you that, right out. I tried really hard when they were little, but as they get older they stop wanting you to know stuff about their lives, and I never had the patience to whittle away at them. And then, before you know it, it's all your fault because you didn't spend three hours a day interrogating them. Besides, when you have three, they form their own gang. You got any kids?'

'No.'

'Thought not.'

'Is it that obvious?'

'I'm good at motorbikes,' says Kay. It's as if she's been starved of the freedom to talk; she unburdens herself, at speed, with relief scored through every word. 'I've got good reflexes, and stuff. I feel free on a bike, free to be good at it. But on a bike it's not always enough to be good. All it takes is some idiot in a car, not looking at a junction, and you're dead. Or out of action for a while. I got hit by a car. Old lady who just didn't see me, and I went right over the top of her sky blue Nissan Micra and ended up in hospital for eight weeks. I promised my mum and the kids – no more.' She is walking faster; I have to break into a trot to keep up with her. 'The thing is, I don't want to be alive just to make them happy. Nothing else does it for me.'

'Was it a very bad accident?'

She slows down again as she describes, lovingly, the broken bones, the removed spleen, the physical cracks that lead to emotional ones, her kids, her mother, and the men who never stuck around. It is easy to admire her stubborn belief that only a motorcycle makes her free.

The main building comes into view once more, a white bulge on the landscape. The lights are off; the island is beginning to look done for the day. I follow Kay back on to the gravel path, through the rose garden, past the glass doors of reception and down the side path that leads to the bungalows. We don't speak again, but it's a pleasant silence; the kind that falls when the curtains go up and the show is about to start.

* * *

The bungalow is one of many placed in crocodile formation, on either side of the path. The interior space is divided by stand-alone partitions, on one side, the basic kitchen with a long wooden table at its centre and two benches; on the other side, eight single beds with duvets with faded green cases. Strings of electric lights hang from the exposed rafters. It isn't homely, but the simplicity is appealing. It's impossible to think of the place as anything other than a temporary stopping point.

The kitchen is already occupied, the aroma of tomatoes, garlic and onion, keeping each other company.

'You've got in there quick,' says Kay to the woman standing in front of the oven, stirring a pan. 'Marianne was going to cook for all of us.'

'I thought I'd make puttanesca,' says the woman, with a beautiful roll of the tongue to her Italian. She has darker skin, and long, hennaed hair, falling in corkscrews. 'There's enough for everyone. Are you hungry? I'll put some pasta on.'

'Great!' Kay sits down on the bench as if she has the right to be served. 'Is there any wine?'

'Some cheap red. I used a little for the sauce.' She gestures towards the bottle. I come forward and take it, then open the coarse pine doors of the kitchen cabinets, hung at head height on the outer wall, until I find three glasses, then bowls and mismatched cutlery. I bring them all to the table, and pour the wine. Kay takes the first glass.

'I've put my case on one of the beds already. I hope you don't mind. I'm Rebecca,' says the woman. She is wearing a loose green dress that falls back from her arms as she reaches up to turn on the extractor fan. The sound of it echoes around the kitchen. I realise she's older than I first took her to be.

'I'm Kay. She's Marianne. I'm usually not that keen on Italian food,' says Kay, 'but I'm starving tonight. It smells great. You're cooking for us too, right?'

'You don't like Italian? That's unusual, isn't it?' says Rebecca. 'I thought everyone liked it.'

24

'And Marianne will cook us something amazing tomorrow.'

'I don't have to,' I say, even though my input does not seem to be needed. 'If you like cooking.'

'No, it's fine,' says Rebecca. She kneels down and retrieves a large saucepan, then takes it to the sink and fills it with water. I watch her complete these homely actions, and wonder who Rebecca would usually be doing them for, and why she feels it necessary to do it for strangers.

Kay carries on talking away, making conversation without needing input. She pours herself a second glass of wine, and I continue to sip on my first until the pasta arrives. It's tasty; the chopped anchovies and olives warm my throat and then soothe my empty stomach. The act of eating is both painful and satisfying.

Kay talks of a holiday she once took to Siena. I try to listen, but my thoughts are on the holiday David and I once took to Lake Garda. I can't remember much of it except the very cold water, transparent to a frightening depth, and the time I had refused to get on a pedalo with David because the idea of being together in the centre of that body of water had been unbearable.

'I'll make coffee,' says Rebecca.

I get up and find cups. At the back of one of the cupboards is an old board game with a ripped lid. I bring it down and put it in the centre of the table, along with milk and sugar.

'Game of Life!' says Kay. She opens the box and takes out the board, then examines the pieces. 'There aren't many pegs left but I reckon we could play a game. It's better than listening to me all night, right?' She rolls her eyes, and starts setting out the little plastic cars. 'So what made you apply, then? For the island?' She doesn't aim the question at anyone in particular; Rebecca is busy spooning coffee into a filter jug, so I reply.

'I didn't.'

'Let me guess – your husband did it for you so he could have a week alone with his mates and his widescreen telly.'

'No, nothing like that. I received the offer of a place without applying. My mother came here years ago. I think maybe it's to do with that.'

Kay nods. 'Did you ask her? Maybe she applied for you. To follow in her footsteps?'

'No, I...' I swallow, hating the nervous feeling in my throat. 'I haven't seen her since she came here, actually, seventeen years ago.'

'She disappeared while she was here?' Rebecca says, bringing the filter jug to the table, along with a packet of digestives.

'No. No, she's in Bedfordshire now.' The ridiculousness of it makes them both laugh. Hearing that sound, I feel comfortable for the first time since that man walked into the library. Time makes the worst things laughable, I suppose. 'She sends cards every now and again and the postmark says Bedfordshire, but she's never given me an address, so I always assumed she didn't want to meet up. She just didn't want to be with my father any more. Or me, I suppose. Something here – something she realised – persuaded her to leave us.'

'So what are you doing here?' says Rebecca. She presses down the plunger on the jug, taking her time, leaning into it. 'Shouldn't you be in Bedfordshire somewhere, asking her why? Or do you want to be persuaded to leave everyone behind too?'

'I want to know why I received a letter inviting me here,' I say. 'I've got no interest in my mother.' It sounds ridiculously untrue. 'The letter was signed by Lady Amelia Worthington.'

'Who?' says Kay.

Rebecca rolls her eyes. 'The founder of the island. The dead founder of this island.'

'That's quite a trick.' Kay takes the green plastic car between her thumb and forefinger and speeds it around the board. 'So how are you going to get your answers? Hunt around in between swimming and yoga? Check the graveyard for signs of recent disturbance?'

'Strikes me as an administrative error,' says Rebecca, pouring the coffee. 'And there is no graveyard here.'

The conversation is running away. I say, 'While I'm here I thought I'd try to find out a little bit about my mother as well. I thought maybe I was invited because she did something interesting when she was here, or wrote a great declaration, or... I don't know. If I could get her declaration, maybe that would tell me something.'

'They don't do that.' Kay puts the car back down on the start square, and fits a blue peg behind the wheel.

'I know, but I thought—'

'Good luck with thinking. It never works for me.' She spins the wheel in the centre of the board; it stops, abruptly, on number three. 'Right. We're off.'

* * *

I wake up.

The enormity of what I've done is upon me, pressing on my chest. I can't remember why I left him; all I can feel is the certainty of guilt. I have become my mother. We have finally been united in the act of desertion.

I should have explained it to him. I should have said, *I need to understand why I received this letter.* I can't understand why I didn't. There is no light. The sea is audible, a murmuring voice outside the windows. I picture myself, how I must look from the sky: a tiny, smothered mass, surrounded by the blue, awaiting my answers, travelling towards a goal that David can't appreciate.

On our fifth date, I told him what it was to be abandoned. We went to a restaurant, like a couple from a romantic novel: an arranged meeting, reservation made, then the slow walk home afterwards, holding hands, a kiss. Containing the relationship within those strictures gave me the much-needed illusion of control. David wore a suit, a tie, aftershave; I found his desire to impress me with his appearance charming and also a little funny. So I responded in kind by wearing a dress to dinner, a different one every time. I liked the idea that with each dress he was getting a different woman. That evening, I had been in a low-cut wraparound dress, offering him more than I had dared to before. But instead of taking it as an invitation to flirt, it had brought out a serious side in him. He asked questions about my life, my past, all the things I hate to talk about.

David likes to search for the bottom of things. *What do you really feel?* he asked me, that night. How very seriously he took my replies, over lamb shanks and strawberry mousse cake, sitting in a deserted bistro on the Swindon road where the waiter strutted by the table, attempting to rise to the occasion.

'What happened on the day she left?' he asked, after three glasses of red wine, just before the arrival of coffee with a burnt aftertaste. I felt so romantic, in a literary sense, with the candlelight between us and Norah Jones on the CD player.

I told him it hadn't been an unusual day. My father had been working as a gardener back then; well, doing any job, really. So I had let myself in after school with my own key.

'How old were you?'

Sixteen. And he had shaken his head at that.

I confided in him, rewarded his desire to know me. I had talked about always feeling that my mother had wanted to leave, to get away from Arnie, with his drinking. Sixteen would seem to be the age when a girl can start to fend for herself; perhaps that was how my mother saw it.

'But sixteen is... at sixteen you're a baby,' David had said. 'You were just a baby.'

I remember reaching across the table and touching his arm. He had said something important, and I had begun to understand, at that moment, that my books were not enough.

Standing at my front door, after the walk home, I asked him to come in, wanting him, and he had said no. A week passed. By the time he phoned I had changed my mind again, decided that I didn't want him, attack being the best form of defence. I would not have returned the message he left on the answer phone if it had not begun with the words, *I've gone and fallen in love with you.*

I didn't believe him, of course. Nobody could fall in love after five dates.

And now I understand, as I lie here in the dark, why I hadn't told him in person where I was going. He has always been the better talker. He would have persuaded me out of it in less than a minute, maybe told me it was my mother I was looking for, and we would be in Bedfordshire right now, searching places together.

I find I'm crying, noisily, competing with the sea, keeping it company.

'Can I get you anything?' says Rebecca, from my left.

I hear the squeak of bedsprings, and then a new weight settles on one side of the bed, next to my knees.

'Do you want to talk about it?' whispers Rebecca. 'Bad dreams? To do with home?'

'I should have told him,' I manage to say.

'Told your husband? That you were coming here?'

'I left him.'

I wait for condemnation, but instead Kay's voice, too loud for the middle of the night, says, 'Yeah, well, we all do something terrible every now and again. That's life for you. Did you bottle it all up for so long that it had to come whooshing out, all of a sudden, like a bottle of Coke that someone shook? You have that repressed look about you.'

'Shut up, please, Kay,' says Rebecca, in what sounds like an amused tone of voice, 'if you don't mind me saying so.'

Kay claps her hands together, says, 'Brilliant!' and then there is the sound of movement, and the overhead light bursts into shocked life. 'Since we're up, I'm getting tea.'

'There's only horrible, cheap teabags,' says Rebecca.

'What would your majesty prefer? Earl Grey?'

'I like Earl Grey,' I say, and the two of them laugh at me. Kay pads away in her zebra-striped pyjamas, and the kettle is soon audible through the partition wall. It works itself up to boiling point and Kay hums along with it, occasionally talking to herself, saying things such as *not even then* and *it's meant to be green, stupid.*

'She's a live wire,' says Rebecca. 'Do you really want to be here?'

'I don't know.'

'You say you want to know why you were given a place here by a dead woman. It strikes me you didn't have to come. You could have simply asked over the phone, couldn't you? And they would have told you that it was an error by some new member of staff. A mix-up of letters. Are you really trying to solve that mystery, or are you after the experience? The experience of being your mother. What it's like to leave.'

I can't move. I absorb the words, until tea arrives. Kay passes around the mugs and sits down on my bed too; it creaks beneath her.

'It's so quiet here, I actually can't sleep,' she says.

'Me neither,' says Rebecca. 'I should say, by the way, I'm a therapist. I'm sorry if I overstepped the mark, Marianne.'

'Why, what did you tell her to do?'

I shake my head at Kay. 'She didn't tell me to do anything. She just pointed something out.'

'I hate it when people do that.' Kay smoothes the duvet with one hand. 'Listen, I've been thinking about how we could get hold of your mum's declaration, if they won't give it to you.'

'You mean break the rules?' says Rebecca. She's in a peach silk nightdress, showing the aged skin at the tops of her arms. Her face is shiny from being cleansed, toned and moisturised before being allowed to relax into sleep. 'They'll kick us off.'

'They'll kick Marianne off anyway, when they discover she never handed in her mobile.'

'It was an honest mistake, I'll hand it in first thing tomorrow.' I lean over the side of the bed and pull my handbag out from under the bed by its leather strap. David bought it for me in Barcelona while on a stag weekend for a work colleague. A coach had been commandeered, and the back rows of the aeroplane given over to their testosterone-fuelled two days. I never asked for details. Instead, I enjoyed a secretive delight at the thought that he had stopped to buy a handbag even though he had been in the midst of a male adventure. I take out the phone from the inner pocket and stare at it.

'Are you going to phone him?' says Rebecca, in a stage whisper.

But the choice is wrenched away from me. I'm grateful. 'No signal.' I drop the phone on the bed. 'I wonder why they make you give up your phone if there's no signal anyway?'

'Psychology.' Rebecca taps its screen. 'Whether the phone works or not, it connects you to your normal life. Once it's locked away, you're going to commit to the week more, to meeting new people, forming new ties. Because on a subconscious level you're much more likely to feel vulnerable, and forget the people who usually keep you safe.'

'Do you think reading your mum's declaration really will help you?' interrupted Kay.

'I don't know.' I slip the phone back into the bag and push it under the bed once more. 'What else could?'

'All right then. Tomorrow night. We'll go and find it. Be ready.'

'Are you serious?' says Rebecca.

'Yup,' Kay tells her, with a level stare.

Rebecca sighs. 'Well then. You'd better try and get some sleep if you're both going to turn into hardened lawbreakers.' She is our mother figure. Kay rolls her eyes at me, then returns to her own bed.

I lie down once more. The rest of the night passes in a deep, deliberate silence. The cold air crackles with thoughts that have no place to go.

CHAPTER FOUR

'So she's gone too,' said Arnie. 'She won't be coming back.' He undid the zipper of his grey ski jacket and pulled one arm free, then the other, carefully, so as not to knock his pint. 'Sorry, but there it is.'

'No, she'll come back,' said David.

Arnie smiled at him, baring his grey teeth. 'Is that right?' He raised his voice to the rest of the bar. 'He's still got hope, this one.'

David remembered a story Marianne had once told him about her father. Her first boyfriend had left a message on the answering machine, dumping her, back at the age when face-to-face talking between boys and girls didn't happen. Arnie had played it for her when she got back from ballet class. He'd also played it for the neighbours, who were round having drinks that night, and they'd had a long discussion in front of her about how she should just get over it and not mope about such a stupid boy. Arnie hadn't considered it to be her private business at all, apparently, and David had wondered if Marianne had exaggerated the story, as she sometimes did, for dramatic effect. But now he suspected it was true after all.

'So what's going on?' said Arnie. He took a long drink of his pint, then patted his thin moustache with his fingers and wiped the moisture on the front of his jacket.

'Did she talk to you? Phone you, at all?'

'No. But I wouldn't expect her to. You, on the other hand, should be her closest confidante. Shouldn't you?'

'I am,' David said.

Arnie shook his head. 'Sorry to be the bearer of bad news here, but it has to be your fault. Your wife's not happy, it's your fault. Trust me.'

So this wasn't about a father protecting a daughter; this was about men being left behind. Abandonment was not the same, however it happened, no matter what Arnie might think.

'Drink your beer,' Arnie said.

Getting drunk in the pub – this was his idea of mutual support.

The Cornerhouse was one of those pubs that people walked past regularly and never went into. It sat where the less developed end of Wootton Bassett high street turned a sharp left into seedier territory, such as DVD rental places with ripped posters in the windows and dry-cleaning places sporting filthy net curtains. There was a sign hung on the roof of the little pub that promised Sky Sports, and then three stone steps down into the barely lit room where a few wooden chairs and thick, round tables squeezed up together to leave room for a skittles alley and a dartboard. David had never been in there, although he had known it was Arnie's second home for years.

At the back of his mind had been the idea that it was a pub by invitation only, for those older men who all knew each other and didn't want to have to deal with young idiots when they socialised. The quiet murmurings, half-hidden under the strains of early Elvis from the radio behind the bar, were not about women or cars or jobs, David guessed. He didn't know what they talked about, and he had a feeling he wouldn't know for another thirty years or so, when, one day, he'd find the urge to step inside a place like this and find a lot of tired old men looking back at him without judgement.

'All right, Mags?' said Arnie, to the woman behind the bar. 'Another two here.'

Mags retrieved two pint glasses from the stack behind her and pulled at the pumps with muscular efficiency. Her arms were bare; she wore a stretchy white top with straps that had entwined with the lace straps of her bra, in a shade of red that clashed with her curly, purplish hair. David imagined her to be in her early fifties, with heavily wrinkled skin under her arms, flapping as she pulled their pints, but her blue eyes, intense in the bristling mess of mascara, looked younger, more alive than the patrons of the pub. She was looking straight at him.

'Here,' she said. 'I'm not a waitress.'

David got up and took the pints from the bar.

'Nine pounds, lovey.' He paid the money.

'Is this your son-in-law, then, Arnie?' she said, not taking her eyes from him.

'That's him. The daughter's only gone off to Skein Island and left him.'

This news was greeted with fresh mutterings from the other men. David carried the pints back to the table.

'Like mother, eh?' said Mags, with some degree of satisfaction evident in her voice as she switched off the radio. 'Right, well, it's eight o'clock.' And that was the end of the conversation about Marianne. How unimportant she was to them. It was a strange relief to not have to field questions, to explain the inexplicable. Apparently this leaving business was something that women did, apart from Mags, who seemed to have transcended female status. Old men knew not to be surprised when women left. Instead they merely nodded, and pulled their chairs closer to the bar as Mags retrieved a small green box from behind the rack of spirits.

Arnie rubbed his hands together and gave David a wink. 'You'd better watch this time, see how it goes.'

'What?'

'The game,' his father-in-law said, as if that explained everything. Mags opened the box, and took out four small painted cubes, one red, one blue, one yellow, one green. She placed them on the bar. David glanced back at Arnie; he was leaning forward, his attention fixed on the cubes. Mags stood back, her hands on her hips. Her expression was difficult to read. There was pleasure there, David thought,

38

but she was trying to hide it under a veneer of watchful superiority. She was in charge, that much was obvious. The men did not move from their seats, but they were all hooked to the cubes, their eyes glued to the wooden sides, lined up in a row.

David felt Mags's attention on him once more. 'You in?' she said.

He shrugged.

'Not good enough. Come back when you're in.'

'He's with me,' said Arnie.

'Not good enough.'

'It's okay,' David said. 'I should go, anyway. I've got a teleconference in the morning.'

Arnie pulled a face. 'Right, well, that's up to you, isn't it?'

'Will you let me know if she rings again?'

'Course.' But Arnie wouldn't look at him. David picked up his leather jacket and put it on, feeling the men around him wishing him gone. Mags had turned back to the cubes, tapping them with a purple fingernail, one at a time, the noise like the tick-tock of a metronome, counting out the seconds until he left.

He walked to the door, stepped outside, pulled it shut behind him. He started a brisk walk back to his empty house, then gave in to temptation, and headed instead for the library.

* * *

David crouched and waited.

Blame was an organism. It grew, and stretched, and multiplied in unexpected directions. Although it had a pinpoint-sharp focus on the unknown attacker, its outer edges also encompassed Marianne's father, and the other women she worked with who had left her alone to close up. He hated himself for letting her leave. He should have leapt out of bed when he first spotted the open wardrobe door and the absence of her suitcase. He imagined, nightly, living that moment of realisation again, acting fast, throwing himself in front of their car.

The library was a small, grey, one-storey building, rectangular with a porch area into which the main doorway had been set. The outside light above the doorway was operated by motion sensor; every time David shifted position it clicked on to throw a sickly bluish glow over the path and the privet where he hid, and when it clicked off again it left David with the temporary illusion of absolute, icy darkness, blanket thick.

And, of course, nobody came.

There was another reason to be here. It made him feel closer to Marianne. She loved her job: the smell and the feel of well-used books, the joy of recommending a tense thriller or a slushy romance to her customers.

He shifted his weight on to his left buttock and stuck out his right leg, flexing his foot. The exterior light clicked on as he worked out the cramp in his calf with his fingers. Agonising, but he wasn't ready to give up yet. In The Cornerhouse, ten minutes' walk away, Arnie would be drinking and watching television, playing the game with the cubes. David wondered what the prize was; it had to be good, to have captured everyone's attention so completely. Or maybe they had nothing else to live for.

He heard the light footsteps behind him only a moment before he heard the voice.

'Stand up.'

It was a woman. Hope leapt in him, but an instant later evaporated. It wasn't Marianne. It was too harsh a voice, too confident.

David did as he was told. The woman must have come from the far side of the library, working her way along the small, gravel path that ran along the back of the building, where the bins were kept.

'Put your hands behind your head,' she said. He linked his gloved fingers around the back of his neck. She sounded so calm. He guessed she was a policewoman, maybe, but still, his major concern was that he didn't move too quickly and frighten her.

'It's okay,' he said. 'Everything's fine.'

'Can I ask what you're doing here?'

It was too complicated to explain. 'Can I turn around?' He didn't know why, but he thought seeing her face might help.

There was a pause. Then she said, 'Yes, all right. But keep your hands up, okay?'

The politeness of it was surprising. He moved around to face her. She was standing underneath the exterior light, eyes hidden in the shadow thrown by the brim of her neat hat, mouth straight. How petite she was, short and slim but with a wide stance, her feet planted in sensible black shoes.

'My wife was working here last night, and she was approached by an assailant. I just thought I'd see if he was hanging around.'

She lifted her chin and gave him a view of her eyes. There was recognition in them. Did he know her? He felt certain he didn't.

'You're Mr Percival?' she said.

'Yes.'

'Have you got ID on you?'

'Yes, in my pocket. Can I...?' He lowered his hands and reached into his coat pocket to bring forth his wallet. She came closer, just a few steps, and held out her free hand in a precise, direct manner, as if she was in charge. Which, now he thought about it, she was. The sensation of her gaze on his driver's licence, then on his face, wasn't unpleasant. He risked a small smile, which she returned. 'I had the same thought,' she said. 'I thought I'd just have a quick check round. Sometimes men like that come back to the same haunts.'

So it hadn't been ridiculous after all. David nodded, trying to keep either vindication or disappointment from his expression.

'How's your wife?' she said.

'She's gone away for a few days.'

She snapped his wallet shut and handed it back. She didn't seem surprised, but maybe that was the training she received, to be calm in the face of all situations. He envied her. 'I think you should probably go home now.'

'Yes.' But he couldn't move, or say more. A knot was forming inside him, a strong, hard knot of despair for this wasted night, for Marianne's refusal to let him help her. It threatened to choke him, drove tears up into his eyes, and the worst thing was that it was happening in front of this tiny, serious policewoman. His loneliness, made visible to a stranger, pulling tighter around his stomach as he struggled for self-control.

'Do you want a lift home?' she said. He shook his head.

'No, I insist, I can't leave you alone like this. You live near the park, right? I know your wife, a little bit. I'm a regular at the library. Come on, the car's parked on the other side of the alley.' She kept talking as she walked away, so David followed her, amazed by how confidently she strode without looking back, as if she didn't realise how tiny and vulnerable she looked to him.

* * *

Her name was Samantha, Sam for short. She was a community support officer. She had a way of talking that didn't tire the ears, even though on the drive back David had not noticed a pause in the flow of her speech on subjects such as the traffic problems of the high street and how the town needed better lighting. It was not entertaining talk, but it was easy to listen to. He could have stayed in the car for hours without feeling any pressure to respond, and so at the end of the drive he accepted her invitation of a cup of coffee. It turned out she lived around the corner from him anyway. He must have seen her around before; that would explain why her face was so familiar, yet utterly unremarkable. He couldn't have described it to anyone else, except to say that it was neither pretty nor ugly. And that, too, was a soothing thing about her. When he looked at her he was not reminded of Marianne's beauty.

Sam's lounge seemed odd to him. It was so different from the cream curtains and wooden flooring of his house. Here, the room seemed crowded by the dark squashy armchairs, the radiator painted red to match the bookshelves and the fringed lampshade. He took a seat in a rocking chair, of all things, next to the small television, and knew straight away that she lived alone. The décor was too individual, and a small cuddly toy, an owl with enormous yellow felt eyes that were peeling around the edges due to age, sat in one of the armchairs, looking proprietorial.

He listened to the sound of the kettle boiling, and waited. Eventually she came in carrying a circular silver tray, her stab jacket undone, her hat removed, but still there was powerful formality in the way she placed the tray down on the glass-topped coffee table and handed him one of the mugs.

'I know your wife,' she said. 'She recommended some thrillers for me. She was really helpful. I've been thinking about what happened to her. That's why I stopped by the library at the end of the shift tonight, just in case there was anyone there. The thought of it makes me sick, someone like that, prowling around the town, looking for a woman who won't be able to stand up to him. This should be a safe place for people, for families.' She sat down in the armchair opposite him, clutching her own mug, her face composed, even though her words had been strident. He couldn't work her out.

'I thought maybe it would be someone from the Swindon estates,' he said. 'Some of those are pretty rough, and we're practically a satellite town for Swindon now, aren't we?'

'It's kept its own personality,' she said. 'You're not from here, originally, are you?'

'My parents still live in Cheltenham, where I grew up. Marianne's from Bassett. Her father's always been here, mainly in The Cornerhouse.'

Sam raised an eyebrow, but didn't comment.

'Are you from here, then?' he asked her.

'No.'

He got the feeling he'd strayed into unwelcome territory. He said, 'She's gone to Skein Island. My wife.'

'No men allowed, right? The feminist thing. She'll soon be back, I'm sure.'

He nodded, but that way she said it made him think of his parents. He had stopped telling them things years ago because they always gave the same sort of kindly, unrealistic reaction to bad news. They lived in sheltered accommodation together, sharing a ground-floor flat that cost him a great deal of money, but their fragility demanded special care. His father had a tendency to forget where he'd put things, and his mother nurtured an obsession with old notes, from greeting cards to shopping lists, for no discernible reason. He never bothered them with the details of his life.

She sipped her coffee. 'Maybe it's post-traumatic stress. She's been through a terrible experience, even if nothing happened. She was very brave at the time, but people fall to pieces afterwards, sometimes.'

'Of course, I've thought of that, but I can't help her through it when she's on an island where no men are allowed.'

She stood up. 'Do you want some more coffee?'

He checked his watch; it was past ten. 'No, I should head off home. I— thanks. For the lift.'

'No problem.'

She led the way through the hallway, which was painted in an oppressive dark green, with varnished wooden banisters that had red wool strung between them, each strand bearing rows of tiny brass bells. David brushed them with one hand as he walked past, and they tinkled.

'Early warning system,' she said. 'In case someone broke in. I know, it's stupid, but in my line of work it can be difficult to relax at night. Thoughts go round your head.'

'Of course,' he said. He pictured her lying in bed, listening for the tinkle of bells.

She opened the front door. 'Listen, David.' She pursed her lips. 'Don't hang around outside the library any more, okay?

The police are handling it.'

He wondered what the difference was between a policewoman and a community support officer. The thought of her standing out there on her own, with nothing to protect her, not even a proper police rank, scared him.

'I can help,' he said.

She blinked. 'It's my job.'

'He tried to attack my wife.'

'Yes, I understand that. But you don't want to get into a situation you can't handle.'

He stepped past her, feeling her flinch away, and then did up his coat in the cold air. The walk would only take a few minutes, but the temperature had dropped further and the pavement was slippery underfoot. Sam was right; the estate did need better lighting at night.

'The same goes for The Cornerhouse,' Sam said. 'That's not a place I'd advise you spend any time in. You know where I am if you need anything. Goodnight.' She shut the door.

David stared at it, then started taking small, careful steps home on the icy pavement. Her last warning made no sense to him. He turned it over in his mind, and as he did so he realised what had seemed wrong to him about her lounge. There had been no photographs in that otherwise homely space: no family, no friends, no scenes from holidays once taken. Didn't women always love photographs? Marianne had covered their own house in them, all framed neatly, all hung in prominent places: the mantelpiece, the coffee table, every single wall.

There had been the bells, a warning for some possible future, but no photographs on show. He realised he had never met a woman before who didn't, in some way, continually reference her own past, through her choice of friends, or through cherished cards, or photos. Maybe she was a different kind of woman altogether.

The thought excited him.

CHAPTER FIVE

Each stroke – the lift of the limb, the fall of drops on the surface of the water – is a soft, slow revelation of relaxation. I am swimming on my back, with my eyes open, devouring my delicious solitude.

Rebecca and Kay opted for a yoga class instead, and I'm glad. In their company I'm a different person, fitting in with their thoughts and ideas. I have never felt so malleable. It is the island, working upon me, taking away everything familiar. I should be shelving books right now. I should be standing behind the library desk, giving out my stamp and my smile. Instead I'm formulating a plan to break the rules. I'm going to read something that was never written to be read.

I reach the deep end of the pool and turn, my body curving like a comma, and start on another length.

The lifeguard sits in the tall chair set back from the shallow end, and I can feel her attention upon me, not in an uncomfortable way, but simply as a bored onlooker, like a housewife watching daytime television. After a few lengths, I notice she has climbed down the rungs and approached the poolside. The illusion of separation between us is broken. I swim up to her feet, taking in the serious blue eyes and the muscular calves as the woman kneels down and leans over to me.

'The pool's closing for lunch in five minutes.'

'Okay.'

'Usually it would be open all day, but the other attendant is off this week, so I don't have cover. For the lunch hour.' She has a Scandinavian accent I think.

'I'll be fine,' I say, 'if you want to go ahead and have lunch. I'm a strong swimmer.'

'It's a question of liability.'

'Yes, I can see that. Okay.'

'So, five minutes, then?'

Something peremptory in her tone forces my hand. I say, 'I'll get out now, if you like,' and pull myself out, my thighs slapping on the cold raised lips of the tiles.

The woman walks away. But she's not offended; she returns with a soft, cream towel from the rack by the changing room door. She holds it out, and I stand up to take it, and wrap it around myself.

The swimming pool is a beautiful space, filled with sunlight from the row of tall clean windows that look out over a stretch of field, and the blue beyond. The roof is a wooden pyramid, very unusual in design, with slats interlocking to form a spire. There are dark blue moulded plastic seats along the wall opposite the windows, lined up exactly, and it feels like being inside a church. I find I'm reluctant to leave.

I could have gone on swimming for lengths that multiplied into miles.

'It's so calm,' I say. 'It must be peaceful, working here.'

'No. We have to stay alert. Ready for anything.'

The cold is setting in. I excuse myself and skitter around the edge of the pool to the changing rooms, where I dress mechanically, in layers designed to trap heat. When I step out into the foyer, with my wet hair soaking into the back of my jumper, the lifeguard is sitting on one of the tubular stools in the tiny café area by the main door. She has a sandwich on the table in front of her, the cling film wrapper partially peeled back.

'What time will you open again?' I ask. I watch her not eat the sandwich. She is staring at it with what appears to be intense dislike.

'A couple of minutes.'

'Is that all?'

'You want my sandwich?'

'No, thanks. Don't you like it?'

'It's got tomato in,' she says, as if that explains everything.

I am caught between my desire to swim and the thought of climbing back into my clammy costume. Eventually she says, 'You picked a really quiet week for your holiday. Usually the pool is so busy. What's your name?'

'Marianne.'

'I'm Inger.' She half stands on the metal bar between the legs of her stool, and holds out her hand. I shake it, and find myself smiling, tickled by the incongruity of the gesture.

'Are you happy?' she asks.

'Um… yes, pretty happy.'

'Enjoying your holiday?'

'Yes.'

'That's good,' says Inger. 'I thought you looked sad, in the pool. That's why I couldn't leave you in there alone. Sometimes people do dangerous things when they're sad.' She says it in such a matter-of-fact tone, while lifting up the corner of the top slice of bread to examine the filling.

'Really? You mean – in the pool?'

She shrugs. 'It happens. I've had four try to drown themselves. Three, I saved. They could throw themselves off the cliffs, but no, they have to come to the pool instead. Off the cliffs would be much quicker and easier for everyone. But they don't really want to die, do they? They want me to save them. Being saved is a good feeling. It gives meaning to your life, I'm thinking.' Inger sweeps up her sandwich and throws it, overhand, into the blue bin next to the main entrance. It's a fair distance, but the sandwich lands squarely in the bin. Inger doesn't look in the slightest bit pleased with herself. Maybe she makes the throw every day.

'That must be stressful, though,' I say. 'Being the one that does the saving.'

'I like it. It's the one I didn't save that bothers me. She drank pool cleaner first, from the storage area. We keep it padlocked now.' She stands up and stretches, then puts her hands on her hips. She looks ready for anything. 'You can get changed again now if you want to carry on swimming.'

'I might leave it for now, actually.'

'I've put you off? I'm sorry. Listen, every swimming pool has a few deaths. Every street, every house, someone has died, yeah?'

'You seem really...' I can't think of the right word and settle, eventually, on, 'Scandinavian.'

Inger laughs. 'It's true. I'm from Denmark. I hope you have a good time while you're here. You should go to the cinema tonight. They're showing Jodie Foster films this week. There's a discussion group afterwards, if enough people come.'

'Are you going?'

'For sure.'

Her casual invitation fills me with the confidence to ask my own question. 'Can I ask – did you know Amelia Worthington?'

'I met her a few times. She was very old when I started here. She didn't leave the white house, and staff don't get invited up there often. Not even now Mrs Makepeace is in charge. She keeps to the house too.'

'Did you have to do a declaration? When you first started working here?'

Inger hesitates, then says, 'I first came as a visitor, for the week. I was a manager at a bank in Copenhagen, and I was interested in Buddhism – this was eight, nine years ago. So I thought a free week, alone, to meditate, would be good. I spent the week trying to sit and clear my mind. Have you ever done that? Meditation? It's very difficult. I couldn't stop thinking. I wrote in my declaration all the things I'd thought about, and when I read it back to myself I knew I didn't want to go home.'

'So you didn't?'

'I talked to Mrs Makepeace – she was Lady Worthington's assistant back then – and she said they needed a pool attendant. I'm a strong swimmer. I stayed.'

'Didn't you have family?'

'I had a boyfriend.' She smiles a little. 'He wanted to see other women anyway. I let him see all the women he wanted. Except me.'

'And what happened to your declaration? Did you finish it?'

'It went into the vault, with the others, I guess.'

'The vault?'

'Up at the white house. The basement is an archive. That's the point of the island, right? These stories, sealed up, like a time capsule. A record of what it means to be a woman.'

'Could you see it again, if you wanted to? Your declaration?'

'Why would I want to?' says Inger, with such puzzlement on her face. 'Once you've changed your life, why would you want to read about what you were before? I don't think that's a healthy impulse. Look, come to the cinema tonight, and stay for the talk, and maybe you'll understand more about making a declaration.'

'Yes, okay, thanks.'

'Back to the pool. It'll be a quiet week for me.'

I nod. 'Hopefully no suicide bids, then.'

Inger shrugs, as if it is impossible to tell when somebody might decide to throw themselves into the deep end.

Outside, on the short walk back to the bungalow, I picture that basement filled with declarations. What do those stories mean? Do they have to mean anything? And yet I can feel the pervasive magic of wanting to put down my own words, separating my life into before and after, altering my ideas about the person I want to be.

Am I turning into my mother?

Or maybe that process has already begun, in the library, in the face of that unknown man. Or earlier still, when my mother left. Yes, people are changed forever when the people they love decide to leave.

* * *

'I think she makes the only choice she can. I mean, she has to avenge him, right? Sometimes we live on instinct and no matter how much we know it's not a good idea, we can't listen to anything but our hearts.' The slim woman in jeans and a cream cable-knit jumper touches the space between her breasts with both hands, and I sit back as the other women in the circle nod. It is the kind of statement that divides people into two categories: those who believe in the all-embracing power of love, and those who think that the first group are a bunch of self-indulgent idiots. I desperately don't want anyone else to work out that I think I once belonged to the first group. Now I'm not so sure.

Rebecca, sitting on my right, nudges me, then says in her loud voice, 'I think you always have a choice.'

'Yes,' says Inger, from across the circle. She is wearing a black dress, which surprises me. It's a sheath, the kind of glamorous garment that belongs to a formal event, not on this island. Still, there can't be many opportunities to dress up. 'I think it's fine to want revenge. It's fine to act on it. But you have to know you'll pay the price for it. Be aware of what it means, yes, and think it through.'

'And that makes it okay?' says Rebecca.

'No, but it makes it methodical,' I say. I like Inger's practical solemnity. Sitting a few rows behind her in the screening room, I found myself watching the back of Inger's head more often than Jodie Foster's deliberations. There had been, in the way she leaned forward during the emotional moments of the film, a feeling of intense concentration emanating from her. I don't think I've ever managed to concentrate on something in that way. Right now, only half of me is in this group. The other half is wondering how Kay is doing on her mission to find a way into the basement of the white house without being detected.

The meeting peters out into general chatting about lives back home, and I am silent once more as Rebecca categorises everyone's experiences and attempts to make sense of them. She really can't help herself. Later, we stand side by side at the sinks in the toilets, and she at least has the grace to look embarrassed.

'Do you know what?' She washes her hands, using the pink soap from the dispenser. 'Other people's problems are much easier to deal with. But I do wonder if my way is the right way.

Who's to say facing up to it and moving on has to work? Why couldn't we all just pretend the worst things never happened and refuse to confront them?'

I'm pretty certain by now that Rebecca isn't a person I would get along with under usual circumstances. 'When you told that woman with the abusive husband—'

'Sophie.'

'When you told Sophie she could leave, you think you could have said something different?'

Reflected in the mirrors are shiny taps, the clean sheets of the walls, and Rebecca's grim smile as she says, 'Do you think Sophie will ever leave him? I wonder if it matters what I say to her. Or if he'll beg, and promise to go to counselling, and next thing you know she'll be in the casualty department with bruises the shape of his fingers around her neck. Again.'

'You don't know that,' I tell her. I have to believe in the possibility of change, it seems. 'You never know. This island has a strange effect on people.'

'Like your mother? You think she hadn't already decided to leave before she came here?'

'I don't know.' I rip a handful of dark blue paper towels from the dispenser, and hand some to Rebecca.

'Was your father abusive?' she asks me.

'He was a normal dad. Until she didn't come back. And then he ignored me, that's all.' I think of piggybacks, of ice creams, of hands keeping me afloat in the swimming pool, locked under my tummy while I kick, and suddenly I feel ashamed of ever forgetting that side, instead of seeing only the shadow of him, lurking in The Cornerhouse. I throw the paper towels in the bin. 'Come on. Kay should be waiting for us.'

'Listen, I'm not sure that this thing with Kay is such a good idea.'

'Let's just see what she's found out,' I say. 'Maybe there's nothing.' But it doesn't feel that way. There is excitement buzzing through me. Something is about to happen.

*　*　*

Standing outside the cinema, under the light from the old-fashioned streetlight placed at a crossroads in the gravel path, Kay hops from one foot to the other in her big, black boots as we walk over to her. 'That took ages!' she says. 'Did you dissect it scene by scene?'

I hear a cough behind me; Inger is approaching in her sheath dress, coatless, with a large bunch of keys in one hand. 'Thanks for coming along,' she says.

'I enjoyed it.'

'Me too. The pool's open from ten tomorrow, if you want a swim.'

I watch her go, sure-footed, swinging the keys. She doesn't seem to feel the cold at all.

Rebecca leans over and whispers close to my ear, very loudly, 'I think she suspects something.'

Kay rolls her eyes. 'Is this whole thing not melodramatic enough for you, then, Rebecca?'

'I just think it isn't a good idea to start doing things that are morally wrong because you happen to both think that the ends justify the means. What happens when you get caught?'

'So we're definitely going to get caught, are we?'

'Yes, actually. Because that's what happens to criminals.'

'Like the Nazis, you mean? Like Klaus Barbie, living out his life in South America, soaking up the sunshine?'

Rebecca flicks back her hair and turns up the collar on her coat. 'There is no point trying to have a rational discussion if you're going to bring up Nazi Germany. That's totally uncalled for. As a comparison. And didn't he get caught eventually?'

'Listen,' I say, before it can get any worse, 'I don't want to upset anyone. I'm not going to torture people or run away to Bolivia. I just want to see one declaration. Just one. I won't look at anyone else's, I promise, Rebecca. And besides, it's probably locked up too tight for me to even get near.'

'Heh,' says Kay. 'That's what you think. Come on. I've had a quick look round the grounds of the white house, and I think I've found a way in. Maybe we'll even uncover the mummy of Amelia Worthington, still signing acceptance letters, with a fountain pen in her bandaged hand.'

'Don't be ridiculous. I'm not doing anything of the sort. And I'd appreciate it if you don't talk about it around me, either.' Rebecca sticks her hands into her pockets. 'I'm going back to the bungalow now. I think you should come back and play a board game and forget all about this, Marianne.

There are other ways to find your answers. You don't have to become your mother to understand her, I promise you.'

It is so polished, such a slick thing to say, that it is impossible to take it seriously. I tell her, carefully, 'We'll be back really soon, okay? We're just going to take a look. That's all.'

Rebecca stares at me, and I return the gaze. She is not my mother, and she doesn't get to tell me what to do. I'm now absolutely certain that I don't like her. Eventually Rebecca drops her eyes and walks away.

'Right,' says Kay. 'It's this way. It gets really dark but I've got a pocket torch.'

'You brought a torch with you?'

'And a penknife. I'm that kind of woman.'

I'm not sure exactly what kind of woman brings a survival kit on holiday but I'm grateful to have that small circle of yellow light from the torch as I stumble along the paths, following, hoping Kay isn't leading us over a cliff. The sea makes boisterous crashing noises below, even though the night is still, and the clumps of wild grass catch at my feet; the thought occurs to me that the island is trying to stop us from reaching the house. I push it away and keep moving towards that bobbing pool of torchlight.

The light splits into segments, fractured by the rungs of a wrought iron gate. Kay moves the torch to the left, along the line of the hedge, to reveal a small hole, maybe made by one of the sheep, only a few yards away. 'Come on,' she says. We squeeze through the privet, and I emerge with the feeling of having been scraped into a new world. The rough grass has become a lawn, and the torchlight reveals the white cube of the house up ahead, with circular black windows, like shark eyes in the deep.

I catch a flicker of light in one of the windows. 'Turn off the torch!'

Kay snaps off the beam. There is no further movement from the upper window. Eventually my eyes adjust to the point where it is possible to move forwards, small steps. I'm grateful for the flat, straight lawn underfoot. The house takes on an iridescent quality, glowing, reflecting the moonlight. We reach the nearest wall and I find myself taking Kay's hand and finding warmth in the corresponding squeeze.

'This way,' Kay whispers. She leads me along the wall, around the corner, to a flight of stone steps that lead down below the line of the lawn to a small door, wooden, with a brass ring for a handle, and a large keyhole set above it. Gathered around the foot of the door are unused terracotta plant pots, arranged in order of height, and a trowel.

I reach for the brass ring and Kay shakes her head. She points instead to a sash window further down, half-open, easy to climb through. She turns the torch back on and shines it through; I see an undecorated room, stone walls and floor, and a washing machine standing in the corner next to a mop and a bucket. There's an archway that leads to what looks like a corridor, and a high shelf, upon which wait bottles of bleach and loo cleaner, and four small tins of paint.

'What do you think?' whispers Kay.

I don't want to think. I want to be done with this, and I want my answers, so I ignore my instincts and climb through the gap in the window, sliding on my belly, feeling the buttons on my coat snag on the ledge, then pull free. I stand up and breathe in washing powder, a chemical brand that irritates my nostrils. I have to suppress a sneeze.

All is silent. I cross to the archway and look down the corridor, which ends in an abrupt flight of stairs upwards. There is a grunt, and then Kay comes up behind me and shines the torch down it, revealing faded 1950s wallpaper, a pattern of huge white orchids against what must once have been a vibrant yellow background. There are three doors: two on the left and one on the right. I walk to the first door on the left and put my hand on the cold brass knob. I decide against it. I don't know why. I'm picturing the library of declarations: a huge space, rows of shelves, alphabetically filed, although I'm probably being old-fashioned and there will only be a broom cupboard with a computer and a hard drive for these many thousands of words. Still, for some reason I turn to the door on the right. I walk up to it, and wait for Kay.

The beam of the torch reveals four squares painted on the wood a little below eye-level – one red, one blue, one yellow, one green – in a row, the lines exact, the paint vibrant under torchlight. I run my fingers over them, feeling the slickness of the paint. They feel familiar to me, these four squares. A logo for some product I have forgotten.

Kay puts her head close to mine. 'What is it?' Her voice contains a tremor of fear that strokes my spine and grabs me for the first time. I manage to say, 'I don't know.' I put out my hand and turn the doorknob. It opens easily, swinging back, and I find myself looking into the large space I had imagined, with tall metal shelves forming aisles, ceiling-high, filled with black lever arch files.

Kay puts her hand around the door and I hear a click; the overhead strip light flickers, then gives out a steady, yellow glow. She switches off her torch.

The room is spotless. I walk down the first row of shelves and see no dust, no disorder. Kay starts down the aisle next to me.

'What's your surname?' she calls, softly.

'Percival. No, wait, that's my married name. Spence. My mother's name was Vanessa Spence.'

'I've found "S",' says Kay.

The surnames are printed on the sides of the files. It occurs to me that she might have made the declaration under her own maiden name. 'Wait – it might be under March as well.'

'You check "M", then.'

I walk down the row, turn the corner, start down another. The 'MA' section is high up; I have to stretch up to read along the row. There is only one March, so I take it down and hold it in my hands. The folder is just like the type I once used at school. I try to slow my breathing, to think about what I want to find out, but it's too difficult to be rational. I give up the battle to control it and open the folder.

A clear plastic pocket is attached to the rings of the spine, and inside the pocket is a sheet of yellow, A4-sized paper.

At the top, like a letterhead for an expensive hotel, are the words

− SKEIN ISLAND −

And underneath

I was born in Padstow in 1953. My father was a butcher. Everyone came to him for their pork chops and ox tongue, and at the same time they'd ask for his advice, about anything, about houses and jobs and their love lives. He gave great advice. To my sisters and to me, too. He'd say, when I came to him and told him what had gone wrong with my latest boyfriend, 'Listen, Jo-Jo, life's all chop and change. Just make sure you're getting enough chop for your change.' I loved him dearly, and when he died, the whole town turned out for the funeral. I've never met another man like him. I don't suppose I ever will, now.

It's not her. This is someone else, some other March. It's the story of a woman who is nothing to do with me.

I slide the sheet back into the pocket and replace the file on the shelf. I walk around to where Kay is standing, and find her sliding folder after folder from the shelf, reading maybe the first line from the paper within before replacing them.

'Nothing,' she says. 'These are more boring than I thought they would be, actually. Did you find your mum's?'

'It's not here.'

'But everyone who comes here writes one. Maybe she used a pseudonym.'

'Or maybe she never came here at all,' I say. If not, where did she go? How can I possibly find out anything, when the one fact I've been holding on to is a lie? I walk through the rows until I find the final files – 'Z'. There are only a few folders there, and then an empty space. Beyond that, there is a brick wall and, set into that, a small cupboard door, perhaps half the size of a normal door. Painted upon it are the four squares: red, blue, yellow, green.

Next to the door, on the ground, is a red plastic tray with three of the black A4 lever arch files in it. I squat, and open the top one. The clear plastic folder within holds a sheet of aged cream, expensive writing paper with no letterhead, and on it, in delicate, looping handwriting, is written:

> *My name is Lady Amelia Henrietta Elizabeth Worthington and I am eighty-seven years old. I am a collector of unique objects. I am the owner of Skein Island.*

I close the file.

I stand up, and open the cupboard door.

Inside is a dark space, a wall of black, and I feel the depth of it, stretching back and back. There is a waft of warm air, musty, over my face. From deep inside, something shifts. It is moving. It moves towards me.

I slam the door.

Kay is standing a little way behind me. She says, 'What?'

'It's a cupboard,' I say. I can't think of any other words to explain it.

'We should get going,' says Kay. 'Guess what I've just noticed?' She points above the cupboard door; in the corner of the ceiling there is, suspended, a small, black camera, with one blinking red light. 'We'd never make professional burglars, would we?'

Rebecca was right. Nothing has been gained, and I have been caught in the act: the act of breaking yet another promise.

'Ah, never mind, we'll just say we were curious. No harm done.' Kay takes my hand. 'Besides, I bet they don't even check it. If they were monitoring it, some security guard would have turned up by now, right? And it's not even pointing the right way. At that angle all it's picking up is this little bit of the room. Come on.'

I hold on to the folder, keep it safe against my chest, as Kay pulls me from the room, through the basement, and pushes me out of the half-open window. All is still.

This kind of darkness, I can cope with. It is not absolute, or consuming, like the black of the cupboard. Something about that cupboard has sparked my imagination, I tell myself, as Kay takes my hand once more and we begin to retrace our steps across the island. Imagination can do the strangest things to a person. It can crawl into a small space and make it grow. I've discovered something that should not have been found. I feel it.

We don't speak, all the way back. We reach our bungalow. The lights are off; I'm sure Rebecca is lying awake in the dark, waiting for us to turn on the bedroom light so she can claim we woke her up and scold us like children. Instead Kay turns on her torch once more and shines the beam at the folder, still in my arms. 'Is that one of the declarations?' she whispers. 'I thought we didn't find one for your mother.'

'This is someone else's.'

'So you're just stealing random ones now? Weirdo.'

'I'll tell you about it in the morning.'

'Aren't you coming to bed too?'

'Not yet,' I tell her. She shrugs, hands me the torch, and wanders over to the bedroom.

I sit at the kitchen table and angle the torch on its surface so I can read in its light. I put the folder in front of me and run my hands over it. Skein Island library has stolen my mother from me, put her firmly out of my reach once more. But I have stolen something from it. Something important. The first declaration.

I open the folder, and I begin to read.

My name is Lady Amelia Henrietta Elizabeth Worthington and I am eighty-seven years old. I am a collector of unique objects. I am the owner of Skein Island.

In 1942 I was the most well-connected socialite in London, and I was in love with a man. He was German, and very rich – a Junker, as they were called back then; a Prince of Prussia. His name was Friedrich. Our wealth allowed us the privilege of not having to choose any side in that war but our own, and so we were following our mutual passion for antiquities through the Mediterranean, with plans to spend a few months in Northern Africa, digging over Carthage. I do not remember giving serious thought to the future. Friedrich was a member of the Nazi party, of course, as everyone was back then, but it meant nothing to him, or to me. You may think that we were selfish, and I wouldn't deny it. But I believed then that every person, rich or poor, should be allowed the right to turn their back on the responsibilities that others mete out to them so easily. It always bemused me that my wealth alone incited others to demand certain behaviours: marriage, children, moral obligations that disgusted me. Some of our ideas change as we age. Only when we are old can we see that this change is not the weakness of humanity, but its strength.

Friedrich made no moral judgements, had no feigned superiority. I admired his tall, straight, thin body, deeply tanned, giving him a swarthy appearance that, combined with his rather large nose, could have led to suspicions of Jewishness in his home country if he had not been related to royalty. He had a deep interest in the Occult, and had spent time with Aleister Crowley and his cronies (a man I never could stand, either in polite conversation or in the bedroom), but Crowley was being kept busy at the time with MI6's ridiculous notions of using astrology in interrogation techniques, and so I had Friedrich all to myself. He really was the most wonderful companion for me at that time in my life. We shared similar passions, including archaeology, tasting of exotic cultures and foods, poetry – he presented me with a beautiful edition of Homer's *Odyssey*, on the understanding that only he should read from it to me.

I do believe I would have married him, although I had sworn against it. Neither of us was new to love, and I had certainly come to view it as an emotion born either of convenience or desperation. His presence was teaching me otherwise, until we arrived on Crete.

We had the intention of finding the Throne of Zeus on that war-torn island. Hitler had expressed an interest, and Friedrich made him vague promises in order to guarantee safe conduct through Crete, by then under Nazi rule, along with a 'protection unit' of thirty men. I am aware that the popular version of events places me on the island before war came to it. This is not the case; I arrived to dig for the Throne at Hitler's behest. You may find this reprehensible and to that I can only repeat my earlier sentiment – back then I failed to see why I should be asked to be more morally upstanding than others on the basis of my personal fortune. If it eases the sting, I could tell you that I had no intentions of giving Hitler the Throne, if I had found it. I would have kept it for myself, as I have done with all my treasures. But we never did find it. We found something much more interesting.

There are a number of caves in Crete, but Pythagoras had described seeing the Throne, a vast construction of ivory and gold, at Zeus' birthplace, and only two caves laid claim to that particular honour – the Dikteon Cave and the Ideon Cave. We started at the Dikteon, our first choice; vast stalactites and stalagmites greeted us, and an eerie, pervading humidity that dampened the clothes and the spirits in minutes. After two weeks in its depths with nothing to show, we moved onto the Ideon, without much hope of success.

Mount Ida, upon which the Ideon Cave was situated, was deserted, apart from the few remaining women in a local village. There were no men to be found; we assumed they were hiding in the mountains, as part of the local resistance, but we were never threatened directly. The women tried desperately to get us to leave, telling us it wasn't safe. They spoke of horrors in the mountains, a monster that incited men to madness. Friedrich started to write down their stories in a black notebook he kept about his person at all times. I thought at first he was horrified, trying to make sense of such savage myths, but he took to reading the book at night, by the light of the lamp in the thin canvas tent we shared, before we made love. His body was gentle as ever but his mind was elsewhere, on a battlefield of its own making, rejoicing in blood and death. He was by no means alone. Half of the men assigned to protect us vanished during our ascent of Mount Ida. We thought we heard them shouting on the wind, from far above us, in the following days. Their words were unintelligible.

Ideon Andron, or the Cave of the Shepherdess, as the locals called it, was not a challenging cave. The large opening, a great ragged hole torn into the rock, led down into a grand space, with crenellated formations running along its sides like liquid. The ground was easy to walk upon, in the main, and there was a sense of peaceful hospitality to the interior. I did not feel that sense of dread that sometimes pervades these places deep under the earth. I felt quite certain that the Throne of Zeus was not to be found there; there was no residue of power, of greatness, in the rock.

The main chamber led into a series of smaller ones, just as benign, making an easy path into the mountain. I felt nothing – I have always put great store in my natural instincts when it comes to archaeology – but Friedrich seemed certain we were on the brink of a major discovery. He claimed to see colours in the rock face leading him, and he found a tunnel, barely big enough to squeeze through. His excited voice floated back to me as he emerged into a previously undiscovered chamber, describing a lake of such natural beauty, filled with red, blue, yellow and green gems, embedded into the walls. Of course, I followed him down – and found nothing of any import. The utter blackness of the chamber fought to overwhelm the flickering light of Friedrich's dynamo torch.

It was possible to make out a small pool into which water trickled from the smooth sides of the natural cavern. Dampness pervaded the rock, lowering the temperature, making my skin clammy. A sense of deep unease, of trespass, overtook me. I am afraid of nothing, but the memory of the feeling that conquered me then still makes my stomach clench. I knew I should not be there, but Friedrich and the men that followed me in did not share my emotion, and I could not explain it to them.

I begged Friedrich to come with me, out of that chamber, but he did not see me, or hear me. He talked only of the colours, of the wondrous beauty he beheld. He, and the eight men remaining in our party, were in paroxysms of delight. They stripped off and plunged into the pool, although it must have been icy. Their whoops and howls, animalistic, followed me as I crawled away, back through the tunnel, and returned to our tent to wait.

I read from my Homer for a while, wishing for Friedrich to return and speak to me of those great journeys. Then I slept, and when I awoke it seemed to me all sense of time had been lost; day, night, hours, minutes, meant nothing. I lay still and listened to the men screaming.

Fear cuts through us, and divides humanity into two sides: those who are paralysed by the terror they feel, and those who must act. I could not have stayed in that tent any more than I could have run away. I had to know, no matter if it cost me my sanity, my life, what was happening in that final cavern. I squeezed into the tunnel, and climbed through utter blackness, too terrified to use a torch, every inch taking an eternity.

A faint light beckoned me onwards, no more than a pinkish haze. As I grew closer it intensified into a red miasmic glow that threw grotesque shadows on the walls. As I moved into the mouth of the tunnel and looked upon a vivid, terrible tableau, I could make sense of only the smallest details: the spray of blood on the lantern, suspended above the pool; the gore that fell from it in slowed time, each droplet like the tick of a metronome to which played the music of madness; a man up to his chest in the water, beneath the flow of blood, his head flung back to catch it in his mouth. He brought his hands to his eyes and groped for the meat of his eye balls, clawing them out of their sockets and smashing them together, then rubbing the pulped remains over his cheeks as if lathering soap for a bath. I saw a group of men wrestling, grunting, writhing in a heap, biting each other, attempting to rip out throats, dismember, pull apart whatever they could find, to leave gouged, lumpen corpses.

And Friedrich – that naked, beautiful body of his, thin and straight and golden in that bloodied light – was locked in a standing embrace with a woman I had never seen before, spilling his essence into her with intense concentration, as she sunk her fingers into his chest, broke his ribs with such ease and reached beyond, taking his lungs and pulling them out, stretching them, so that they formed great veined and patterned wings, undulating in the air, spreading out from his coupling like a butterfly on the brink of first, trembling flight.

He came to fulfilment, an expression of blind delight I recognised, and then dropped to his knees and fell backwards. The wings fell with him, splattering the rocks and earth. His head moved; he lived, for a time.

I moved forward, intent on running to him, but the woman— the woman—

She looked at me.

She was very young, no more than sixteen, an Aphrodite with limpid eyes and a mass of long white hair that flowed over her thighs. With Friedrich's blood glistening on her, she held out her hands to me, and I thought it was not a summons so much as a supplication. Did she ask for help? I shook my head, crouched low; my instinct for survival held me close. I felt the power of her, and yet she wore the expression of an innocent, even as the men screamed around her and ripped each other to pieces in her presence.

And then she changed. As I watched, she aged, to a woman in her thirties, a fuller body, plumping out into fecundity before my eyes, her breasts heavy, the line of her chin thickening. Her attention did not waver from me as she clapped her hands together, once, twice, three times, and the sound, like thunder, reverberated in the cave, so loud, so loud, that the remaining mutilated men dropped to their knees and covered their ears with their hands.

She lifted her eyebrows at me, as if to say: You see how it is? And she smiled. There was such boredom in that smile, a terrible, tired, mirthless expression. This meant nothing to her. Friedrich meant nothing. My fear underwent a sudden transformation into rage, vast and overwhelming.

I found myself shouting at her, shouting Friedrich's name, what she had taken away from me, the things we had done, the love we had shared. I wanted his meaning restored to him. I came out of the tunnel and stood tall, not caring to survive in a world in which someone so fine could have been used as a momentary indulgence and then destroyed. I told the monster of that mountain – this is love. This is suffering, and this is life. This is a tale worth telling.

And she listened.

The men died in quiet groans, taking their time, and she listened to me with the intense eyes of a starving child. I talked on, my tongue freed by my terror, and I told her of the world outside, of the war, and before then, the men I had known and the beautiful items I had found in the earth and brought home to the quiet chill of England in autumn. I talked until my throat was hoarse, and my breath came in gasps, and still she listened. She never moved. The last man sounded his death rattle and she did not move, although she seemed smaller to me, her expression hardening, hardening, until I realised she was no longer flesh, but a statue, encrusted in my stories.

I stopped speaking, ran my swollen tongue over my lips, felt the desert dryness of my throat. The light from the suspended lantern had turned a pure, clear, yellow, and the bodies of the men, including Friedrich, were intact, without blemish.

I crawled away, back through the tunnel. I climbed into my tent, found my canteen of water, and took a long, long drink, until there was no water left. Then I fell asleep.

The women of the local village tell me they found me on the slopes of Mount Ida, but I do not remember getting there. They took care of me for many weeks until I returned to sanity. They were a soothing balm on a distraught mind, and I never learned their names, or even how to tell them apart. They made up a community without men. It came to me over time that the men were not away fighting for the resistance;

they did not live on this mountain, for a man who got close to the monster would most assuredly be driven to insanity. I began to understand what the monster was, and it came to me that I had found the most unique and precious artefact in the world, perhaps the one I had been searching for all along.

I decided to capture it.

I used only women. I waited out the war, and then I arranged, with the help of the Greek and the English governments, for my treasure to be transported to a place where I could keep it powerless, unable to affect the male sex.

I don't suppose anybody will understand my decision to bring the monster to Skein Island. I've never really cared for what people thought of me. But I do wish that I could tell the women who make their earnest declarations that I did not set up this retreat for them. I set it up so I could be alone with the monster who murdered my love, and so I would always have new stories to tell her.

I keep her trapped in my words. I hold her prisoner, and that is what she deserves.

I switch off the torch and the darkness reaches out to me, wraps me up. Outside, the wind blows, loud and lonely, over the emptiness of the island: the bungalows, in which a few of us, strangers to each other, sleep; the still, blue depths of the swimming pool, untouched by the wind and rain; the rough grasses that cover the cliffs, giving way to a long gravel path that leads up to a blue front door of a silent white house.

I creep into the bedroom and undress. I slide under the duvet, and lie there, listening to my breathing, trying to make my body relax into sleep, unable to cast the images of Amelia's story from my mind.

A thought occurs to me.

Someone pointed a camera at the door in front of the cupboard at the back of the library. My heart tells me it is not to stop people from getting in. It is to stop something from getting out.

CHAPTER SIX

David didn't change clothes after work.

He Googled 'Skein Island', read the Wikipedia entry and found a few old photos from the sixties of women holding hands in a circle, and of the outside of the chalets where they stayed. As the evening drew in, he made an omelette, then watched a documentary about the Arctic Circle. He sat very still, on the sofa, listening for sounds outside the front door such as the scrape of a key in the lock, the drag of a suitcase up the path. Eventually, he picked up his wallet and left the house.

At The Cornerhouse, Arnie was in his usual seat, sipping a pint. David raised an arm at him, then dropped it. He walked across the room, weaving around the tables and the other men in their small, huddling groups, and was greeted with an expression of surprised dislike.

'I thought this place wasn't good enough for you.'

'I wanted to ask you something,' David said.

'It'll have to wait. Game's about to start.' Arnie pulled out a seat and nodded towards it. David sat down and looked back at the bar; Mags was there, her hands on her hips, and the four cubes were already lined up on the counter.

'I'm not serving,' warned Mags.

'He knows,' said Arnie.

'Is he playing, then?'

David opened his mouth, and Arnie laid a hand on his arm. 'Course he is. Why else would he be here?'

'Right.' She fixed David with her gaze. 'You're after Geoff, then. Come on, Geoff, get yourself up here.'

One of the men sitting by the bar stood up and fiddled with his striped tie. He wore thick bifocals that magnified his gaze. Even without them, it would have been impossible to miss that his attention was fixed on the cubes. He crossed to them, and stood in front of them, blinking. His hair was sleek and black; combined with the glasses, he reminded David of a mole.

'Go on, Geoff, make a choice, there's a dear.'

'I, um, don't know.'

The tension in the room was growing. There were perhaps ten men sitting at tables, fanning out in a semi-circle from the bar, nursing their pints, leaning forward.

Geoff moved his hand towards the cubes, then withdrew it. David heard the men's exhalation of breath, and realised he'd been holding his own breath too. He whispered to Arnie, 'What's the game about?' but Arnie flapped his hand until he was quiet again.

'What did you choose last time, love?' said Mags, crossing her arms under her breasts, displaying her cleavage in her sheer blouse like a bird fluffing out its feathers.

'Blue,' said Geoff. He had a gruff voice, but the tremor within it was easily audible.

'And was that lucky for you?'

He flinched, and said, 'No.'

'Well then, probably best to keep away from such an unlucky colour,' she told him, with a conspiratorial raise of her eyebrows.

'Right,' he said. 'Right. Green.'

Mags picked up the green cube and turned it over and over between her long, painted fingernails. 'You sure?'

Geoff pushed the bridge of his glasses back up his nose with one finger. Nobody else moved. 'Yeah,' he said, eventually. 'Yeah.'

She handed him the cube. He held it in the palm of his left hand and touched the top surface with his right index finger, then squeezed it between finger and thumb.

The lid of the cube popped open.

Geoff reached in, very carefully, and pulled out a small white square of paper.

The room sighed, a slow release of excitement. David glanced at Arnie, and saw a strange mixture of sympathy and relief on his face as he sat back in his chair, his shoulders slumped.

'Another IOU, is it?' said Mags. She plucked the white square from Geoff's hand, along with the green cube. Then she popped the paper under one bra strap, and gave Geoff a big smile, her teeth bared to the room. 'I'll have to think of something else you can do for me. Right, who did I say was next?' David watched her head turn toward him, and she fixed him with a calm, superior gaze. Some sort of power emanated from her; the power of a High Priestess at an ancient ceremony, he thought, or maybe the power of an aging diva, on stage, certain of the undivided attention of her audience.

He broke the gaze, and appealed to Arnie. 'Listen, all I want to know is what happened on Skein Island. Did your wife's letters ever mention what took place there? Why she decided not to come home?'

'Why do you want to know? Marianne will tell you all about it when she gets back, won't she? Or are you not so sure of that any more?' He chuckled, a sound like a dry cough. 'We'll talk about it after.'

Mags tapped each cube with a long fingernail, three times each, like a summoning ritual.

'I don't have time for this,' said David.

'Then get out.' Arnie stared him down.

Mags called, 'Come on, handsome, get up here and pick a colour before closing time. You can't do any worse than Geoff, can you?' She pointed to Geoff, who had retreated to a far table, slumped over, his chin in his hand. Still he watched Mags and the cubes. David got the feeling that if Geoff had been given the opportunity to guess again, he would have taken it, no matter what it cost him.

'How much time do you think we have?' said Mags.

David stood up. He walked over to Mags and the cubes. He had the strongest suspicion, from the way she held her chin high and grinned at him, that it wouldn't matter what colour he picked. She already had the result planned, and, whatever it was, she was looking forward to it.

But the cubes were close now, and they exerted a pull that he hadn't experienced before. He wanted to touch them. And he wanted to win. It was an exciting sensation, this desire to play. For the first time since Marianne had left he felt in control once more.

It was purely his decision – to play, to guess, to name the colour. He looked at each one in turn, and thought through his options, forcing himself to take his time.

The cubes had markings on them. Carvings. Intricate work. The red one bore a shield, the blue a short sword, or a knife perhaps. The green had one long straight line on it, and the yellow had a scroll. They looked heraldic, or maybe older. Classical in design.

It would be too obvious to go for green. Yellow or blue, perhaps? Blue was the colour of truth, of sunny skies and deep seas. Marianne loved blue. The night before she had left for Skein Island she had been wearing her favourite dark blue waistcoat.

Yellow, then – a scroll could contain answers. But the pull to the red cube was too strong to deny.

'Red,' he said.

Mags lifted her eyebrows and opened her mouth. It was such an artful expression of surprise that he felt sure it must be fake. 'Sure?' she said.

He wouldn't give her the satisfaction of changing his mind. 'Yes.'

'Right then. Bit of an action man, we've got here. No messing. Here you go.'

She picked up the red cube and he held out his palm for it, just as Geoff had done before. It was warm and wooden. He felt around the top, found a small depression and pushed it in, and the lid popped open.

Inside was one black marble.

David took it from the cube and held it up. The intense concentration of the men as they focused on the marble was overwhelming; he felt them lean forward, yearning for it.

'First time lucky,' said Mags. 'Come on.'

'Where?'

'A trip to the back room,' she said, as if he should have known. She adjusted the ruffles on her scarlet blouse and smacked her lips together, and a mixture of terror and sexual desire swept over him, horrified him. He was a prisoner to it.

'No, I don't need it. One of the others can go,' he said. He put the marble back in the cube, closed it up, and put it back in line with the others.

'Doesn't work that way, dear.' She grabbed his hand. He felt the points of her fingernails pressing into his skin. 'You play, you pay.'

'No, I—'

Arnie came up beside him, patted him on the back, and David found himself walking around the side entrance of the bar, the other men crowding around him, pushing him onwards.

'You always win first time out,' whispered Arnie, in his ear. 'To give you the taste.'

'Just relax and enjoy it,' said Mags. She held out a shot glass, half-filled with a brown, viscose liquid. 'A shot of brandy. To get you going.'

'Going where?' he said, and everyone laughed. Reality was fading; everything was moving more slowly. He couldn't remember why he was afraid. He took the glass, drained it, said, 'That wasn't brandy,' as he tasted oranges and something fresh, like mint. He was getting an erection.

One of the men said, close to his right cheek, 'I don't know anything about Skein Island. She never talked to us again. All she left was a note.'

'But the letters,' David said. Was it Arnie talking? 'The cards. Birthday cards.' His voice sounded deeper, like an echo in a cavern, the sound spreading low, through the muscles of his abdomen.

'I've got a lady friend in Bedfordshire. I asked her to send them.' There was a snort, and hot, beery breath filled David's nose. The smell was unbearably potent and for a moment he couldn't breathe. 'Couldn't let Marianne think she'd been deserted. But that's what happened. Gone, she was. She wanted to be gone.'

Mags shoved Arnie and the other men back, flapping her hands, then led David down the corridor that ended in a windowless storage room, filled with orange crates of empty bottles, cardboard boxes and silver kegs.

Set in one wall was a small, white door with four coloured squares painted upon it: red, blue, yellow and green. Mags opened it with a large brass key, attached to a gold chain around her neck, and it swung back to reveal a total, consuming blackness from which palpable warmth emanated. From within the dark, David sensed a want, a need. Something called to him. It was as if Marianne had said his name; he felt his erection twitch in response.

He stepped through the doorway.

The men were cheering, very far away. A sweet smell enveloped him, like a cloud of perfume left behind by a beautiful woman at a party. He wanted to find her; he pushed through a crowd of faceless people to reach her. The cheering grew louder, ahead of him, becoming the rise and fall of many people. His legs were being pushed apart and he felt something large between his knees, under his buttocks. He fell backwards, ended up sitting astride it, and it began to move at speed, towards the thin, horizontal strip of intense blue daylight – the purest, cleanest sky he had ever seen. His body shook under the pressure, the sensation of speed, and the cheers became deafening, drowning out his own heartbeat as he crashed into the living picture at the end of the tunnel.

His hands were full; he looked down, and saw a long wooden pole and thin strips of leather. The horse upon which he sat had a black mane that was streaming in the wind, and when he looked up he saw the enemy, ahead, dressed in black and thundering towards him on an enormous charger.

There was nothing else for it but to lean forward, brace himself for impact, and swing around the lance, aiming for the breastplate, trying to block out all other thoughts but to win.

The collision was the most intense delight of his life; he felt his lance crack into the chest of his opponent, who reeled back and fell to the ground. The crowd roared their approval, banging drums, clapping hands to make a cacophony of elation. He dropped his broken lance and saluted them, over and over. The cheers only grew louder. A pink haze filled his vision, then encased him in slick, warm wetness. It was her, his prize.

He was soaked in the ecstasy he had won, drowned in it, pulled down and through, for the longest time. Then the pink haze of her love withdrew, along with her scent, and that final loss caused a crescendo of intense pain. He was a hero no more. Just plain old David, abandoned. Lonely. It was more than he could bear.

After an age, the visions receded just enough to bring him back to his body. He got to his feet and staggered forward until he collided, hard, with a solid wall. The shock of it brought tears to his eyes. He put his hands against freezing brickwork and crouched down, making himself as small as he could manage, hoping she wouldn't find him again and take away everything he had ever known, ever loved. He had been aware of that power in her, so much greater than his own, so different from the soft, tentative touches of women he had known.

Like Marianne – so tender, so hesitant to let him possess her, to find enjoyment in sex, at the beginning. Then that last night, when she had demanded pleasure. And he had given her what she wanted, but it had made him uncomfortable to be her object. That unsettled feeling had turned out to be the first tremors of the earthquake that now shook him to pieces, left him unsalvageable.

The thought of Marianne flooded into his emptiness. He punched the wall – once, twice. Again. He felt the pain, the blood on his knuckles, but the pain was welcome. It reminded him of what he was, of his ability to protect himself, to overcome, as a man should. But the wall did not shrink away from his fists. There was no way out of the darkness.

A bright light switched on overhead.

David looked up, squinting, and made out the plastic casing of a security light. A cobweb was strung between it and the wall. A light film of drizzle hung on the strands of the cobweb. The banality of it was bewildering.

'I told you not to come back,' said a woman, near his right ear. He flinched away from her voice, and she said, 'What have you done? Jesus.' She knelt in front of him. He managed to stay still as she picked up his hand and examined his knuckles. 'Can you get up?' She was surprisingly strong, pulling him up to his feet, and her black jacket, white shirt, neat black hat, suddenly became familiar.

'Sam.'

Under the security light she was as bright as an angel. 'I told you he wouldn't come back here.'

He couldn't understand what she meant. Then, in a rush, he placed himself outside the library, and the confusion hit him hard, gave him an attack of shivers. How had he got there? He had no memory of leaving the pub. 'I didn't…'

'Have you been drinking?'

He remembered the glass Mags gave to him, and nodded. 'The Cornerhouse.'

'Right, well, you've had enough.' She tugged his arm, and he followed her to her car. During the drive, he kept getting traces of the distinctive perfume, but every time he turned his head towards it, it disappeared again. It hadn't been real, not real in the way that Sam was. He began to understand that he'd had some sort of hallucination. Never had feelings been so intense, so painful, so pleasurable.

Sam pulled the car up outside her house, and he followed her inside. She motioned for him to follow her upstairs; he brushed the string of bells hanging from the banisters, and the tinkling noise was pleasant, restful. How amazingly tired he was, but Sam steered him into the bathroom, and got him to sit on the side of the bath as she dug out antiseptic, cotton wool and plasters from under her sink. She examined his knuckles, then began to dab at them with the antiseptic.

'She's not coming back,' David said. He wasn't sure if he was talking about Marianne or the woman who had encased him in the vision. He wanted them both.

'Of course she is. It's one week at a holiday camp. She'll be back, and she'll be so pleased to see you. That's how a holiday works.'

'Not this one.'

'What makes you think Skein Island is any different?' Sam peeled the backing from a large fabric plaster and smoothed it over his middle knuckle. 'It's just middle-class, middle-aged women discovering themselves. Am I doing the right things? Living the right life? Who the hell knows? Seven days on an island off the coast of Devon isn't going to tell you, but it's free and it's better than getting drunk and punching walls.'

'I'm sorry,' he said, automatically, to the bitterness in her voice. He reached out and touched her face. She looked so angry, so young. How could she be so dismissive? She let him cup her chin, and the anger faded as he told her, 'I'm so sorry that you found me like this. I don't understand what's happening. I've had some kind of... dream.'

'I told you to stay away from The Cornerhouse. The men who come out of there are wasted, and they can't wait to go back again. It was investigated a while back. We thought maybe they were drinking home brew, something really strong, but we didn't find anything. You don't want to end up like that. You're freezing. Come on.'

'No, I need to tell you—'

'Come on,' she told him, and he got up and trod along behind her, across the corridor to a darkened bedroom, warm from the radiator under the window. She drew the purple curtains and pulled back the duvet on the neat bed. 'Take off your clothes and get in.'

'No, I should go...' But he couldn't find the will to move, and when she crossed to him, crouched down and started to remove his shoes, he had the strongest desire to cry. It was all he could do to stand there and keep his face still, in case she looked up.

She put his shoes neatly against the skirting board, then took off his socks and slipped them into each shoe. Then she stood up and started on his shirt. He let her work the buttons, pull it from him, and when she put both hands against his chest the warmth of her was astounding. 'Get into bed,' she said.

'No.'

He stared at her, watched her take in his denial. He couldn't obey her instruction; he had to find control once more.

'Get in.'

'No.'

'Please. I... Please, get warm.'

He put his hands over hers, then led her to the bed, and pulled her down with him. Underneath the duvet, he wrapped his arms around her; she moved back against him, her bottom pressed into his groin.

'There,' he said.

They didn't talk. Although he was tired, he couldn't get close to sleep. It evaded him every time he grew near to it. He matched his breathing to Sam's, in and out, and he thought of how quickly everything had changed. He could not have imagined, only a week ago, that he would be in bed with another woman. Only terrible men did that, not men like him. And yet it did not feel wrong to be there. Sam was fully clothed, and he still had his trousers on, and it wasn't even about who was wearing what. It was a comfort at a terrible time. It was as if a death had happened, and those left had to find a way to carry on. How they carried on mattered to nobody any more, nobody important.

'This is really happening,' she said. 'Yes. It's okay.'

'You don't get it. Nothing ever happens to me. I feel like I'm always waiting for something, a moment.'

He put his hand on her breast. He wanted to show her how easy it was to change fate. 'I know how it feels. To want things to be different.'

'No, you don't,' she said. 'I don't want things to be different. I want me to be different.' She touched the back of his hand, and he took it as a sign that she wanted him to continue, to stroke her nipple, bring her to feeling. He touched her with the curiosity of exploration, without sexual thoughts in his head, and remembered the girl who had lived down the road when he was little, and the games they had played together – looking at each other, wondering how it all fit together. The delight in the fact that people fitted together at all; that was what came back to him through the night, and even the next morning, as he watched her make coffee and toast in her tiny kitchen, and realised he couldn't wait for the end of the week. He had to see Marianne.

* * *

'It doesn't mean anything,' said Sam, once they had eaten.

'That's not true. I'm just not sure what it does mean, that's all.'

'It means you were lonely and drunk.'

'No, I wasn't – listen, I have to go. God, that sounds awful, but I really do have to go.'

'You're going there, aren't you? Skein Island? There's no way to get on it. They don't take men.'

'I'll find a way,' David said. The thought of persevering, and accomplishing, was all that was keeping him going. He needed to see his wife, to tell her what he had learned last night. Maybe her mother had never gone to the island after all. Maybe she was dead, had been dead for years. That could be the starting point for solving the mystery together. The case of the disappearing mother, and the father that covered it up for years.

He could picture it clearly, and how it would play out. At the end they would be the triumphant husband and wife.

'Go on then,' Sam said. 'Just forget about last night. That'll be easier for everyone.' She had curled in on herself, her lilac dressing gown pulled tight over her breasts, no strength visible in the dropping lines of her tiny body.

'No, I don't want to forget it, okay? I'll come and see you when I'm back. We'll talk properly.' But he did want to forget it, was already filing it away as a stupid mistake after some sort of hallucination that he never wanted to think about again. Except that the two things had become linked in his mind. Being wrapped up in his vision, and in her. Being the centre of a fresh, clean world.

He kissed her on the cheek, and she pushed him away. 'I hope it all works out for you.'

'You too.'

He let himself out of her house, and ran home, pumping cold, cold air into his lungs, calculating what he was going to pack and how much money he would need to find a way onto Skein Island.

* * *

Nobody would take him.

The afternoon sky began to darken, and the few fishermen left on the quay all told him the same thing: men weren't allowed there; it wasn't worth the money David was offering to break the rules; couldn't he tell that a storm was coming? They were battening down the boats, and heading inside for the evening. But when David followed them into The Ship and Pilot, a small, grey pub set back from the harbour wall, he found a mass of old men with grizzled, suspicious faces, eyeing him as he stood in the doorway.

David took a few steps forward. The small fire in the grate was barely flickering, and the wood upon it hissed. Hanging from the ceiling, suspended with catgut, were dusty bottles containing delicate sailing ships built from matchsticks and tiny scraps of cloth. On the mantelpiece – one long stretch of dark, uneven wood – sat four small cubes. Red, blue, yellow, green. He felt the pull of them.

He stepped back, nearly fell over his own feet, and hurried outside, to their laughter.

In the harbour, the solitary boats were pulling at the hefty blue ropes that moored them, tossing their heads like horses at the approaching rain, visible over the channel. David stood against the thick sea wall and looked around, at the hills, pressing close. He couldn't return to Wootton Bassett, not now he'd seen the cubes here. They were a secret that every other man somehow understood, and from which he had been excluded. Finding Marianne, conquering this adventure, was more important than ever. If he could solve one mystery, he could solve them all.

'Night's getting in.'

So he had been under observation; a young, heavy-set man was watching him from a small, blue fishing boat. A stuffed doll, like a scarecrow, was tied tight by its waist and neck to the prow. The man was heaving up a rope, hand over hand. David watched as an empty, crusted lobster pot, stinking of the bottom of the sea, broke free from the waves and was tossed on to the deck.

'Will you take me out?' David said. The scarecrow had been dressed in a blue overall and a sou'wester. In contrast, the young fisherman wore black jeans and a grey ski-jacket, modern, stylish. His long curly hair flopped around his ears in the wind.

'I'm just putting her to bed.' He didn't have much of a local accent.

'I'll pay anything you like.'

'Where do you want to go, eh? Night fishing?'

'Skein Island.'

The fisherman laughed without making a sound. 'You can't get on there, mate.'

'Just to look. From the boat. Just to sail round it once and come back again.'

'It'll be a rough ride.'

'That's fine,' David said. He got out his wallet, sensing victory. 'How much?'

'We'll do that later. Come over and put on a jacket.' The man set out a metal walkway from the side of the boat to the quay, and David edged across its slippery surface.

He had sailed before, at South Cerney, when he was a teenager – a friend's father had kept a boat moored there – but this grey sea, choppy with intention, was very different from that calm stretch of water. The boat bucked underneath his feet as they hit the mouth of the harbour, and as the rain picked up so did the swell of the waves. David stood next to the fisherman at the wheel in the tiny cabin, undecorated apart from a small ceramic mermaid placed on the sill of the window, her arms stretched up, exposing enormous breasts with red-tipped nipples. The wheel was turned first one way, then the other, apparently without thought, somehow making sense of the ocean.

'Your wife out there, is she?' The fisherman nodded. 'We get 'em every now and again. Lovesick types, jealous types. You don't look like the usual.'

'What do they usually look like?'

'Thick. It's no good depending on women that way, is it? Either you're on top or they are. Dog eat dog. Eat bitch.'

In a fit of pure malice David said, 'Married, are you?' already knowing the answer.

The man gave his silent laugh, shoulders shrugging. 'You won't catch me playing that game.'

'That's what they all say.'

'You mean that's what you used to say.' He was right, of course. During A Levels, sitting around in the common room with their legs slung over the frayed arms of the chairs and a ghetto blaster playing rap or indie as loud as they dared, he and his friends had talked about girls as the enemy. To be overwhelmed, taken, given what for, then left if they became too demanding in some way that was never specified. It had felt expected of them to talk that way, no matter what they felt inside about themselves or their sexuality, which had to remain hidden from view. Women were seen as a mysterious foe back then, lying in wait across a wasteland of years, shrouded in fog. Not quite real.

'There it is,' said the fisherman.

Ahead, cliffs rose from the sea, close and dark. David watched the fisherman turn the wheel, and the boat struggled against the surging waves, drawing parallel to the island.

'Once around and we're heading back.'

David nodded. 'I'll just go out on the deck, get a better look.'

'Hold on to the rail, then.'

He slid back the cabin door and stepped on to the deck. The rain and wind hit him like an attack; he braced himself, managed to close the door behind him, and gripped the rail, feeling terror of the deep seep into him.

Marianne was on that island, and he couldn't get any closer. He had harboured visions of diving in, swimming across clear water with powerful strokes of his arms, to find her on the shore, waiting, with a look in her eyes that unmistakeably meant *I love you*. But the walls of the cliffs, the black rocks that surrounded them, were a rebuttal of his imaginings. He couldn't see anything but the rock face.

He looked at his hands on the rail. The strength of them, holding on.

The man at the library had tried to make Marianne obey, bend to his will, and she had told him no. How had she done that? All the power in his body was nothing compared to her – her ability to change the situation, take life and shake it out, make it work out differently. His hands couldn't hold her; the cubes had shown him that. A woman's power to control men – Marianne, Mags, the damsel from the back room of The Cornerhouse – beat back the strength of his grip every time.

He let go of the rail.

At first he kept his balance, tilting his body to keep upright, riding the motion of the boat. Then it bucked, so hard and fast, like a bull underneath him, and his thighs hit the rail and his body went over, turning a full somersault into the rain. The liquid ice of the water encased him and froze him, instantly, leaving no way to move, no way to think. When he surfaced, sucking up a breath as huge as the sky, he realised his lifejacket was the only thing that had saved him, bringing him up to the surface.

What are you doing? said Marianne, quite clearly, in his ear. He couldn't reply. The waves slapped his face, ripped at his hair and throat. The boat wasn't close; he couldn't see it anywhere. He tried to swim in a circle to catch sight of it, and couldn't even manage that. The sea kept dragging him onwards, insistent, and suddenly a black rock loomed up at his face. He threw out his hands, caught it, felt the slam and the scrape of his body against it, couldn't hold on, and was tossed back. Stinging ribbons of pain twined around his palms and wrists, and then he was thrown at the rock again. This time he didn't get his arms out; his head connected with the rock, and there was no pain, no sea, no island. Just the sense that something had to be done, didn't it have to be done? And Marianne saying, *David, David, what are you doing?* over and over in his left ear, her voice so sad, so sorry, that all he wanted was to hold her and tell her that everything was going to be—

PART TWO

CHAPTER SEVEN

The swimming pool is closed.

Maybe it's too early. But my watch says ten minutes past ten. And I couldn't wait around the bungalow any more, sitting at that table surrounded by toast crumbs and cups of cold coffee, watching Rebecca pace and listening to Kay read aloud from the declaration I stole.

Something is wrong on this island. Something that lives in a small room next to the library of declarations, behind a door marked with four squares. I don't know what it means, and I don't know what to do. I can't run; there's nobody to take me from this island.

Rebecca doesn't believe it, anyway.

'They'll find out that you broke in, and they'll come for you,' she said over the noise of the rain. She was applying jam to her third piece of toast with absolute precision, up to each corner. Behind her, Kay stopped pacing and pulled a face.

'Maybe she's not dead after all,' she said. 'Maybe Amelia faked her own death. For some reason. Maybe she's crazy.'

'She was obviously crazy,' said Rebecca. 'But that declaration could have been written years ago. Does the handwriting match the signature on the letter you received, Marianne?'

'I don't know. Maybe.'

Rebecca raised her eyebrows at me. 'What are you trying to convince yourself of? There's no conspiracy. There's you and Kay, breaking the rules. And they will catch you.'

I thought she was right. But I waited for hours. Where are they, the nameless 'they'? When are they coming? Eventually I couldn't wait any more. I came here, to the pool, wanting the empty expanse of the water to hide in. I can't deny that I'm looking for an ally, and Inger looks like just the kind of person who might step in and save me, if saving is needed. Would she turn her calm, capable face to them, and tell them that they can't take me?

I'm letting my imagination run away with me. I've always loved a good story, and now I seem to be spinning one for myself. There has to be a simple explanation for all this. A confused old lady with Alzheimer's. A fable, a figment of imagination, someone pretending to write like Amelia would have. There are many alternatives, but none of them work at driving out Amelia's words. Of dispelling the feeling that crept over me as I stood next to that small door marked with four cubes.

And the swimming pool is still not open.

I knock on the glass door, but nobody comes.

I start a slow walk up to the white reception building. If there's no swimming today, perhaps there's an alternative

– yoga, or creative writing. The rain is, unbelievably, intensifying, but it doesn't matter; I'm already soaked through. The drops are smashing into my face like a punishment. By the time I reach the reception I have been hammered into a wet mess, my clothes sopping, my head and hands numb. The automatic doors admit me, and I squelch over to the main desk and look over the laminated timetable that is pinned to the display board.

The receptionist emerges from the door behind the desk and glances at me. She stops walking, and the glance becomes a stare. I can feel her deciding on what she's about to say. This is it. The moment is here.

'Marianne Percival?'

'Yes?'

'Mrs Makepeace is looking for you. She's just gone over to your bungalow, about ten minutes ago.'

'Mrs Makepeace?'

'The director. Of the island.' There's a flurry of rain and noise behind me. A woman is standing by the entrance, her long blue raincoat dripping, her hood pulled up, obscuring her face. She's a few inches shorter than me. Her raincoat skirts the ground, and the sleeves cover her hands. It was made for a much larger woman.

'Here she is,' says the receptionist, with acres of relief in her voice.

'I'm sorry,' I say to the woman in the raincoat. 'Is there a problem?' Now the moment is upon me, I'm determined to play it cool, to not admit to anything.

She pinches the hood between her thumbs and forefingers and slowly pulls it back before giving me a good look over. She's older than I expected, with big brown eyes and a blunt, businesslike fringe to her short hair. She has lines on her face, visible even from across the room. They run from the corners of her eyes to the corners of her mouth, as if she has spent years doing nothing but smiling. She looks intelligent, and charming, and like she could hold her own in an argument.

'Hello hello hello,' she says, staccato-fashion, 'I'm so delighted you're here. I was just about to organise a search party, which is ridiculous on an island this size, really, isn't it? I should be able to just go and stand outside and whistle, and everyone should come running. But, of course, I can't in this rain, can I?' She moves closer to me. 'I tried your bungalow but they said you were at the swimming pool, and then the pool was closed, which it's really not meant to be today, so that's something else I'm going to have to look into. But it turns out you're here! How lucky! You're soaked through. You really could do with a better coat for this weather. I need a few minutes of your time, Marianne – would that be okay?'

About halfway through her speech, I realise that she's nervous. I also remember that her name isn't Mrs Makepeace, whatever she might claim. Her name is Vanessa. Vanessa Spence. Or it was on the day I last saw her.

I'm looking at my mother.

Funny, but even as one part of my brain keeps repeating that fact, the other part manages to respond, in a perfectly normal voice, 'Yes, that's fine,' and my feet are following her around the reception desk, and into the small office behind it. My mother is saying, 'Oh good, well, let's not drag ourselves up to the main house right now, not in this weather. Why don't we just come through here, will this do?'

'Yes,' I say. I take off my coat and put it on the back of the seat on the nearside of the desk. She unbuttons her own coat quickly. Underneath she's wearing a double-breasted jacket with a short skirt in matching blue – another outfit that looks too big on her. She sits down opposite me and clasps her hands, interlacing her fingers on the desktop. Her fingernails are very short and unvarnished.

'You broke into my house last night,' she says. 'What were you looking for?'

I have no idea what to say. She's suddenly direct, and dynamic. She looks like she wants an answer, and quickly, but I can't provide it. Eventually, I manage one word. 'You.'

'I thought so.' She nods. She doesn't speak for a long moment. 'There's a lot to explain,' she tells me, as if I didn't know. 'I've tried to get it straight. When I heard you'd arrived I wanted everything to be clear, in my mind, so it would be ready for you. It would make sense. But I couldn't decide what bits I should tell you.'

'Tell me all of it.'

She smiles. 'I don't think that would be a very good idea.'

I can't call her mother, but I need to be sure. No – it's not that I'm unsure. It's that I need her to acknowledge it too. So I say, 'Vanessa?'

'Yes, I know, you want to be told what happened. That's why you're here. I never came back because I got a better offer. You're a wife now, too, aren't you? That's what you wrote on your form. You can't have been married for long so perhaps you won't understand this yet. Or perhaps you're just beginning to see how reductive terms like wife and mother can be. Is that why you acted on the letter I sent you?'

'You sent it?'

'Well, really, it's from Amelia, I suppose. The spirit of her. But I wrote it and signed it. It's difficult to explain. But it's all very important, so I'm going to have to try harder, aren't I? I've been waiting for this moment for years, and, forgive me for saying so, but you're not making it any easier.'

I don't remember hating her, before, but it would be very easy to start hating her now. She doesn't even pretend to care. She uses a slightly disappointed tone of voice on me, as if she deserves to. 'You waited for this? While you were in Bedford?'

'Bedford? Why on earth would I be in Bedford?'

'You wrote and said—'

'Ah.' She holds up a hand. 'Arnie. I'm guessing Arnie set that up. I should have realised he'd feed you some lies rather than let you find out what happened for yourself. Always attempting to control the situation, that was Arnie. Too clever for his own good.'

I bite back the instinct to remind her that he's not dead yet. I dare say she doesn't actually care. 'You never wrote any letters to me from Bedford? None?'

'I couldn't explain it in a letter. Not then, not now. It's the kind of thing that has to be done face to face.'

'So here I am. Better late than never. Perhaps you'd like to get on with it.'

She takes in a breath, as if I've shocked her. I'm glad. It makes me feel like her equal. 'All right,' she says. 'It's like this. Last night you took a declaration made by the founder of this island. So you know she was an amazing woman. I'm here because she asked me to take over the task of caring for this island, and reading aloud to the statue in the basement. I wouldn't choose to start there, but you saw the door with the four painted squares. You even opened it, didn't you? So it seems ridiculous to start anywhere else.'

I should feel something, but I can't conjure an emotion. Too many shocks in one morning, perhaps. 'You keep the… statue down there?'

'I go down to it with a pile of newly completed declarations from the week before, and I read the words out loud. Amelia always believed it prefers fresh stories.'

'So Amelia is dead? And you read to a statue because she asked you to?'

'Yes,' she says. 'Well done. You've got the basics.'

I look around the office: the white walls with one framed picture, a Vettriano print of a dancer in a flame-red dress; a traditional grey filing cabinet in the corner next to the window, where the venetian blind has been pulled, leaving the room in grainy semi-darkness.

Would it be better to simply walk away? I wish I had less self-control. Then I wouldn't have to rein in this instinct. I would leave the room and never talk to her again. But first I would say, no, shout—*You let a statue take priority over your child? Over me?*

'I know what you're thinking,' she says, 'and I certainly wouldn't have picked that as the first piece of information I'd give to you. Not if you hadn't read it for yourself. But you did, didn't you?' She sits back in her chair.

There's a light tapping at the door, and the receptionist pokes her head around. 'I just wanted to check if everything's okay?'

'Yes, thanks Carol.' My mother's pleasant face is back in place. 'We won't be much longer.'

'There's tea and coffee making things in the top drawer of the filing cabinet, if you want drinks.'

'Lovely, that will warm us up. You get on now, I'm fine to make it.'

Carol closes the door, and we're alone again.

'She's wondering what's going on. It's a strange day,' says my mother. She stands up, opens the drawer and brings out a small travel kettle. She checks it for water, then puts it on the carpet next to the skirting board and plugs it in. While it boils she fetches two mugs from the drawer, and shakes instant coffee from a jar into both. I watch her perform these actions as if we sit together this way every day, knowing each other, perhaps working together in this office, comfortable in this sudden silence.

The kettle boils. She pours water into the mugs and hands one to me, not even asking how I take it. She takes a sip of her own and sits backs down, leaving the kettle on the carpet. 'I came here for a week off,' she says. 'To sit around, do nothing, meet other women in unhappy marriages and have a good moan about it. Moaning is therapeutic, did you know that? I've seen it work here. A week of dedicated moaning about the sheer awfulness of their husbands, fathers, sons, and they're quite happy to take the ferry back to it all. I would have been too. I could have gone back to your father and stuck it out for decades. I might still be there now. I really mean that.'

I try to keep up with this monologue. She's beginning to relax into it, to say things the way she wanted to. We must have hit on how she pictured this meeting – her talking, me hanging on every word, mugs of coffee in hand. 'Back then, Amelia – Lady Worthington – still lived in the white house. She had built up this collection of rare things, beautiful things, that she loved to show off. I'll give you the tour, if you'd like. She held drinks twice a week, up at the house. Buying Skein Island from the government, setting it up, that was all her. It was a feminist statement back then, to come to the island. The world's most intelligent and dynamic women came here to talk to each other, to learn, and to be able to say that they'd been here. She was disappointed with how it ended up. The island became a joke, didn't it? People laugh about the idea of the place? They poke holes in it. No politics. No reality, I suppose they say.'

She sips her coffee, seems to remember the thread of her story, and her voice lowers once more. 'So Amelia asked me if I was enjoying the week, and I said yes, and we talked. Mainly small talk. It had been a hot week, and the other women had tans. She asked me why I didn't, and I remember I told her that nobody ever discovered the meaning of their existence whilst sitting on a sun-lounger. She thought this was hilarious. She never went out in the sun herself. She asked me about Arnie, and I described him. I told her Arnie would have loved to have been in charge of the world, with all his big ideas, and having to be a gardener in a small town outside Swindon was slowly killing him. And that's why she offered me the job. To be her Personal Assistant.'

It's as if the story has skipped forward, leaving out a vital piece of information. 'Sorry, why?'

'Because I understood what type of man he was, and what type of man he was never going to be,' she says. 'It made the whole process easier for Amelia to explain. As soon as she told me, I knew I had to stay, you see. I gradually took over running the whole operation. The island, the statue, the cubes. Amelia told me there are only four types of men in the world: red, blue, green and yellow.'

There is another light tap at the door. Carol appears once more. 'I'm really sorry about this,' she says. 'The coastguard is on the phone again.'

'No probs, Carol, we're done here,' says my mother. She gives me a kind, impersonal smile. 'Listen, Marianne, I'd love it if you could come to dinner tonight, up at the white house. We can carry on chatting. I really have to take this call, you see.' My mother stands up, and picks up her coat from the back of her chair.

'They're looking for someone,' says Carol, with an excited squeak in her voice. 'A man was out fishing yesterday and went overboard.'

'He won't wash up here,' says my mother, throwing Carol a look. 'The tide will take him on to the rocks further up the coast, past Allcombe. Shall we say five o'clock, Marianne? I've got into the habit of eating early. Yes, okay, Carol,' she says, as the receptionist flaps her hands at the thought of the coastguard waiting on the phone. The two of them bustle out of the office in a tangle of wet coat, leaving me alone.

I stand up, leaving the coffee untouched, and put on my sopping coat. As I walk past the reception desk I hear my mother in business mode, saying, 'I can appreciate that, but the rules here are absolute, and we have a number of influential backers who would be most upset to hear that we were being forced to… Yes, it would be much better if you were able to manage to conduct the search without landing, unless you have female crew members? No, of course not, so in that case we should aim to keep disruption to a minimum—'

The double doors slide open and the sound of her voice is cut off by the wind and rain. It's so fierce that I can't think of anything but the struggle to stand up, to walk forward, to make it back to the stillness of the bungalow so I can try to find the words for this evening, so I can try to understand why my mother left me for the sake of an old lady, a statue, and a scary story.

CHAPTER EIGHT

David woke up in a soft bed, a pastel blue duvet pulled up to his chin, the thick noise of rain on the roof overhead, and for a moment he thought he'd dreamed the boat, the quay, everything. But then the pain in his head stamped down and told him it was all true. It had happened.

He couldn't imagine how he was alive. But he was, and so he tried to be thankful for the headache. Even so, he wanted strong paracetamol, and some answers. He threw back the duvet and found his boxer shorts and trousers, freshly washed and dried, on the end of the bed. The room was another one of those feminine sanctuaries, with cushions and mirrors and an embroidered throw arranged over a small chair. The wooden roof sloped, and a skylight overhead gave him a view of dark, fast-moving clouds. He dressed as quickly as he could, heard a sound at the door, and realised a blonde woman was standing there, watching him. She was very attractive in a serious kind of way, with a straight line for a mouth, and frosted pink lipstick. Her white T-shirt and navy blue tracksuit bottoms looked like a uniform.

She held out a glass of effervescing water and said, 'Soluble aspirin.'

He took the glass and pressed it to his forehead. The icy touch of it made him gasp.

'It works better if you drink it,' she said, with her perfectly straight lips. So he drank it, the whole glass, in a few gulps, and then handed it back to her.

She nodded, and said, 'You shouldn't be alive.'

The phrasing was odd. Did she mean he was lucky to be alive? He said, 'Yes. Where am I?'

'Do you remember any of it? You were confused when I found you.'

'On the rocks?' he ventured.

'Yes. You were on the rocks. I swam out to you, helped you to the beach. I saved you.'

'Thank you,' he said again.

'It's my job.'

'Sorry?'

'I'm a lifeguard. Here on the island. My name is Inger.'

He noticed she had an accent, and put it together with her height and her white-blonde hair. He didn't understand what was happening, but at least he felt he had the measure of her. 'I'm on Skein Island, then?'

'Of course. You must be the first man to stand on this island for years. Although you shouldn't be standing at all. After what happened to you. You look very... healthy.'

'I don't feel it,' he said.

She touched his head with the back of her hand, like a nurse.

'I'm certain you shouldn't be walking around. I thought you had a concussion.'

'I've got a tough head. Actually, I'm starving.'

She assessed him with her gaze, then nodded. 'Come to the kitchen, then.'

He followed her out of the bedroom into an open-plan space, wooden and echoing. At the far end was a fitted kitchen and a rough oak table with two low benches. He sat on one of them, and watched her retrieve eggs from the fridge, and a saucepan from an overhead cupboard. Her capability, her economy of movement, was very calming. He could have watched her for hours.

'How did you – you couldn't have carried me?' he asked her, once the eggs were cooking.

'No, no, you were conscious when I found you. Just a little confused. You called me Sam.'

'I'm sorry if I was—'

'No,' she said. 'It was fine.'

He didn't want to think about what it meant to have said Sam's name. He hated that he could remember nothing about it.

Inger had somehow managed to deal with him, get him here, take off his clothes, put him to bed. 'Did you call a doctor? There's a doctor on the island, right?'

She slid his omelette onto a blue-rimmed plate, then took cutlery from a drawer and handed it to him. 'Yes, there's a doctor, but I— Men aren't allowed on the island.'

'Yes,' he said. 'But... yeah, okay.'

'I could get into trouble. For helping you. There are strict rules. I shouldn't have touched you. But I had to help you.'

'You're saying you should have left me?'

'I'm saying I know I couldn't leave you.' She enunciated each word precisely. 'And you're fine. Because I didn't.' She turned away and washed up the frying pan: the hot water tap, a squeeze of fairy liquid, the dishtowel rubbed around the pan in smooth, circular motions. He recognised her compartmentalisation – what she could handle, what kind of conversation she was prepared to have.

'So what now?' he said.

'It's getting late. Stay here tonight. Think about it in the morning.' She dried her hands on the dishtowel. 'But I think I might be able to get you on board the ferry on Saturday. There's a half-hour window after the boat docks before the guests are taken down to board. I can probably sneak you on, if the Captain is amenable. I think he will be.'

'To bribery, do you mean?' He thought of his backpack, his wallet, lost to him. 'I don't have any money. Anything.'

'I know. Don't worry. I have.'

'Why? I don't understand why.'

'Because I save people,' she said, as if that made everything clear.

The greyness of the day had thickened into early evening. Before long it would be dark. It was difficult to see Inger's expression clearly as he said, 'I need to get to my wife.'

She turned to him. 'Is that why you were out on the boat?'

'She's called Marianne. She's here.'

116

'Yes, of course. Marianne.' She smiled. 'So you both like the water, then.'

'What?'

'She comes to the swimming pool. Where I work. You'll see her on Saturday.'

'I need to see her now.'

'That's really not possible.'

'Please,' he said. He couldn't take her objections seriously. 'Please, if it could have waited until Saturday don't you think I would have taken a rain check on jumping into the sea and getting smacked in the head by an enormous rock?'

'That would have been the sensible course.'

Despite her resistance, David found he liked her – her calm way of handling things, thinking them through. 'Please,' he said. 'I'm begging you.'

'Perhaps I can persuade her to come here. In the morning. But only if she wants to see you. Now I think you should go back to bed and rest.'

'That's fine,' he said. He got up, fought a moment of dizziness, then went back to the bedroom and climbed under the duvet without removing his clothes. He felt the need to be ready, ready for something. Sleep seemed like an impossibility. It was an unwelcome surprise to feel his body relax into the mattress so willingly.

* * *

He was woken, in the dark, by the sound of a shutting door, and wondered if Inger was on her way to find Marianne.

David turned on his side, felt the tender muscles contract, but even as he winced the pain lessened, faded away to nothing. What would Inger say to Marianne? Would she tell her that he had thrown himself into the water? He couldn't imagine what words she would use.

His body was filled with energy, crackling, fizzing. He got up, stretched, walked around the bed, walked back. He had to do something. The thought that Marianne might refuse to come to him was unbearable; he had never even considered it until Inger had put the idea into his head. But now, for the first time, he wondered if he had really committed an act of intrusion, of violation. It was agonising to think she might consider this to be another example of the male need to dominate, to control, just like the attacker at the library. All he wanted was to hold her, to take her home. It was impossible to change his desire for her, and he couldn't escape the thought that to come this far and not see her would damage him permanently. Making sense of everything depended on her – surely she would see that? And yet, Inger's calm face would not stress the urgency of it. It would be easy for Marianne to dismiss Inger, to decide that real life could wait.

He found himself jogging out of the door, into the night. The cold and the rain did not change his mind. He shrugged them off, ran faster. He felt stronger, more powerful, for moving, making his lungs and legs work. The gleam of Inger's torch was his beacon.

CHAPTER NINE

'Amelia's collection of Egyptian artefacts is really stunning, and it's amazing how few women choose to come and visit it, really. I mean, the details are in reception and it's open at all times, just upstairs. I'd be happy to take you around the upper floors later. It's a museum dedicated to her and there's so much to learn, there really is...'

Finally, Vanessa takes a breath. I'm so grateful for that pause; my ears were beginning to hurt. She talks too loud on this, apparently her favourite subject. She's been talking about it ever since Rebecca brought it up, which was the second we got here.

'What's wrong?' Vanessa says to me. 'Don't you like Greek food?' She's put together a spread of Greek meze: dolmades, stuffed olives, hummus, souvlaki, rice salad. It covers every inch of the enormous, rectangular glass table. I've no idea how she managed to get the ingredients, but the food is abundant and the four of us will never make a dent in it. When I think of the fact that Vanessa was not actually expecting Rebecca and Kay to turn up as well, this banquet becomes inexplicable. Is it meant to be a sign of wealth? Of her ability to spoil herself? Or perhaps she's like a nervous mother who has overprepared for her child's birthday party, laying on far too much food and too many games, determined to do too much rather than not enough.

'It's lovely,' I say, not able to think of anything else that begins to cover it. Kay, sitting on the opposite side of the table, has adopted a bemused, entertained expression, barely on this side of polite. I wish I could do the same.

'Did you recognise the quote on the letter? And in reception? Homer. Quite significant.'

'Of what?'

'The male sex.'

'So, Vanessa,' says Rebecca, 'I think it's so great that you're really happy to open up about the statue monster thing. When did you first meet it?'

'I can tell that you don't believe in it, and really, I can understand that,' Vanessa says to her, meeting her eyes directly, 'because you aren't important, are you? I don't mean that in a cruel way. It's just very obvious to me that you're a bit player in this story, trying to elevate yourself to centre stage, hopping up and down in your desperation to control everything and failing quite dismally. But really, you're too old for this shit, aren't you? If I can be forgiven for that cliché.'

Kay makes a coughing sound through a mouthful of dolmades.

Vanessa turns to me. I get a sense of her frustration and annoyance in the way she leans over the table, her hands clenched. I recognise myself in her body language. 'I don't know why you found it necessary to invite your new friends.'

I'm not sure either. I don't think that I did, exactly. When I got back to the chalet they were waiting for me, the two of them, desperate to tell me that the manager of the island was looking for me, that I was in serious trouble, and what was I going to do? Their excitement, their tension, was the reason I told them about meeting my mother, and that act seemed to have established an inviolable group, whether I liked it or not. It was taken as read that they would accompany me to dinner. I can't say I don't want them here, exactly. They are muddying things, perhaps, but it's beyond me to judge it. I had no idea what to expect from tonight. The Greek food alone has thrown me completely.

'As you say, it's not about anybody but Marianne, is it?' says Rebecca. 'Marianne asked us to be here. So here we are. For her.'

My mother looks at me and raises an eyebrow.

'Lovely meal,' says Kay. She's the only one left eating. 'Did you have all this stuff delivered?'

'The *Sea Princess* brings over the supplies every Saturday. I sometimes put a few bits and pieces on the list. Perhaps I went a little overboard when I found out Marianne was coming.'

'You wanted to impress her?' said Rebecca.

'Is that so strange?' Vanessa snaps back.

'After eighteen years, some would say so.'

Vanessa falls into a thwarted silence. Does Rebecca see herself as my champion? I can't stand the thought of it.

'It worked,' I say. 'I am impressed. It's very tasty.' This awful repetitive circle we're following: the food, the food, the food. Suddenly I hate myself for playing by the rules. 'If you wanted me to think of you as a good cook rather than as a good mother, then yes, it worked.'

She says, without any hesitation – I suppose this is more like the kind of conversation she prepared for in front of the mirror – 'Well, at least I'm a good something.' And I find myself liking her, just a little, in the way that I might like a stranger who has said something witty and cool back to a rude acquaintance.

But then I remember her choice to stay here, and I'm wary of her all over again.

Kay has finally stopped eating. She looks around the dining room as if seeing it properly for the first time: the long purple curtains, the table, the chandelier and the obediently burning fire in the fireplace. There is, unbelievably, a stuffed white cat on a tasselled red rug before the fire. It is curled into a ball, but also elongated and flattened, as if it has been sat on a few too many times.

'This place is bizarre,' says Kay. 'I love it.'

'I wouldn't have felt comfortable changing things,' says Vanessa. 'I didn't feel it was my business. Everything is just how Amelia left it. It really reflects her personality, you know, precisely. The... rich, illusory bravado of it.'

'What an interesting description,' Rebecca says to the stuffed cat. 'Illusory.'

'Old women living alone like to pretend they're still young.'

Vanessa sighs. 'I find the photographs the most interesting part – pictures taken of her with so many rich and famous people. She knew everyone.'

'Sounds like you should open this place up properly. To the public, not just the women here on holiday. You'd make a fortune.'

'Oh, we could never have that. Besides, we don't need the money.'

'Ah…' says Rebecca, as if a locked door has just been thrown open wide. 'Of course. No men allowed. Because of the monster. Can I call it that?'

'I prefer to think of it as a statue.'

'Why? You know Amelia's story. You're reading to it, you're refusing to let men near it, so obviously you believe in it.'

'It's not that simple,' says Vanessa, wincing.

'Why not? It's only your emotions complicating it.'

I want to shout at Rebecca, make her stop this attack, because all it is doing is making me feel sorry for my mother, defensive towards her, and that is the last thing I want.

'The statue is— It's not just a statue, that much is plain, but I never experienced anything like—'

'So you think Amelia made it up? In that case, don't you need to admit to yourself that you're using this statue as an excuse to not face up to the consequences of your actions?'

'That's it.' Vanessa stands up. 'Come and see it.'

'Pardon?' says Rebecca.

'The statue.'

It's the first time I've seen Rebecca lost for words. Perhaps nobody ever called her bluff in a counselling session before. She blinks, and shakes her head.

'Seriously?' says Kay. She stands up too, and scratches her neck, a masculine gesture, like a builder being asked to give a quote. 'I'm up for it. In the library, right? Through the door with the four coloured squares. I have to tell you, I believe in monsters, but I don't expect to see one down there. Still, I'd like to have a look, if that's okay.'

Everyone turns to me. I have become the focus of the room.

The unspoken question is – do I believe in monsters?

I know there is something behind the white door with four squares, and I don't want to face it.

I could side with Rebecca. She's waiting for me to announce that I won't be buying into this delusion, that my mother needs professional help, that we need to get her off this island before we can even begin to form a normal mother–daughter relationship. Where does that kind of help get you? The kind where somebody takes your own ideas from your head and stuffs in fresh ones instead?

Do those new, shiny thoughts mean that monsters no longer exist? Does it mean the rapist isn't breathing hard outside the door?

I don't believe that every monster, real or imaginary, needs to be faced. But the one in this house does.

So I stand up. 'Let's go.'

For one moment, it looks as though Rebecca is going to cling to her principles and stay at the table, but then she pushes back her chair and smoothes her skirts. 'Perhaps this is the best course of action,' she says. 'Facing it head-on.'

'The monster?' asks Vanessa in an amused voice.

'Whatever you think it is.'

'What a very delicate way of putting it.' Vanessa strides out of the dining room and we follow after her in a snake: Kay, Rebecca, me. We march through a minimalist living room, the fire unlit, into a long draughty hall with black and white tiles on the floor and walls. Underneath the wide staircase, carpeted in a scuffed and faded red, is a door, painted black. Vanessa turns the handle and we follow her farther, down into the basement. The stone steps, so bare in contrast to the décor of the house, are lit by small electric lights running the length of the sloping ceiling, strung on two bare wires, but even though the way is clearly visible, I can't bring myself to close the black door behind me. I don't want to lose that opening, that possibility of escape.

At the bottom of the steps we enter familiar territory: the corridor, and then the library, with the rows of shelves holding empty declarations. Vanessa slows her pace, and strolls down the 'A–G' aisle, running one hand along the folders. She reaches the small white door with the four squares, then takes off her green jacket, folds it and puts it on the floor, and rolls up the sleeves of her cream blouse, even though it's freezing. She picks up a folder from the tray next to the door, then traces her finger along the squares. 'Red for heroes. Blue for villains. Yellow for sidekicks, and green for wise men. Or wizards, if you like. Sages. Sage green. I've often wondered if that's where the saying comes from. Amelia told me they were as old as the statue, those definitions.' She swings back the door and steps into the darkness.

Kay is the first to follow. Rebecca looks at me. I return her stare calmly, much more calmly than I feel, and then I walk through the doorway too. I hear Rebecca following after me. She manages something I could not; she shuts the door behind her. The light of the library is snatched away, and Kay makes a small hissing sound. I stop walking and wait for my eyes to adjust. I have no idea if I'm in a tiny room or a cavernous space. Although I know there can't be a lot of room down here, under the house, I have the idea that if I lift up my hands I wouldn't scrape my knuckles across a low ceiling, but would find only air.

There is a greenish glow coming from the wall on my right. As the seconds pass, I make out more colours, coming from where the walls give way to natural rock. I see red, blue, and yellow too, faintly, giving just enough light to let me see the outlines of shapes, and to stop me from stumbling as I walk forward to stand next to Kay. Vanessa is ahead, turned towards us, her face barely visible. There is the sound of water, trickling. I shiver, and there's the sudden sensation of pressure between my shoulder blades.

'I can't see anything,' whispers Rebecca, next to my ear. She is holding on to my jumper, I think; I can picture her fist bunching the wool.

Vanessa turns around, shows us her upright back, her blouse reflecting the dim light. 'Hello, Moira,' she says.

The sound of trickling water is not strong, but I have the impression we are close to the source of it. There's dampness in the air, and I think the uneven floor might be wet. I feel as though I'm standing in a shallow puddle, but my walking boots protect my feet. Isn't Rebecca wearing high heels? She's still holding on to me. I resist the urge to turn to her, to ask her if she's okay, if her feet are wet, anything at all just to get her to let go of me.

'It's a woman,' says Kay, and her voice trembles, resonates with fear, and that tone would be enough to make me run if Rebecca wasn't pressed up against my back. Her grip is relentless.

Kay has stopped moving. I manage to walk up to stand beside her, and she whispers to me, 'It's a woman. Is it?'

In front of us, in an alcove set in the back of the rough cave, she stands. Behind her the rocks glow red, yellow, blue, green, dimly. I can only just make out her features; she is beautiful, I think. She radiates age and intelligence, and it is humbling to be near her.

'Meet Moira,' says Vanessa. 'That's the name Amelia gave to her.'

The statue doesn't move. Of course. How could it move?

And yet my strong feeling is that she's not carved from stone. She is encased in it, a thin layer of it; it has grown on her. The reality of her is just under the surface of the rock. Very close to waking, as if she could stretch and the stone would fall from her. She is waiting.

I don't know what she's waiting for.

'It's a statue,' says Rebecca, and the fact that she really believes that shines through her voice. She just doesn't get it. 'It's just a statue.'

I say, 'No.'

But now she has planted the doubt, it begins to grow inside me. What is Moira? Are my senses lying to me? Why should my perception be different to Rebecca's?

Moira's face alters. Not discernibly, not so a person could take a photograph and point out differences, but there is no mistaking a change from beautiful to ugly. The nose is now severe rather than straight, and the mouth is loose rather than generous. I now feel I'm looking at an older woman, one whose hard life has written itself on her face.

'She changes all the time,' says Vanessa. 'I watch her for hours.' She walks up to Moira with a nonchalance that shocks me. Has she really been in Moira's company for so long that she is able to touch her without feeling profoundly uncomfortable? But Vanessa stops short of touching her. She walks behind her and taps something attached to the wall. I take a step to the right and see a length of pipe jutting from the rock, leading down to a squat barrel from which the trickling sound emanates.

'We sell it,' says Vanessa.

The piping runs around Moira's feet, like manacles, and seems to come from inside the rock, just below her knees. There is a sense of wrongness to it. I have to fight the urge to attempt to rip it from her.

'Like a spring?' says Rebecca. 'A natural spring, on the island?'

Vanessa doesn't bother to reply. She pulls something from her pocket and a moment later there is a pinpoint of light in her hands – a miniature torch. She puts it between her teeth so she can open the folder she brought in from the pile by the door. Then she shifts the torch to her left hand, holds the folder in her right, and begins to read aloud.

I'm not a good mother, so how can I raise a good son? I shout when I should be reasonable. I can't help it. It's so much easier to let it out, all the frustration, that I've had a bad day. I'm annoyed at everyone, including him. Kyle should have a bad day too, he should suffer too, that's how I feel. I'm suffering so he should too. But I'd swear it doesn't bother him, and that makes it worse. He looks at me like he's meant to be shouted at, like that's what life is about. Like I'm teaching him something he needs to know. He's only eight and I've already taught him how to be horrible. How to take it, and how to dish it out.

Maybe this is what all men are, deep inside. They are here for us to fight, so we make each other suffer. Being on this island makes me wonder if we could really do without them. Aren't they responsible for all the crime, anyway? All the violence? People say – oh, he must have had a violent father. But maybe their mothers taught them to be that way. I'm teaching Kyle to hate me already.

Vanessa stops reading.

When she spoke those words, they made a different sound.

Resonant. Deeper and stronger. Not like it sounds when Vanessa says, 'She's feeding off them now. Off Kyle. The idea of him. What he could have been. All these declarations, and so many women find themselves writing about what men want, what men need from them.'

Flat words; they have no substance. I don't believe them, and Moira is disinterested in them. But when Vanessa read to her, there was avidity. The ugly face was intent. Now it is serene and heavy with age.

'This is elaborate, isn't it?' says Rebecca. 'This act. All the things you're doing to make Marianne believe you.'

'Rebecca, can you really not feel it?' says Kay.

'Feel what?'

Kay flips her hand at the statue, at Moira, and in response Rebecca's tone hardens into belligerent, obstinate belief: 'You're seeing a carefully prepared room. You know that, right? Lighting, effects, like a film. It works on you, just like a film does, standing here in the dark. But it's not real. It will do you no good to believe in this. If it was genuine, don't you think Vanessa would turn on all the lights, show it to you properly? Everything always looks different in the light, doesn't it?'

'Women never mattered, did they?' Vanessa says. She is warming to her subject. She gestures with the folder and the torch, and throws back her head as her voice gets louder. 'Not in the great tales of heroes and villains. Women were the prizes and the punishments. Moira isn't interested in us, you see. Men feed her, make her stronger, so that the entire world gets caught up in her.'

'Let's go back upstairs,' says Rebecca.

'Don't you see? She's real. She's real. I had to be here. Don't you understand, Marianne?'

'There's a crack,' says Kay. Vanessa drops her hands.

'What?'

'A crack. In her neck.'

Vanessa puts her face next to the curve in Moira's throat. When she shines the torch upon it, I can clearly see the crack that runs through the stone, from below the left ear to the clavicle. There's a soft sound, like a ripe fruit hitting a hard floor, and as I watch the crack widens, deepens, approaching the breastbone.

'What's happening?' says Rebecca.

'I don't know.' Vanessa switches off the torch. There is a tremor of movement under my feet. The ground is trembling. A noise is building, a low roaring. The piping behind Moira groans and begins to rattle against the rock. 'I don't know. This is wrong. There must be a man nearby. Amelia said she would only change if there was—' She pauses, head tilted to one side, and then she turns around and looks straight at me.

'Run!'

The ground splits apart.

There is no time to react, to think of what should be said or done. I push backwards with my legs as the floor begins to give, and my head hits something hard as I fall. I scrabble behind me, touch the door, grab the handle – how did I get so close to the door? It can't be real. But it is solid, it stays solid, as the rest of the room sags, drops away, screaming, grinding, shouting so loud at its disappearance. I can't see Kay or Rebecca, but I can see Vanessa. She is holding on to Moira, who remains upright, an island in the centre of the moving ground. Vanessa's terror is palpable, and so is Moira's amusement, written on her face, and through the fretwork of cracks that now cover her, life pulses, reaches out: more than life, more than flesh. She glows. Vanessa is shouting something at her; I can't hear. Moira's hands are golden, and they move, they move, so slowly, up to Vanessa's open mouth, and they close around her lips and pull apart, stretching, stretching the skin until they are ripped free of Vanessa's face, and there is so much blood, and then the door swings back, into the corridor, and snaps from its hinges, so that I am shaken free of the handle to land on something cold and hard underneath me.

I realise I'm shouting the word no, no, no, over and over. I can't hear myself but my own lips are saying it. I'm in the corridor, the lines of the walls are angular, sloping inwards to meet just above my head, and the stairs at the far end have formed a concertina, squashing, shrinking, and then I can't see them any more as the air thickens with dust, and breathing becomes so hard that my mouth stops moving and my chest hardens into a stone of pain.

CHAPTER TEN

He watched Inger knock on the door of the wooden chalet, wait, then knock again. She moved to a darkened window, cupped her hands to the glass, and looked inside. Then turned, and saw him. She pulled a face: a caricature of the disapproving mother. He couldn't help but laugh.

She stamped up to him. 'I don't find this funny.'

'Sorry.' But David couldn't stop smiling at her. The night was so clean, making his skin tingle with its freshness. He had never felt so well. Maybe this was a by-product of all he had gone through in the last few days. Catharsis had taken place, and he was now a better version of himself. He felt it.

'She's not there, anyway,' said Inger, putting her hands on her hips. 'Nobody's there. She was sharing with two other ladies. The only organised activity on a Monday night is massage therapy with Janet. Could she have gone to that?'

'She's not a massage person.' He'd tried to rub her feet when they first got married, and she'd clenched them up into birdish claws and told him she was far too ticklish to enjoy it. Could that have been a lie?

'I don't know, then,' said Inger. She puffed out her cheeks, then said, 'We should go back.'

David looked around. Something was building. He felt it in the darkening sky, the curves of the ground. He remembered the round, white house, visible in the distance. It had struck him as the hub of the island, around which all things rotated. He'd felt the pull of it. It would sound ridiculous to Inger, so instead he said, 'Come on,' and set off back the way they came, following his instincts, wondering where this new confidence in them sprang from.

'No—' said Inger, and he heard her running after him. He felt the strength of it, being in charge, making the decisions once more. She wouldn't be able to stop him for all her heroics.

When she caught up to him, David said, 'What's in the white house?'

'Mrs… Makepeace…' She was out of breath already. He realised he was jogging. It put no strain on his lungs, his body.

'I'm not meant to be here, I know, but I just need to look through the window. Nobody will know, and then I'll come back with you and lie low, I promise, honestly.'

'But—'

'Honestly,' he said. He didn't slow down. The night was no impediment to his speed; his feet found the right path, even though Inger stumbled. He saw the white house up ahead and aimed straight for it, faster, stretching out his legs.

'I can't…' Inger fell behind. He found he was sprinting.

The sleek strength of his muscles was a surprise; he felt like an animal. He found he had rejoined a path that led up to a wrought iron gate, which he simply climbed over, not bothering to check if it would open or not. The path widened until it formed a semi-circular gravel space in front of the pillared facade and a large, blue front door.

David looked behind him. Inger was nowhere.

He ignored the door and moved to the nearest window. Inside was a pattern of black and white tiles covering the walls and floor. David put his hands to the glass and it trembled at his touch. No – the glass wasn't trembling. Something else, something under the ground, had come alive. It shuddered and squirmed at his touch, then groaned, so loud, so lonely.

He pulled back his hand and covered his ears.

The house reared up, and the windows split apart with great cracks, the glass falling into splinter shards that pelted down in dust and tiles and plaster.

And the ground opened.

It swallowed half the house in a second. The rest of the house fell over and lay on its side; David watched it, felt certain it would attempt to get up. It creaked and complained on, and gouts of steam erupted from the black mouth of moving earth into which the house had fallen, just beyond his feet.

Inger was pulling at his arm. He realised she was shouting at him.

'What?' he said.

'Come back! Come back!'

She was strong – he could feel her muscles pulling against his – but he didn't step away. There was something he was here to do. It came to him as a revelation. He had to go down into the hole. Marianne was in there. He was not about to be defeated, not when he was so close to her.

'I have to go in,' he said.

'Back!' shouted Inger, still tugging at him. He turned to her and saw enormous eyes, fear-filled, liquid. Beautiful. He took her hand from his sleeve and kissed it.

She snatched it back, and David stepped forward, felt the earth begin to slide under his feet. He kept his balance and rode it to the tilted house. The window he had been looking through had lost most of its glass and shape to become a squashed rhombus of an opening. He climbed through, felt the remaining shards catch on his tracksuit bottoms, and then he was in the black and white tiled hall, turned at an angle so that, to stay upright, he had to lean against the wall and crab down the corridor to where the next doorway lay, burst outwards, with only rubble piled high beyond it.

'Marianne?' he said.

He listened, and heard nothing beyond the groans of the dying house. Shouting seemed ridiculous; he was certain she was there, so he put his hands on the stones and started to throw them behind him. More flowed out of the gaps he made, and he suspected it was an endless task, but he knew it was the right thing to do. He would have done it for eternity.

Inger was calling his name. He didn't turn around. After a few minutes of shovelling with his hands, he heard her scramble down the corridor, and say, 'Oh my God, oh my God,' at his back, as if that meant something.

'Marianne,' he said again, and Inger said, 'No, no.' He felt irritation at her decision to react rather than act; wasn't she meant to be a saviour of those in distress? But then she knelt down and started to pull at the stones around his feet, and he realised all she had needed was a moment to read the situation.

They worked together.

'It might collapse,' she said, after a while, in between breaths.

David concentrated on the rhythm of his hands. Someone was screaming outside.

'I'll go and see,' said Inger, and started back down the corridor.

He pictured a group of women standing around the house, their hands over their mouths, portraying shock and terror. Soon, with Inger's help, they would get over it, start to organise themselves, build themselves into a team of good intentions. He suspected they would attempt to pull him clear for his own good. And his hands were a mess of cuts; his blood was making the stones slippery. The window of opportunity to save her was closing. What would he do if he couldn't save her? He would be a waste of a man, a dead end of the possibilities he had been born with. He thought of Arnie, and the other men who slumped in The

Cornerhouse, waiting for a win on the cubes for a few moments in a dream.

He heard himself saying, 'I won't, I won't,' in time to the widening of the hole, each stone in turn. He had to save her. It was his destiny.

A hand poked through, clutched at his. A voice he didn't recognise said, 'Please,' and he squeezed the fingers, felt the skin, realised it was Marianne at the moment she said, 'David?' How could he not have recognised her? He felt hot, feverish with guilt, as he scrabbled at the stones until they gave and he pulled her up and out, falling backwards, so that she came into his arms and he was holding her, listening to her cry, wanting her to cry because nobody else had ever cried like her. She yelped and snorted, and always got the hiccups afterwards, and David waited for the hiccups to start, then stroked her face as she alternated between them and trying to talk.

'How—you—you—you,' she said. He picked her up. She felt heavier than he remembered, and there was no blood on her, no rips on her clothes. She seemed intact, weighed down by the dust that cloaked her. Every second that he held her cemented her back to him. He could feel her, prickling, singing with life, like a part of his body waking from numbness after too long being still. Life was returning to them both.

Inger awaited them on the other side of the window. David helped Marianne through, watched a knot of women tie themselves around her with towels and torches. A light rain was caught in the beams of light, like the moment was frozen.

'Come out,' said Inger.

'What's happening?' he said.

'The emergency services are on their way. But it's going to take time, coming from the mainland. Ten minutes for the helicopter. They said stay out of the house. It's unstable.'

Marianne was being led away by the women. He watched her shake her head, turn, point at him. No, not at him, at the house, her gaze rigid with fear, expectation. The women piled towels on her shoulders and dragged her on.

'Are there others?' David said.

'Come out,' said Inger, again.

He said, 'I'll be careful,' not meaning it. He had no intention of doing less than any hero should. He ran back to the remains of the doorway and squeezed himself through, into the darkness beyond.

CHAPTER ELEVEN

Now the island holds men. They walk around as if they're stepping on any normal, sane stretch of land: hillocks of wild grass, dark brown crusted turds of sheep. Their feet squelch these things down, and they don't understand they are violating this place. Or perhaps they know and don't care. There are more important things in life than the sanctity of Skein Island. This is, after all, an emergency.

I'm aware that, in my head, I sound like my mother.

But Vanessa is being put in a helicopter right now, so maybe I feel like I should step into her shoes until she can resume her responsibilities. She was carried out by David, unconscious, but now she is awake and annoyed, her eyes stretched wide, making frantic statements at me over the top of the plastic mask they've clamped over her nose and her intact mouth. Whatever I saw down there wasn't real. Her mouth is proof of that.

The paramedics have tied her to the stretcher. She was clawing at them, and she even scored a cheek with her long nails. She looks fine, if furious, but the way the two paramedics have marked her as a priority, even before Rebecca with her broken leg, is giving me the feeling that her outrage is a blanket under which is hidden all manner of failures – failure in her body, in her duty, failure to keep us all safe, failure to keep this island under her sole control. Perhaps this is a long enough list of failures to defeat her.

She clenches and unclenches her fists rhythmically, so I take one of her hands in mine and walk alongside her stretcher as they take it to the helicopter, away from the crater that was once her house.

She doesn't let go of me, and she has a grip like steel. The paramedics turn, and the stretcher is taken to the right, away from the helicopter. My wrist twists awkwardly as they put Vanessa down in the field, then step away and begin a quick conversation, their mouths close to each others' ears. I look behind me, putting more pressure on my aching arm, and I see another stretcher, other men sprinting with it to the helicopter.

One of the paramedics follows my gaze, and beckons to me. I lean over, and he shouts, 'Worse off.' It must be Kay. But I find myself considering the possibility that it's Moira, revived to flesh under the rubble, and I feel such fear, strange fear, as I imagine what she might be about to do to these men surrounding her. Moira, kept prisoner for years in that basement, chained to the wall, encased in stone. Turning men mad in her presence so they rip each other to pieces. But why would she need hospitalisation? She's not human, is she? And besides, I tell myself, she's a statue, a statue, a bloody statue.

Vanessa is watching my face. She opens her mouth under the mask and then can't seem to shut it again, because her tongue is protruding through her lips, just the tip of it, as if she has just eaten something spicy and is waiting for a glass of water to arrive.

I picture the meze: dolmades, olives, scattered food, thrown over the wreckage of the floor, being trodden into the remains of the carpet by the men, who are everywhere, swelling in numbers, multiplying in response to this emergency. I find myself retching. I shake free of Vanessa's grip, crouch down and lean over the grass, but nothing comes up. Have I already digested tonight's meal? Are we already moving on in time, skittering away on an icy sheet of minutes spent?

'You're not empty,' I hear myself say. Or maybe I just hear the words in my head, because the helicopter is taking off and the wind is fierce and deafening. I stand up and watch it go, and as it becomes smaller, shrinking to a speck, the world is returned to sound, and Vanessa has somehow got her mask off and is trying to speak, but her lips slap together without form, without control. The paramedics are moving around me with a new urgency. They snap the oxygen mask back over her face, so I can no longer clearly see the struggle in the lines of her mouth, even as she fights on.

Does she want me to find Moira? I turn around and scan the crowd, half-expecting to see the living statue standing there, smiling. The ground is an open wound, bleeding clots of dirt, spurting steam. The house is a weapon jutting from the gash. I've never seen anything so horrible. As I watch,

David emerges from the wound. He is filthy, his clothes are ripped, his hair is plastered to his head. He looks alive. I see the other women – the island visitors now gathered in a knot to this tragedy – watch him too. I'm not surprised. He is no longer the David I knew. He's a golden icon of a man. We women are now beneath him.

Once I saw potential in him, a greatness glimmering under the surface. Now he has unfolded into a hero. He comes to me and puts his arms around me, wrapping me in the smells of mud and smoke, and I love him again, oh I love him. He kisses me and he is reverent. It is like the kiss he gave me in front of the altar. We have resealed our bond, and I could never leave him again. I don't want to be anywhere else.

He says, 'Thank God, thank God. I'm here. I've got you.' I realise I'm telling him I'm sorry.

'No, don't be sorry. I found you.'

'My mother.' Why has she worked her way into this moment? But it seems vital to say, 'She's been here all the time.' Calm now, prone, on the stretcher she lies. I look at his face. I can tell he's moved by the sight of her. He saved her too, brought her out of the ground, carrying her.

'She was trapped,' he says.

'Under a statue?'

'It was heavy. I managed to move it eventually.'

'You touched it?'

'I was amazed she was alive at all.'

Something in his tone alerts me to what I should have seen.

143

I make myself examine her face. Her eyes are open. Her chest is still. She does not fight any more because that option has been removed. She has been overcome, and conquered.

'We had to prioritise the other woman,' says the businesslike paramedic, who is suddenly at my side.

'No,' I say, 'she hasn't explained it yet, not properly. I don't understand it yet. No, that's not how this is meant to be.' My voice is so loud, getting louder. I'm never normally this loud. I'm a softly spoken person, that's who I am, but these words just won't come out quietly because nobody seems to be understanding them and I have to be louder, louder, louder, so I am shouting in the face of something that's not listening to me.

David pulls me closer, shushes me, rocks me, until something clicks shut inside me.

We have reached the end of a pattern, a cycle of discovery. It's time to go home and take slow, deep breaths until the meaning of all this becomes clear.

I take in the morning sky. It is clear and pink, and the rain clouds have disappeared, for now.

PART THREE

CHAPTER TWELVE

'She never said all her children were girls,' says Rebecca. 'What are the chances of that? All four of them, mini-Kays.'

'Why would she?' I ask.

'No reason.' Rebecca shifts in the wicker chair and pulls at the deep V-neck of her black dress. Her encased left leg sticks out to rest on a matching stool, the plaster a grainy white. 'It just makes me feel worse. Stupid, I know.'

I know what she means. The four girls had taken up the front pew of the church, with the eldest on the end of the row. A hymn had been chosen, one I didn't know, about God accepting my heart, and during it the eldest girl had thrown back her shoulders and sang to the vaulted ceiling, and the pit of my stomach had moved in recognition of Kay's genes, Kay's mannerisms, living on.

But maybe Rebecca doesn't mean that. Maybe she thinks that bereavement is harder on women than on men. I don't know her well enough to understand her, and what I do know of her irritates me.

She pokes the strap of her black bra back underneath her

dress – she can't seem to stop fiddling with it – and takes a sip from her glass of lemonade. I would not have chosen her as a companion for this funeral. I didn't even know that she was going to attend; we've not spoken since the island. I wasn't certain I was going to attend until the last minute, but David persuaded me in the name of closure, and I had a new black suit for Vanessa's funeral, so I thought I might as well get some mileage out of it.

How practical I am about these things. My father wouldn't attend Vanessa's funeral, and so I organised a bouquet of white lilies and signed his name on the card. Whilst performing these administrative tasks, I thought only of myself. It was an act of make-believe, the fantasy of a small child who can't bear the reality of quarrelling parents. Even a pretend pact, signified by white lilies of all things, made me feel better, just for a moment.

But now, here, at Kay's wake, that illusion has passed. There are no reasons or reconciliations in this death. I thought I might come to understand why Kay's decision to get back on that motorbike, to live her life no matter what the consequences, became worse than inconsequential in the face of a statue, in a basement, on an island. I have been looking at her mother and her girls, to see if they have understood how ridiculous their arguments were. They all begged her not to buy another motorbike.

Standing here, in the conservatory of Kay's mother's house, I keep Rebecca company as we look out over the ordered garden, watching the rose bushes in the December rain.

There's an arbour, and beside it a large pampas. The empty raised beds are a churned dark brown, and the shining stones of the rockery look as if they would be so slippery underfoot. I turn and observe the mourners hold their faces rigid and whisper as if they are slowly turning to stone too, from the neck down. David is standing next to the buffet table, beside a metallic red plate that bears delicate slices of garlic bread. He's nodding his head as Rebecca's husband talks to him. Their eyes are locked, their body language engaged. They are obviously enjoying the conversation. I wonder what they are talking about. The husband is a surprise to me. Rebecca never mentioned him on the island. How is it possible to have a husband and not talk about him?

If I had my way I suppose David would not be here, and then Rebecca would have thought that strange, no doubt. So perhaps it is as well that he talked me into letting him drive. The fact that he is willing to stand a short distance away from me today is a step forward. Since he rescued me from the basement he has not left me. He loves me, and I love him, of that I have no doubt. That has never been in question. But he is no longer just my husband, and of that I have no doubt either. Touching the statue – touching Moira – has changed him.

'You're still thinking about it, aren't you?' says Rebecca. While I watched our husbands, she was watching me. I feel ashamed of whatever might have just passed across my face. But I'm glad Rebecca has raised this topic; I realise I have something I want to say. 'Thinking of Moira, yes. I'm having the house rebuilt. The basement will be excavated, if possible.

If she's down there, I'll find her.' Settling my mother's estate is ongoing, but everything will eventually pass to me; the solicitors who held her Last Will and Testament have made that clear. The island will become my property.

I can't get my head around that, but I'm certain that the house must be restored.

'Are you thinking she's still down there?' Rebecca says, in that voice she uses – the patient tone of a therapist to those lowly individuals who don't understand their own motivations. I wonder how her husband stands her. She must dissect every meal, every word, every sexual encounter they share.

'Are you asking me if I think stone statues can move?' I say, calling her bluff. I keep my eyes on David, wondering if he will look at me. But he's talking, arms moving, making compact gestures as if describing an object. If he was the kind of man who cared about cars, I would say he was having that sort of conversation: how fast, miles per gallon. But he really never seems to care about such things. Maybe Rebecca's husband does. I have to search my memory for his name; we were introduced before the funeral, briefly. It finally comes to me. I say to Rebecca, 'Does Hamish like cars?'

'What?' she says. 'No. Try to concentrate. This is important.'

'At least we can agree on that.'

David and Hamish are smiling at each other, both talking, mimicking each other's movements. They are in complete agreement about something. Around them, others are having the stiffer conversations that suit funerals better. If Kay were here she would have wanted to drive a motorbike through the living room and upset the carefully laid plates of garlic bread and sausage rolls, spilling them over the floor.

Kay's mother is circulating through the crowd. She's a tall woman with good posture, and she wears her white hair in an angular bob that looks fresh and glossy. She's holding a silver tray upon which cluster flutes of white wine. Every time she stops at a group, the mourners draw together. She nods and smiles at them, and they respond in kind, but nobody takes a flute. As she crosses my field of vision I see annoyance flash across her face – *Will nobody take a bloody drink?* She is thinking. *This tray is getting heavy.* Why doesn't she set it down and forget about it? Walk out of here, return later when everyone has left her house? Somebody would probably even do the tidying up and the dishes, out of guilt.

But mothers don't leave, do they? Not even after death. Not the good ones.

'I wish you were able to talk about this,' says Rebecca. 'Because— Because I really need to talk about it too. Hamish tries to understand but he's...'

'A man,' I finish for her, and I know she hates it, the thought of this unbridgeable divide between man and woman that Vanessa has placed in our heads. But she doesn't contradict me.

'Since it happened he seems dead set on protecting me. Perhaps it was the thought of losing me. Everything we do now, every time I attempt to get up, he's there, wanting to be my crutch.'

'That's pretty normal, surely?'

'Of course,' she says. 'But before, if he was having protective impulses, we could talk about it. He'd be happy to admit it, to see that it was irrational. Now we can't even have a conversation. Whenever I raise it he doesn't listen. It's like I'm of the utmost importance in his life, and at the same time, totally irrelevant.'

Rebecca has a way with words. I recognise this feeling, this marginalisation. I feel it every time David looks at me.

It would be so good to tell Rebecca my thoughts and fears about this. But I know what she wants is to cast me back into the role of patient so that she can make herself feel better. So instead I say, 'The preliminary reports on the house show the foundations were weakened by a natural spring that runs under the island.'

'Really?'

'Vanessa was tapping it. In the basement. Diverting the flow of the water and collecting it. Barrels of it. Don't you remember the piping? It wound around Moira.'

'The statue,' Rebecca corrects me. 'I don't remember that. What for?'

'I don't know yet.'

'A natural spring,' she muses. 'One pound fifty for a small bottle of Malvern water nowadays. She was sitting on top of a gold mine and died because of it. An expensive way to go.'

Vanessa filled those barrels for a reason. I wonder to whom she sold them, and what purpose they serve. It's been intimated to me that I will soon become a very rich woman.

Is it all left over from Amelia's enormous fortune? Or had Vanessa found another way to add to the island's wealth? Financial records – those not destroyed in the collapse – will eventually come to me, and then I will get some answers.

'So what did you see?' I find myself asking Rebecca, before I can stop myself. This is the conversation I didn't want to have. 'What did you see, down there? If you didn't see the piping, or the barrels, and you didn't see Moira?'

'I knew it,' she says. 'You still believe it. That parlour trick Vanessa pulled.'

'Forget what I believe. What do you believe?'

'Your mother had real problems. I'd maybe characterise it as Stockholm Syndrome. She met a rich, brilliant, troubled woman who had lived through wars, seen terrible things, and that woman bound your mother to her, with lies. With stories. Then she died, and left your mother alone, and she wanted you back. To continue those stories. Keep them alive. So she set that whole thing up to manipulate you. She wanted you to stay there, on that island, with her. If you're not careful, she'll get her way. You'll end up back there forever. Maybe not physically, but mentally.'

'She never asked me to stay.'

'She was getting to it!'

'It took her seventeen years to get that far.'

'People spend their whole lives preparing for certain moments, Marianne.' Rebecca scratches her knee just above the cast. 'Only those moments count, for them. The stuff that happens every day, that's just marking time until the big scene. The reveal. We all live that way sometimes. Working towards a wedding day, the birth of a child. We imagine it, and prepare for it, even if we're not engaged or pregnant. Perhaps it's a female thing. We just don't live in the present, do we?'

I think perhaps she's right. But if Moira was an illusion, clever trickery with lights and effects, then what was my mother hoping to make me think?

'I never should have gone to that stupid island,' says Rebecca. 'I knew it wasn't going to teach me anything useful about myself. All I've learned is a phobia of damp basements.'

'Here's hoping that's a life lesson that stands you in good stead.'

'Marianne, I come from Yorkshire. All the basements are damp. I can't even make it down the stairs to grab a bottle of red wine from my cellar. Now that's an issue.'

I can't help it. I laugh. She laughs too, the guilty sound of survival, and we don't stop until David and Hamish come into the conservatory and stand beside us in a flanking manoeuvre.

'We really should get on the road,' says Hamish. He's aged less well than Rebecca, a wiry, pale white-blond with a slight physique and very blue eyes. Beside him Rebecca looks more vital. 'It's a long drive back.'

'Yes,' she says, meekly.

'I suppose we should as well,' I say, and David nods. How handsome he is in his dark suit. How glad I am that he's beside me, so that I don't have to face these conversations alone.

Hamish says, 'Great to chat with you,' to David, and David replies, 'You've got my email?'

'Yes.' Hamish pats his breast pocket, where I assume he keeps his phone. 'I'll be in touch.'

'We should all say goodbye to Kay's mother,' says David. 'She's done a wonderful job here. Maybe we should check if she needs a hand tidying up.' We all agree, and David turns to look for the poor mother, the right words no doubt already forming on his lips, taking the sting out of the situation for us all.

* * *

David and I travel home in silence. It's not a strained silence. It's comfortable, companionable. We are so pleased to have weathered these two funerals, and we are looking forward to recommencing our old life.

He's driving. With the radio on soft jazz and the night already upon us, I remember the trip to the police station. That night feels so very long ago.

As we get closer to our junction on the M4, David takes one hand from the steering wheel and clicks off the radio.

'How are you?' he asks.

'Good.'

'Me too.'

'Good. I'm glad.'

I think we can do this. I can go back to work in the library. They've rearranged the shift patterns so that nobody is ever left alone to lock up. I can work there, and look forward to a takeaway on a Friday night, and maybe I can give David children because there's no doubt that he'll make a wonderful father. We can be content, our family, in the knowledge that we've had our adventure and no more shocks await us.

'What was Kay like?' he says. 'If you don't mind me asking.'

'She didn't want to live for other people. She was taller than me, and she walked really quickly. She wasn't keen on Italian food.' It's an odd list, and it includes everything I know about her. Suddenly I feel the movement of time, a jolt, like riding a galloping horse towards a fence, far in the distance, and realising that the jump is coming, coming, is so very nearly upon me.

We are home. David reverse-parks the car and then we get out, to a darkened house warmed through by the silent, pumping radiators. The neighbours have their Christmas decorations up, multicoloured lights strung around the small, bare cherry tree they keep in the middle of their front lawn. Already we have moved on. My mind turns to presents, and food, and the beginning of a new year. I want to get something special for David. I can't think of anything that would do. Clothes, music, films: all too mundane. If he were a woman and I were a man, I'd buy him a ring. An eternity ring, worth a month's wages at least, to seal the deal.

I follow him into the living room and watch him draw the curtains. Then he sits on the sofa and I sit next to him, side by side, our coats and shoes still on. He pulls me into his lap, and I kick off my shoes and relax into him. We are wrapped together in our womb of a house, and the certainty hits me that this is not the beginning of our happily ever after. We will have to grow up soon, up and apart, and face the truth about the divergent paths of our lives. I have things I have to do, mysteries that still need to be solved. I push that unwelcome revelation away and sigh into his neck.

'While you were away I met someone who said she knew you,' he says. 'She's a Community Support Officer.'

'How did you meet her?'

'Outside the library.'

'What were you…?' I didn't finish the question. I'm certain I'd rather not hear the things he's trying to tell me.

'He started all of this, you know that, don't you?' says David. 'He would have—'

The words spring out of me. 'Raped me. Burned me. Hurt me. Used me. Killed me. Fucked me. Cut me.'

'Stop.'

'I'm here with you. I'm fine. You need to let it go,' I tell him.

'Sam – the woman I met – she was desperate to catch this man, to stop him from hurting others. And you can come out of an attack, an earthquake, a meeting with the mother who abandoned you, her death, and you think you can simply let it all go?'

'Not me,' I tell him. 'I can't let it go. You can.'

He is quiet for a moment. Then he says, 'I think I need you to accept that when things happen to you, they happen to me too. Maybe not in exactly the same way, but they do happen to me too.'

'Yes. All right. I can see that.' I move from his lap to the other side of the sofa. 'So tell me. Tell me what you went through.'

'It's not a competition, Marianne.'

'Then why do I feel like I've got a rival? This woman – Sam – who wants to be a heroine. Do you prefer that? What is she trying to prove?'

David crosses his legs. 'I'm not interested in what she's trying to prove.'

'I don't think that's true.'

My body has become used to the heat of the house; I'm no longer warm. I take the throw from the back of the sofa and wrap it around my legs.

'I think you need help,' says David. He leans over and puts a hand on my thigh. 'To talk this out with someone. Not just the library thing, but the thing with your mother as well. And I need the same, maybe. There's too much to take on. So much has happened, so fast. There's so much you're not telling me.'

'Can't we just not talk about it? I think if we just…' I make a smooth line with the flat of my hand, like a journey on calm seas.

'Do you think that'll work forever?'

'It'll work tonight. Tomorrow night. Maybe all the way to Christmas. That's what I want. A happy Christmas. Can we have that? Please?'

'And then?' David takes his hand away and stands up. 'Will you be ready to deal with it after that? If we do this entirely on your terms, because it seems that's how everything has to be?'

His words, and the pain behind them, hurt me deeply. He's right, then – we are interlinked. We have grown together, and any time those strands get pulled there is a twinge, a soreness, to the movement. 'I'm selfish. Yes, I know it, and I'm so sorry. I can't blame you for anything that happened while I was away, and I won't. I won't, as long as I don't have to talk about it. Don't tell me any more about your friend, or how you met her. All that matters right now is that you came for me. Everything else can wait. Because we love each other, it can wait. Right?'

He nods, and says, 'Cuppa?'

'Lovely.'

Normality is restored so easily. He wanders off to the kitchen, shedding his coat, and our love is a given once more.

CHAPTER THIRTEEN

Time passed for David in a slow haze. The bubble of life with Marianne protected him from the worst – and best – of his emotions. They both returned to work. She resumed library duties and he went back and forth to his office with no real understanding of what he was doing. He couldn't remember the conversations he had there, or the daily commutes in the car. It seemed beyond trivial to him. If he had gone on making no effort and taking no interest at work, he was certain he would have lost his job, but in the final few days before Christmas it seemed that nobody was concentrating on such things.

Even The Cornerhouse was decked out with tinsel and paper chains, and a row of orange fairy lights ran along the optics, giving out a glow that could almost be described as welcoming. Although an effort had been made with the decoration, the place was deserted. The usual crowd of old men was missing, and a weary silence hung over the rough tables and chairs. The pull of the cubes had left David completely. He wondered if the other men felt the same.

162

David was about to leave when he heard a cough, and realised Arnie was still there, in his usual seat at the back by the fireplace. At the next table along was Geoff, the perennial loser at the cubes, still wearing his striped tie and nursing his pint with a bruised expression. David's eyes caught a movement behind the bar, and Mags came forward, and leaned against the pumps with a raise of her eyebrows. She wore a black blouse, her hair loose, her breasts hanging low. She looked older and smaller without her usual audience.

David felt her watching him as he crossed the room to Arnie, tapping the envelope he held against his leg. He stopped in front of the table, not knowing how to begin.

'What now?' said Arnie, as if picking up a conversation from minutes earlier.

'Marianne asked me to give you this.' David held out the envelope. Arnie reached over without enthusiasm and took it, breaking the seal, sliding the Christmas card into view. It was the expensive type, stiff cream paper, with a picture of a holly leaf embossed with green and silver glitter, golden calligraphic greetings of the season surrounding it.

'Nice,' Arnie said. He didn't read the message inside. 'She's still not keen on seeing me, then?'

'She explained it,' said David.

'Yeah, it was a lovely telephone conversation. To be fair, I think she covered everything. Not a word was wasted. A talent she got from her mother.' He put the card down next to the dregs of his pint of beer. Mags came over with two full pints, and said, 'Pay me later,' before stomping away with the old glass in hand.

What had Marianne said to her father? The night after her mother's funeral she had taken the phone upstairs and locked herself in the bathroom with it. From downstairs, all he heard was the soft rumbling of her serious tone of voice. No shouting, no shrillness. Had she told Arnie that she couldn't ever forgive him for his refusal to come to the funeral? Or was it the secrets he had kept from her that had led to this break from him? Did she tell him she never wanted to see him again? But no, David was certain that Marianne would never say anything so permanent. Right now, they were living their life here in Wootton Bassett as if it were only a temporary arrangement. Besides, the giving of a Christmas card suggested nothing so extreme.

After Christmas, that was when she wanted to talk about facing the past and constructing a future. Until then they were all just treading water. The metaphor made him think of Inger. David wondered where she was now. He hoped, for her sake, she wasn't alone. She was the kind of person who needed someone to be strong for.

'You been down the gym?' said Arnie.

David shook his head.

'I hear you pulled them out of an earthquake.'

'A house collapsed.'

Arnie nodded, as if such things happened every day in his experience. 'I'm not such a bad person, you know. I would have done the same thing. I would have pulled Marianne out of an earthquake. And Vanessa, too. Even Vanessa. So a house fell on her.' He took a sip of his new beer. 'Like the Wicked Witch of the Wotsit. Did her toes curl under? I'm just joking. It's dead here tonight.'

'No cubes?' said David. He kept his voice as casual as he could.

'Given up doing that,' said Arnie, glumly. 'Haven't we?'

Mags called, 'No more cubes, you bloody lot,' from her usual place behind the bar. 'Bloody men.'

Geoff stood up, and wobbled over to their table. He sat and scraped his chair right up to David, so close that David could smell the mustiness and old, dried sweat of his clothes.

'What are we gonna do?' he said. 'Hm? What? She's taken the cubes down. They're not on the shelf any more.'

'They stopped production,' called Mags. 'No more barrels. No more cubes. Not anywhere. Besides, you lot don't need it any more. Busy making your own plans, aren't you?' She muttered something, then picked up a tea towel and ran it up and down the bar, forlornly, like the proud owner of a failing vintage car.

'And no more favours for poor old Mags,' said Arnie. 'We all knew she was rigging it, a bit of sleight of hand to get her favours. She had us all cleaning her windows, getting her shopping, anything she wanted, just so she'd let us win every once in a while and have a taste of the stuff.'

'But now you don't want the stuff.'

Geoff shrugged. 'It doesn't seem so important any more. We don't need to pretend, do we? We just... are.'

It was a difficult thing to take on board. The cubes had been bigger than The Cornerhouse, than Mags or Arnie or the old men who had based their lives around it. David thought of the pub in Allcombe, on the quay, with the fisherman sitting so still, and the cubes on the mantelpiece, the only decoration not covered in dust. How many pubs had played the game of the cubes?

'What do we do?' said Geoff. 'I've been waiting for you to come back. I knew you'd know what to do.'

'So why did Marianne run away, then?' said Arnie.

'I don't know,' David said.

'It wasn't because of that attack? It was in the paper about it. Some bloke's been hanging around the library.'

'When was it in the paper?'

'Four or five days ago. Mags, have you still got it? I read it and thought – I wonder if that's Marianne. But I'm always putting two and two together and making fifty-eight. Mags, the *Gazette*, it was, have you got it?'

'On the pile,' she said, pointing to the small round table next to the slot machine. Geoff got up and wobbled over to the stack of papers upon it. He riffled through them with surprisingly quick flicks of his fingers.

'Got it,' he said. He came back to them, and put the paper in front of David. Arnie snatched it up, licked his thumb, then turned the first page and pointed to the top of page three. It was a small article, only one column, with no picture.

Appeal for Information

Wiltshire police are asking for witnesses
to come forward regarding an alleged
sexual assault that took place outside
Wootton Bassett library on the night of
Thursday 15th October.

If you were in the vicinity or have
any information that you think might be
relevant, please contact—

David stopped reading. 'No. That's not her. She wasn't
assaulted.' He worked backwards in his head, checking
the dates. This attack had happened while Marianne was
away on the island. The man she had faced down had
escalated his game. He felt a strong urge to tell her. 'I have
to talk to Marianne.'

'You sure it wasn't her?' Arnie folded up the newspaper.

'Certain. Look at the dates. She was attacked the week
before. But she stood up to him, and he ran off.'

'Ahh,' said Arnie. 'I knew it. I knew it. Same bloke, then.
That explains why she ran away. All these poor women
getting raped right here in our town.'

'She wasn't raped,' said David.

'Rapist living in Wootton Bassett and nobody tells us, do
they? You'd think they'd give men the chance to deal with
it themselves, protect their women. He could be out there,
doing it again, right now, and he loves that library, doesn't
he?' There was a malicious enjoyment to Arnie's voice.

David stood up. Marianne was in the library, the quiet, bright library, a shining beacon in the darkness. The ugliness of the world was becoming so very clear to him. It had been moving into focus since he talked to Hamish at the funeral.

It's all so wrong, Hamish had said. *Criminal out on the streets, you know. I found out a paedophile lives down the road from us. Rebecca's very sensitive to things like that; how can she relax, knowing he's in the street too? We never had kids because of people like that. I know it's really upsetting her.*

How horrible to be in that situation, David had thought. He remembered feeling guilty over how relieved he was not to be in that situation himself.

But that situation was everywhere. That blackness of broken, selfish, dangerous souls had spread all over the world, and nobody was doing anything about it. 'Pliers, that's what you need,' said Geoff. 'Take a pair of pliers to the bastard's testicles. Doing that to your wife.'

'I've got to go,' said David.

'You don't want to believe everything Marianne says,' said Arnie. 'She was always a good liar, that one. All of them are. And they all leave in the end.'

David strode over to Mags, laid a ten-pound note on the bar and met her gaze. She gave him a small smile, apologetic. 'You don't need any cubes now,' she said. 'Look at you.'

He left The Cornerhouse and ran for the library.

CHAPTER FOURTEEN

'Can I just say…' Patty hesitates in the doorway. 'That we all think you're really brave and when you feel ready to go back out on the front desk again, you just let us know.'

'Great,' I say. 'Thanks. I'm still a bit…'

'Yes, of course.' She looks at the kettle on the work counter, as if it is deeply interesting. Eventually she points to it. 'You want?'

'No, thanks Patty.'

'Okay. I'll be out the front, then.'

'Give me a shout if there's a rush,' I tell her, safe in the knowledge that a rush of customers at 7:45 on a Thursday evening is the most unlikely of things to happen in this library.

'Okay. You do your—' She points at the spreadsheet I have open on the computer screen. She's in her sixties and says she'll never get comfortable with electronic systems. I have always liked that about her. She is determined to remain immune to modern life, and her vision of the world is intact, frozen, formed from *Coronation Street*,

Panorama and the Silver Jubilee. I can feel, in her presence, that maybe everything isn't out of control after all.

After she has left the back office, I switch from the spreadsheet to Google once more.

The news has become a code to crack. I start every day on the BBC website and I hunt for articles, through the *Guardian* and the *Independent*, on through CNN and Al Jazeera, even the *Sun* and the *Star* and the *Daily Mail*. The stories give me clues as to whether Moira escaped the island, where she might be, how her power to affect men is changing everything.

Because around the world, men are changing. They are becoming heroes, villains, sages and sidekicks. Today, in Kentucky, a fireman rushed into a burning orphanage and saved sixteen children, one after the other. Police think the fire was started deliberately by a serial arsonist who is now operating in the area. Today, in Lancashire, an old man lay down on train tracks and had to be forcibly removed. He had written on his face in indelible ink:

I DON'T WANT THIS

Today, in Kenya, Somalian pirates attacked a holiday resort. They rounded up all the men and divided them into four groups. They killed every member of the smallest group, and kidnapped the men in another. Two groups they left alone. Five men dead, six missing. Forty-eight ignored.

Were these things happening before? Not like this, not in such clear delineations, I don't think. Or am I catching Amelia's madness?

I think Amelia knew what unique and special thing she was hiding in that basement. That's why she named her monster Moira. By doing that she left a clue that was easy to follow. All it took was a quick internet search to find the truth.

I looked up the derivation of the word monster. It comes from Middle English, leading back to a Latin root: *monstrum*. A portent, an unnatural event. Whatever Moira is, I don't think she's unnatural. And if she's part of the natural order of this world, then that means men are meant to be more important than women.

I click on the bookmark to my favourite page: the Wikipedia entry on the Moirai, the Fates – the Greek idea of incarnations of destiny. Three women who control the threads of life for all men. Clotho, Lachesis and Atropos. But in Homeric stories and Mycenaean myths there aren't three women who perform these roles. There is one.

Whenever I consider this, my hands begin to shake. It's a terrible piece of knowledge to possess.

I look up Lady Worthington on Google. There are many sites that mention her; she is a romantic historical figure, I suppose. I click on one devoted to feminist pioneers:

Born into the heart of the English establishment at the end of the nineteenth century, Lady Amelia Worthington was niece to the fourth Earl of Stanhope, and heir to the Worthington fortune, a trove of priceless Roman artefacts collected in Northern Africa by her father, the Victorian explorer, Lord Percy Worthington.

Upon her father's death, Lady Amelia used her vast wealth to travel with a freedom and independence that women were just beginning to explore after the end of World War One. She participated in archaeological digs in Egypt, and was a close friend of Lord Carnarvon. After his sudden death in 1923 in Cairo (some say due to the Curse of Tutankhamun, but nowadays widely attributed to blood poisoning), Lady Amelia left Egypt and travelled extensively in Turkey, the Greek Islands, and the Mediterranean. She was heavily involved in the British dig in Thermi, on the island of Lesbos, conducted in 1933, that uncovered extensive pottery and figurine remains from the fourth century BC, along with rich mosaics and impressive sculptures.

Her whereabouts are undocumented during World War Two, rising to speculation that she remained on the Greek Islands and was involved in the resistance movement. Cretan resistance fighters later recalled reporting to a female British secret agent who lived and worked amongst the Cretan women without arousing Nazi suspicion.

In 1945 Lady Amelia conducted a deal with the British government, aided in part by an unlikely friendship with Foreign Minister Ernest Bevin (with whom she shared a political belief that the days of empire were over, and a penchant for Webster Cigars) to purchase Skein Island, lying only eighteen kilometres from mainland Devon. She then used her vast fortune to set up the world's first feminist retreat, offering a week of free board and lodging to those who needed a period of reflection or to escape difficult domestic circumstances.

The rest of the piece deals with things I already know. She lived as a recluse, and lived on the island she dominated. And then she passed the reins on to my mother.

I sit back from the screen. I can't control my thoughts any more. Everything I learn sends me a new message I can't ignore. The world is being filled with the stories of men: heroes, villains, sages and sidekicks. Women will be marginalised into minor characters once more. We will lose the freedom we never knew we had – a chance to make our own stories.

Moira is Fate. The Fates. Three women in one, making heroes, villains, sages and sidekicks in order to weave a tapestry of stories. Were all those myths true, after all? Odysseus, Hector and Achilles, Perseus, Theseus? And others, later: King Arthur, Mordred, Lancelot, Merlin. Thousands of stories, shaped by Moira for her entertainment. Weaving together the strands of men's lives.

Each man delights in the work that suits him best, Homer wrote. They are all born with the seed within them to become one of four things. And now those seeds are growing.

David will think I'm crazy. But, after Christmas, I must attempt to explain it to him. And he will react as a hero should, he will attempt to protect me from myself. His desire to do this, to take control and make the decisions, will only get worse.

The feeling of foreboding, of dread, knowing that I'm

about to be controlled, dominated – I am familiar with this. I felt it that night the stranger walked into the library and said, *Get in the back. Take off your clothes and lie down.*

I can't bear it, can't sit here waiting for this to happen all over again. A part of me thinks my fear of it is the reason for its creation. I must be making this whole thing up in order to bring my fear to life. This is an elaborate construction of explanations, assurances, abandonments; is it of my own doing? Am I mad? Rebecca would find a textbook way of putting it. I've had a break with reality. I've rationalised a traumatic experience.

I push the doubts away. I am the strong one. I have worked so hard to be the strong one. I can't even begin to rationalise it, but I know I have to tell myself that I am indomitable, have been ever since the day he came into the library and said *Get in the back. Take off your clothes and lie down.*

And I said— I said—

I wrench my mind away. My heart is a runner on a long, straight road. I am prickly with sweat, on my scalp, under my arms. The world is out of control, doesn't anyone see it? Men set buildings on fire and other men run into those buildings. Men are divided and killed and born and they must be men of action, while I must lie down, take off my clothes and lie down, take off, lie down.

'David's here,' says Patty. 'He's early.'

I am amazed at myself. I say, in a perfectly even tone of voice, 'Oh good, I'll come out to the front. You can take off now if you like, Patty, and I'll lock up.'

'Are you sure?'

'Absolutely. David's here.'

She accepts that with a grateful nod because, after all, David is a man. She knows he will protect me. She gathers her things – anorak, umbrella, woven shopping bag – and says, 'Have a good Christmas, then.'

'Are you working on the twenty-seventh?'

'No, twenty-eighth I'm down for, afternoon and evening.'

'Great. I'll see you then. Are you cooking for everyone?'

She sighs. Every year Patty buys an enormous turkey and invites all the lonely members of her extended family to her house for Christmas dinner. She has a number of unmarried cousins and widowed aunts, along with an ancient grandfather who ruins everything if he gets the chance. Last year he spat his false teeth into the gravy boat. I wonder if Moira will have an effect on his villainous behaviour this year, and he'll have some macabre masterplan in mind, such as demanding to carve the roast and then stabbing someone with the meat fork.

'Good luck with that,' I tell her, sounding so much like my old self that I have to resist the urge to reward myself with a smug smile.

Patty leaves, and I close down the computer. Then I follow her out. In the bright library, standing alone in front of the rotating display of slushy paperbacks, is David. He faces the window that looks out over the car park. I can see his reflection in the glass, his lips pressed together, his eyes moving over the darkness, as if scanning for something or someone.

'Nearly ready,' I say. 'You're a bit early. I've still got to shut down.'

'I was with your father.'

Is that why he's so anxious? 'I know, I'm sorry, I will get round to speaking to him. I just can't face it now, but I will go and make it up with him after Christmas, okay?'

David turns to face me. The way he looks at me is disquieting. He wants something from this conversation, and the energy in his expression scares me. 'Arnie said another woman was attacked. The week after you. In the car park.'

'The library car park?'

'Right outside the building.' He jerks his thumb into the darkness. I realise he's angry. Beyond angry.

'That's terrible, but it's the responsibility of the police to—'

'She was assaulted.'

I wait for a moment, then say, very carefully, 'That's terrible. I gave the police a description of him. It's up to them. If it's the same man.'

'I need to stop him. I want you to tell me what happened. Every detail. I know it'll be difficult for you, but I'm sure you understand—'

'I told you already.'

'So he came in, you said no, he left? What was so different the next time, that it ended up in an assault?'

'I don't know! These people… progress. On to worse things. They get up courage. I was lucky. If you want to call it that.'

'I just... I get the feeling you're not telling me the truth. I feel like you haven't told me the truth in a long time.' He looks sad, so sad, and it's terrible to realise that I have done this to him. Not deliberately, never that, for he's still my husband, but I should have realised that he would know on some level that I was feeding the world a pack of lies.

There must be a way to find words for the truth, for all that has happened to me. It would be impossible to spit it into sentences, recreate it in syntax, grammar, punctuate it with exclamation points. I did this, I didn't do that. All those declarations on Skein Island, all the words that Moira took into herself – what did they mean? How can we tell the truth when it will change the lives of those who listen? 'Are you ready?' I ask David. 'If you want the truth, I'll give it to you.'

'Will you?' He sounds doubtful.

'If you want me to. It won't be— It's horrible. The words don't even begin to describe it.'

'I need to understand it. Then I'll know how to stop him.'

So I turn out the library lights and lock the door. We are shadows, lit only by the bulb from the back office, and I tell him, 'It started like this. It was closing time. I was about to lock up when he came in, and stood in the doorway. He told me to go into the back office and take my clothes off. He wanted me to lie down.' It doesn't sound right to me. My voice is different, strained, with a saw-edge of fear. It's the memory of it, coming to life, taking me over. The edges of that night and this night are bleeding together.

David stands perfectly still. He says, 'No. Right? You said no.'

I shake my head.

'What did you say?'

'I asked him not to hurt me.'

David pauses, swallows. 'What then?'

'Then I did as I was told.'

I lead the way into the back office. We stand together under the strip light.

'I took off my clothes,' I say. I don't whisper, or shout. I am calmer now, emptier. This is the moment I have been dreading, fighting against, but now it's here and I am ready for it.

'All your clothes?'

'Everything. I folded them and put them on the desk.' My white knickers, folded, on top of the trousers, the waistcoat, the shirt, the bra, in order: so neat. I don't look at David. I don't want to get caught up in his emotions. It is so much easier if I pretend this is not something that happened to me. I, I, I. It helps if I picture this as a story. So I find myself changing into a different form of speech. 'She took off her clothes,' I tell David. 'But that's not where the story began.'

I am a distant measurer of words as I tell him:

There was once a man who was born evil.

He knew it from the first moment he knew himself. He was meant to do no good. He was certain of it. And that thought made him proud and excited and sad and lonely, all at the same time. But there was no way to express it, because the wrongness within him was palpable. Whenever he tried to talk to anyone about the evil inside him, even his own family, they refused to listen. They didn't want to spend time with him, because they were afraid of what was inside him too.

So instead, when he was old enough, he bought himself a camera. It was a digital camera, small and easy to use, but he had opted for one with a very powerful zoom, so that he could sit in public places, like a park or a coffee shop, and take out his little camera, and pretend to be cleaning it or photographing ducks when really he was zooming into the face of a woman, right up into her eyes, her lashes, so close that every pore was captured. He didn't just want their faces. He also took photographs of the soft skin at the back of their knees, the casual overlap of nail varnish onto the cuticles of their fingers; arms, legs, hair and cleavage and anything that wasn't covered by clothes, he shot.

Then he took the camera home, laden with hundreds of images, and enjoyed each one in turn.

This is not a man you should feel sympathy for. He was not just lonely. He didn't imagine these women were his friends or his lovers. He imagined they were his slaves, and that he was making them lie still under his gaze to pay them back for seeing his ugliness in return. He was not a man who could be fixed by a real relationship, and he did not want to be fixed. He wanted to get worse. He wanted his obsession to define him, and so he started to plan his escalation to a new level of evil. He came up with a way to make a real woman suffer the worst humiliation possible, and he looked for an opportunity to implement it.

The local library provided him with that opportunity.

He wasn't a member of the library, but he passed it occasionally on his walk into town. It closed late on a Thursday, and from the darkness outside it was possible to see the lone woman who worked there. She would be shutting down the computers, and shelving the final returns of the day. What she looked like wasn't important to him. All that mattered was her vulnerability. She was alone, a shining light in the black pit, as fragile as a candle.

He watched her for months before making his move, and it was much easier than he had ever dared to hope for. He simply stood up from his hiding place behind the hedge and walked into the library. She looked up with a welcoming smile, and he told her what he wanted from her, wondering what she would do.

To his delight, she simply obeyed him. It was as if he were a god and she was a mere mortal. He didn't even need a weapon; his voice was enough. Her fear gave him power, and he had never felt so wonderful. The next ten minutes were the best of his life.

He made her undress, and lie down on her back. Then he took out his camera.

He started by taking headshots, then torso, keeping the delicate shell of her navel in the centre of the picture. He moved on to her limbs, trying to make sure the images would overlap so that he could piece her back together like a puzzle later, back in his flat. He wanted to make a complete map of her: her veins, the path of her arteries.

That was the beginning.

Then he told her to open her legs. He knelt between them, taking care not to touch her, and he photographed every fold of her labia, every line of her tight, puckered anus.

He told her to kneel, and to lift her arms. She had a small mole under her left armpit, from which three fine, barely visible hairs grew. He photographed them in an ecstasy of discovery.

Finally, he told her to open her mouth.

He photographed her tongue, her throat, her tonsils. He photographed the glistening droplet of her epiglottis, and the slippery descent that led to her stomach. Her teeth were creamy yellow; he thought maybe she drank too much coffee, and told her to drink more water in the future. She started to cry, making an ugly, desperate expression, and he photographed that too, and the slow trickle of tears into her open mouth.

Then he told her to stay still, and he left. He didn't even bother to check if she obeyed him. What she did no longer mattered. He had captured the essence of her. He took it home, the purity of her, and downloaded it, and looked at it ceaselessly, remembering how it felt to be a god.

But soon his ability to remember that feeling wore off.

Within a matter of days he began to plan again.

I stop talking, and the room is silent.

I am serene. I have never felt relief like it. The words are out of me and I have claimed my mouth as my own once more.

'Is it true?' says David. He has collapsed inwards, and looks like a smaller man. I never thought I could feel so good as he stands opposite me, deflated.

'Yes.'

'Why didn't you tell me? Don't you know you can tell me anything? It wasn't your fault, no matter how you reacted. There's no reason to feel that you weren't brave enough. There's no shame in being a victim of somebody like that.'

I shake my head. 'You don't understand. There is no shame. I lied for your sake. Because I knew it would become all you would see when you looked at me. I knew you'd be consumed by it.'

'You did it for me?'

I put my arms around him. The moment that I knew was coming is here. I had hoped it would not appear until after Christmas, so that I could have that memory, but it's too late for that now. We have tasks to do, and I must tell him where his future lies. 'You need to find him. You need to deal with him. And I need to go back to Skein Island.'

'No,' he says, 'No. I need you here. I can stop him. I understand that I need to stop him. But I need you here, to help me. To be waiting for me, after I've done this thing. Please.'

'I can't. Don't you understand? I can't be the victim at the beginning and the prize at the end of your story. There are things I need to take care of. The island needs me. There's nobody there to run it.'

'So what? Let it stop.' He holds me, strokes my back through my dress and it feels so good. 'We're finally getting through this, all of this.'

'No, David, we're not. Trust me. On the island, things happened to me. My mother showed me a woman. A monster.' I try to explain it, as best as I can, and I appeal to his bravery, to his desire to solve the problem. I do this deliberately, and not without guilt.

After I've finished, he says, 'So you think I'm turning into a hero? A proper hero? Like in stories of old?'

'You already are a hero in your own head. But I think that – if I don't find a way to stop her – you'll have no choice but to act like one all the time.'

'So you're trying to save me?'

'Yes. Not just you. But mainly you.'

He kisses me. 'Thank you, but I really don't need saving.'

'We might have to agree to disagree on that.'

'A few weeks ago I would have assumed you're having a breakdown, you know that, right? But something happened to me while you were away.'

'Something... with Sam?'

He frowns, and says, 'Sort of,' and it hurts me so deeply that I can't breathe. 'She found me here, outside the library, waiting to kill him, that man who...' He swallows, and continues, 'I'd been in The Cornerhouse with Arnie, and they were playing a strange game. I had a... hallucination of some sort, and I was a hero in it, a knight, and there was a woman there, a... goddess. Like you described.'

'A game?'

'With four cubes, coloured cubes.'

I have no idea how this can be, but I'm already sure of the answer as I ask him, 'Were they red, blue, green and yellow?'

'How did you know that?'

So I tell him every detail of my week on the island, and he tells me about cubes, and the game, and the liquid he drank before he had dreams of Moira. We swap information, trade notes, and by the time we finally lock up the library, I think I understand the world a lot better.

We go home together, taking a slow walk, hand in hand. There is no reason to pretend that we can be together, no matter how much we might want that. We're part of a pattern that must be played out. He will be the hero he was born to be, and I will attempt to find the monster from Skein Island.

PART FOUR

CHAPTER FIFTEEN

'I was certain someone would come,' says Inger. 'I have to say, I'm surprised it's you.'

'Hello,' I say. 'I thought I'd be alone. I'm so glad I'm not. Can I come in?'

The light shining from her cottage window had been the first good moment in a terrible day. Packing, saying goodbye to David, driving for hours in heavy traffic on the last Friday afternoon before Christmas, and then arriving at Allcombe and having to find a fisherman to take me over to the island as heavy drizzle blanketed the Bristol Channel: I had done all of these things, all the while thinking that an empty island would await me. I expected to sleep that night in my ancient threadbare sleeping bag from university. But in the shroud of late afternoon, the lights of the staff cottage had sung out to me. I had no hesitation in making for it.

Inger says, 'Yes, come in, come in. I'm sorry, I've not seen many people for a while.' She steps back and I enter. The heat hits me. It's cosy inside, a tiny living space leading into a kitchen, much smaller than the guest bungalows. There's a squashy white sofa, anglepoise lamps, and patchwork covers on the cushions. There is a pot-bellied stove in the hearth from which warmth is emanating at a ferocious rate. I put down my rucksack and strip off my coat, then my jumper.

Inger closes the door, and says, 'I don't really understand anything that happened. You're Mrs Makepeace's daughter, have I got that right? So that means you must own this island now?'

'Yes, I, um, own it. I'm sorry, do you think I could have a coffee?'

'Yes, all right.' I follow her into the kitchen. She's dressed in a grey tracksuit, her blonde hair scraped back. I watch her fill the kettle with water from the tap. 'Nearly everyone left. There was no word about reopening, or getting paid…'

'Do you have contact numbers for staff?'

'They will be in the reception office. Why? Do you need to talk to them?'

'I don't know,' I say.

Inger takes two mugs from an overhead cupboard and spoons in instant coffee. I can see she's thinking hard. 'I hope you decide to open the island again. I think it would be a good thing to do.'

'Why did you stay? Even without pay?'

'I was hoping that the island – what it stands for – could be salvaged. I'd like to help with that.'

'Another thing that needs saving from drowning?' I ask her. She smiles, and the kettle clicks off as the water boils for a furious few moments, then settles back down into stillness.

* * *

There are a hundred empty beds to choose from on this island, but I am glad to be on Inger's sofa, listening to the crackle of the fire in the belly of the stove, feeling my body relax into sleep.

Inger has put up no Christmas decorations, and that is another thing I am grateful for. It reinforces my belief that this island is separate from normality, kept free of the usual demands that life places upon us. It is suspended in salt solution, an embalmed island in time, and the fight to keep it preserved in this manner is about to begin.

I wonder if David is alone in bed tonight. I hope so. Maybe it's selfish of me, but I want him to spend at least one night missing me before he turns back to Sam for comfort. For some reason I'm certain that he will; it was a promise in his face when he talked of her. There is unfinished business to be taken care of between them, I think.

Since I've given up all rights to him, I shouldn't mind. But I do. I do. So I allow myself to feel grief and guilt for a few minutes, safe in the knowledge that Inger won't come down to ask what's wrong, even if she hears me. She's not that type of woman, not like Rebecca. Rebecca's interest lay in examining problems, and Inger is interested in solving them single-handed. If she can't do that, then she doesn't want to acknowledge the problem in the first place.

But who am I to criticise her, or Rebecca, after all the things I've done? I wallow in self-loathing for a moment, like a pig in mud, and then I tell myself that I no longer have the luxury of hating myself because I have to be better than that. I have so much to do, and I don't even know where to begin.

I am terrified. The basement will be excavated – I've paid a fortune for female workers to come here, claiming it's in the spirit of the island, and I might find Moira waiting for me under the earth. If not, if she somehow escaped, as I suspect she did, then where do I look for her? How do I catch her when I know what she could do to me? She dismembers, she destroys. She is a monster.

Perhaps it's easier to be a man. If I'd been born a hero, I would have no doubts now. But I'm weak, and scared, and still a victim.

But I'm also a survivor. It is a thought that comforts me and moves me towards sleep, further down, until I close my eyes and leave all the unanswerable questions until the morning.

* * *

'What are we looking for?' says Inger.

'Not sure. Invoices. Receipts. Letters. Personal documents. Anything.'

I wish I was better at coming up with ideas. It was Inger who pointed out that maybe all the paperwork hadn't been kept at the white house, and maybe we should look at our immediate surroundings. To do something manual, to throw around paper rather than merely ideas, is a relief, even if we're only finding thank you notes from past visitors, and ferry timetables stretching back to 1978.

'What's in that one?' I ask Inger. We are sitting cross-legged, facing each other, on the floor of the back office. A stack of documents from the bottom drawer of the filing cabinet sits between us. She's holding a vinyl ring folder that looks a lot more exciting than the weather print-outs from the Meteorological Office that I'm examining.

'Receipts from the mainland for fresh fruit,' she says. 'I have a new understanding of how many pears we all ate last year.' She puts down the folder and stretches, raising her arms above her head as she yawns. I catch her yawn, and return it. I'm tired too, even though it's still early in the afternoon. But I'm not despondent. Even if we don't find something here, a clue to help me understand this place better, we'll find it in the remains of the white house, I'm sure. The excavation has been completed; nothing was found, apart from a few intact barrels of water and some lucky declarations that escaped destruction. The white house is now being rebuilt. The basement has been filled in with concrete.

'Look,' says Inger. She holds up a few sheets of yellow paper, stapled in the top left corner. 'It was underneath the receipts. It doesn't have a red file, but it looks complete.'

It's a declaration. I recognise that type of paper, and the letterhead. It should have been lost with the other hundreds, thousands, of declarations that Vanessa kept in the library. I can see the loops and lines of a neat, sure hand, setting out a life story in black.

'What does it say?'

Inger purses her lips, then reads aloud, '"I'm not going to give her a second helping. She takes all of my time and energy as it is. Instead I'm going to keep this all to myself. It's the story of how I came here, and why I stayed. My very own—"' She stops reading. 'It's a proper declaration. It's private.'

'It's Vanessa's declaration.'

'Yes, I think so. The handwriting…' Inger looks up at me with her steady eyes. 'Do you think we should destroy it?'

'Destroy it?'

'Declarations weren't written to be read.'

That's true. The authors never dreamed that their words would be read aloud in order to feed a monster, but that is what happened. And I know that, no matter what the reason behind my mother's decision to record her past, she wouldn't want me to read it. But I don't really care whether she'd hate it or not.

'Inger, would it bother you if I asked to keep that?'

'Are you going to read it?'

'Yes.'

'Why? What do you think you'll learn?'

'I don't know.' I feel tempted to lie, to say I'm hoping to gain some sort of empathetic and wonderful insight into my mother's choices, but I suspect Inger will see through such bullshit. So instead I tell her, 'I already know why she abandoned me, and that she thought it was the right choice. I suppose I just want to own something that was personal to her. To feel I have a right to it. I already have her money and the island. Now I want a little bit of her voice.'

Inger considers this, and nods. 'That makes sense,' she says. She folds the paper once and gives it to me. 'Do you want to read it now? Shall I give you some time?'

'No, thanks. I'll do it tonight.'

'All right. Tonight.'

So we spend the rest of the day sorting through a history of bungalow allocations and staff holiday requests and coastguard reports, and I feel like I'm on the edge of a precipice, teetering, toeing the chalky, ragged drop into a cold, blue sea below.

* * *

The day is done; the night is here. How strange time has become to me. It is disjointed, unconnected to the slow sweeps of the hands of the clock. I could almost believe that I am not aging at all.

The dim light of Inger's anglepoise is casting a circle over the sofa, where I lie in my sleeping bag, with my mother's declaration in my hands.

Outside, all is calm, still and cloudless, the iciest of nights. In the morning all will be frozen, but in here the stove gives out glad heat and the spicy, warming smell of burning wood. Inger has gone to bed, and the moment has come.

I lift the declaration and read:

I'm not going to give her a second helping. She takes all of my time and energy as it is. Instead I'm going to keep this all to myself. It's the story of how I came here, and why I stayed. My very own declaration. Not like the first one, when I came to the island for my week away from the world, and wrote about how my husband and my daughter failed to appreciate me. That was how I felt back then, no matter whether it was true or not. Doesn't everyone fail to appreciate everyone, after all? But I had my predictable moans to get off my chest, and that's what I did.

Predictability – that's a terrible way to live. In all the years that have passed since my arrival, I never woke up knowing exactly what was going to happen.

Perhaps I always craved an element of danger, but I don't remember being an adventurous child. I liked dolls and cuddly bears, and I kept all my toys throughout my teenage years, right into marriage. I only got rid of them once Marianne came along. I wanted everything that belonged to her to be brand new.

When I applied for Skein Island I never thought I'd get a place, so when the acceptance came through, I decided to go immediately, before my nerve deserted me. It was going to be my personal adventure, probably the only one I ever experienced. I was ready to have my week of self-discovery, and then return home forever more. But I'd be lying if I said I wasn't hoping for something more than that. In retrospect, what was I expecting to happen? On an island in the Bristol Channel with no men, I harboured some overblown romantic fantasies. I think one involved a dashing pirate kidnapping me on the beach. Too much Daphne du Maurier is to blame for that. Of course, as soon as I saw the beach I realised how ridiculous that idea had been. Not only were there no pirates off the coast of North Devon, but the beach was a small patch of grey shingle strewn with smelly seaweed – hardly the golden stretch I had envisaged.

I remember checking into my bungalow. The décor was utilitarian, the other women uninteresting. The first two days of my holiday were spent taking part in macramé and yoga workshops. It didn't occur to me to not attend the meditation sessions or the knitting circles, even though I hated them and still do now. I didn't want to draw attention to my differences by refusing. The truth is, I've always imagined myself to be less of a woman for not liking such things, and I've never wanted anyone else to find out.

This is a strange thing to admit. I've been denying it to myself for years, but I'm just not fond of the company of women. Ironic, I know. When I was younger I thought maybe I hadn't met any of the right sort of women yet, and that one day I would find a whole pack of them, just like me. I hoped they would turn up on Skein Island. But now, after years of waiting, I've begun to accept that all women are the same. I include myself. Didn't I simply go along with the herd? Didn't I make the choices that were easiest for me? When did I ever stand up and say, actually I don't give a flying fuck about yoga or manicures? I only ever thought it. There must be millions of us thinking it. But we never act on it, do we? We never take over the magazines or shoot the fashion designers. We're all too goddamn good for an actual war.

I've only ever met one woman who took on the world, and that was Amelia Worthington.

I met her on my third night on the island, and was enthralled by her. We all were. By sheer luck I'd been given the seat next to her at dinner in the white house. She was elegant and loquacious, charming enough to accept my gushing speeches of adoration with good grace. At the end of the meal she offered to give me a personal tour of the house, and took me around the upper floor, where the artefacts were kept. It was an exhibition of pieces she had rescued from around the world: Egypt, Greece, Turkey. 'Rescued' was the term she chose to describe them. Others were not so keen on her euphemism. When I became her personal assistant, just two days later, the first task she allocated to me was the answering of letters from collectors and curators, often demanding that she release details of her hoard and return those that she had stolen. I responded politely. It was never going to happen, of course; she had so many powerful admirers, celebrities and politicians who kept her safe. It was a protected, cosseted life by then, but she had earned it. At least, that was what I thought back then. I saw her as a woman who stood alone, fighting the establishment, carving out a haven for all women. I didn't find out the truth until six months later.

So I took the job under the illusion that I'd be doing some real good, I suppose. But it was more than that. A seduction took place. Amelia told me that she needed me, that nobody else could do the job, and I wanted so badly to believe her. Years later, towards the end, I asked her what she had seen in me that hadn't been present in all the other women who stayed on Skein Island. She said, 'Nothing, my dear. I picked you at random.' That's a difficult thing to accept. Like winning the lottery or surviving a concentration camp, it's these things that happen out of the blue, without any logical explanation, that never make sense to us, that puzzle us to the end. The guilt of such luck is enormous. But Amelia always liked to tell stories, right until the very end, so I like to imagine that just wasn't true. Maybe she said it just to shut me up, so she could get on with her nap. I wouldn't put it past her. No, she must have seen something special in me. My tenacity, my ability to do the worst jobs, make the tough decisions. My gullibility.

That first time, when she took me down into the basement and introduced me to the statue, I didn't dare to question her story. I never have. Of course, the business was up and running by then, and my role within it was laid out for me. I had to change the barrels once a day. That was my first duty. They had become too heavy for Amelia.

'Her essence leeches into the water, dear,' said Amelia, over consommé later that evening. At that point I had already moved into the white house and had become used to listening to her stories every day, so this seemed no different to me. She often talked of her travels, her lost loves, and her brushes with death in the same dreamy, half-remembered tone. 'It makes the liquid from the spring potent with possibilities. We fill the barrels, then ship them out to a farm in Barnstaple. They prepare it for sale, with love and care...' She made it sound like a rural smallholding, with rustic charm. Five years passed before she entrusted the accounts to me and I discovered the scale of the operation. Her personal fortune, inherited from her father, had dried up decades before, but the spring had made her a millionaire anew, keeping hundreds of people in jobs, allowing the island to run comfortably. Clubs, bars and pubs all over the country bought that liquid, paying a fortune for the smallest of bottles.

'It brings happiness to all men,' Amelia told me, in between mouthfuls of consommé. 'They get a little taste of Moira, and she shows them what they could have been, in another era. Those dreams only last for a few minutes, but they will keep coming back for more.'

I asked her how much these drinking establishments charged for the pleasure, and she replied, 'Oh, my, they don't charge money for it,' as if that would have cheapened the transaction. To this day, I still haven't found out what happens. To be honest, I don't think Amelia ever knew either. She wasn't particularly interested in how the liquid was used. It was always the declarations that held her attention.

She kept reading them to the monster until her voice gave out and she could no longer make it down the basement steps. I think it had been the most pleasurable aspect of her old age, reading aloud the words of so many women, like eavesdropping on thousands of private conversations. I didn't understand it. The monster had to be fed, but I always felt it was a betrayal of the visiting women. A necessary one, but still a betrayal.

'I caught Moira with the stories of my life, and now I tell her the stories of other lives,' Amelia would say to me. 'Isn't she beautiful?'

I've never found the monster beautiful. She is a statue: cold, sharp, carved, no softness in her. Every time I look at her, her eyes seem different, but the expression remains serene. She wants to be free, I think. Maybe she's had enough of the stories of women, and she wants to put them back in their place, as prizes or distractions in the kind of stories she used to create. But I get the feeling she'd like to do something personal to me, something awful.

I think she wants to kill me.

I think she had a better relationship with Amelia. Perhaps she admired her cunning, her skill in trapping. Amelia was an adventuress, with a thousand stories to share. I'm just an administrator with one sad tale to tell. More of a whine, really, about how I gave up everything for someone who doesn't appreciate it.

In the minutes before she died, Amelia knew exactly what was happening to her. The pneumonia had grabbed her hard, squeezed her dry, punched her beyond breathless. It took her an age to wheeze out that she wanted to be taken downstairs one last time. I helped her. She was so small and frail by then that I thought it would be easy, but she leaned against me with all the weight of death in her. As we struggled down the stairs I remember thinking that I would never be able to get her back up again, not without help. I put her in the wicker chair next to the monster, and I left them alone. I left the door ajar, and didn't go back up the stairs. I waited without much patience, even tried to listen in for a while, but I couldn't hear a word.

When I came back in Amelia was dead, and Moira was motionless. Of course she was motionless. But if I had ever expected her to move, it was then. Just to look at me, to acknowledge the moment, the realisation that we were now stuck together for good.

Skein Island had become our mutual prison.

Of course, nothing melodramatic happened. An old lady had died of natural causes, that was all, and I dealt with the paperwork, because that was my role. I read one declaration to Moira every day, and changed the barrel, and dispatched it to the farm to be bottled. I kept everything going, just as it was.

Lately, I find myself accepting the fact that I won't change anything now. It was never my job to be a bringer of change, I think. Maybe women are born into roles, too. But still, I did one revolutionary thing in my lifetime. I had a daughter of my own. I never realised it before, but it occurs to me now that she might reach a point in her own life when she begins to feel unappreciated, and to wonder why that is. I have her address. Such things are easy to find on the internet nowadays – electoral rolls and so on. I might write to her, give her a mystery to solve, a quest on which to embark. If her life is boring, she'll grab that quest and let it bring her here.

If she comes, I'll be able to explain myself to her. I think I might manage that, if I work it out in my head beforehand.

I suppose that's what this declaration is, really. Practice at explanation.

I'd love to be able to see an understanding of my predicament dawning in another human being's eyes. Maybe, if she can grasp it, it will start a new chapter in my story, and in her own. Perhaps I could even return to Wootton Bassett, if she will take my place, just for a few days. If there's one thing I've learned from reading declarations, it's that every woman deserves at least a few chapters of her own in the story of her life.

I put down the paper on the floor beside the sofa, and settle myself for sleep. It's easy to relax into the pillow, to feel lethargy seep into my arms and legs, to snuggle into the warmth of the sleeping bag.

I know them now: Vanessa, Amelia, Moira, Skein Island. I understand that Moira makes men strive to go forth, to fulfil their destinies, while women go round in circles. They return to what they understand, and surround themselves with the familiar, even if those familiar people and places hold terrible memories for them. They hold close the things that they detest.

And now I hold the thought of Moira close. I will find her, and bring her back, so that I don't have to be anyone's victim.

But, just like all the best heroes, I can't undertake this adventure alone. I'm going to need help.

I know exactly who to ask.

CHAPTER SIXTEEN

Being a hero was not as easy as it sounded.

David had only one place to look for the man who had violated his wife, and that was the library car park. But hiding in the bushes for three hours a night was not an option; the police regularly patrolled the spot now. And he was fairly certain he wasn't dealing with a stupid adversary, so why would the man turn up here anyway? He had considered going to Sam, asking her to somehow lower the police presence, but the pain of Marianne's departure was too acute. He couldn't picture himself on Sam's doorstep, begging for entry, with things leading in a direction he was not ready to revisit. So he kept his distance from both her house and the library, and as a consequence had nowhere to go and nothing to do except despise his own uselessness.

But then, one cold, dark January night, there was a knock on his front door, and time started to move forward again.

Arnie and Geoff stood there, holding each other upright, trying not to look drunk, and failing. David checked his watch. 11:48 p.m.

'Cornerhouse just kicked out, has it?'

'We heard a little birdie saying my daughter's pissed off again.'

'Who told you that?'

'I've got a library card,' said Geoff, in a very loud voice, standing to attention.

'Is it true?' said Arnie.

An upstairs light in a house across the street winked on.

David said, 'You'd better come in.'

Arnie and Geoff wobbled into the living room, not taking off their shoes and coats, and David shut the door and followed them. They sat side by side on the sofa, hands in their laps, attention fixed on the television screen and the end of the film David had been watching.

'*Rocky*,' said Geoff. 'Brilliant.'

Sylvester Stallone was sweaty, desperate, having his eye cut so he could continue to see the killer punches coming. David took the remote from the arm of the chair and switched it to mute. 'Marianne's gone back to the island,' he said. 'She'll probably write to you, once she's ready.'

'I'm not reading any letters from that place,' said Arnie. He had a patchy grey beard that made him look even more unkempt than usual, and the smell of beer wafted out from him in waves. 'Listen, come to the pub with us.'

'It's closed.'

'Not now, boy.' Arnie shook his head at Geoff, who tittered. They had become a circus double-act, stuck together, gurning at each other for their own amusement.

'Listen,' said David, 'it's really late—'

'The way I see it,' Arnie said, 'that bastard hurt Marianne, am I right? He hurt my daughter. I'll be honest, I might not have cared about it much five or six years ago. All I cared about was the cubes. I've mowed Mags's lawn, if you get my drift, every Saturday for the past decade because of losing on the cubes. But I don't owe her any more favours now and I don't need the cubes any more. I used to need them to know stuff, but now it comes to me anyway.'

David sat down in the armchair. Rocky had just lost the match and was calling for Adrian, his pulped wreck of a mouth hanging open. 'What kind of stuff?'

'Other people. I'd drink the medicine down, and then I'd go in the back room and see other people living their lives. Marianne, in her library. Vanessa reading, in the darkness, always reading. Like mother like daughter. And now I see it in my dreams, at night. I saw what happened to her. I saw that man come into the library. I know his face. I know how to get him. Into cameras, isn't he?'

'Once, with the cubes, I was watching a big fight,' said Geoff, his eyes still fixed on the screen. The credits were rolling. 'There was one in red trunks and one in blue, and I was in the corner, with the stool, waiting for the bell to ring. I don't know what it meant.'

'We can stop him,' said Arnie. 'Well, you can. With our help. Before he does it again.'

'He won't use the library,' David heard himself saying, while another part of his brain shouted about the ridiculousness of it. 'The library staff are never alone now. And it's being staked out by the police.'

'It's not bloody America here yet, mate. They don't have the staff to keep that up for long. Give it two weeks and they'll have to call it off. Then you'll be ready to step in.'

'What makes you think he'll come back anyway?'

'That's what he does. Besides—' Arnie tapped his nose. 'He won't be able to resist it. We'll make sure of that.'

David stood up. He couldn't reach a decision. Was some sort of plan forming? Arnie and Geoff were the last companions he would have picked for this mission, but they did seem to be committed. They were both sitting up straight now, looking more focused. Maybe having something to think about other than the cubes was doing them good.

Arnie raised his eyebrows. 'Well?'

He could tell them to go, and they would. Probably without much of an argument. But did he really want to do this alone?

'I'll put on some coffee,' he said. 'You'll need to sober up if we're going to really talk about this.'

'White, two sugars,' said Geoff.

'I'll take it as it comes, son,' said Arnie, with a smile. 'And then we'll talk about what you need to do tomorrow to kick this thing off.'

'Isn't tomorrow a repatriation day?'

'It is. It's too much for him to resist. You'll see.'

The credits had finished rolling, and the late news had started. David turned the volume back up, and let the sounds of battles and blood from around the world reach him as he went into the kitchen, switched on the kettle and waited for it to boil. Things were escalating. It wasn't his imagination. Hatred was growing, proliferating, and it was his job to stop it.

* * *

The feeling in the crowd was different.

Usually, on repatriation days, there was a quiet air of solemnity over the town. People spoke in lowered tones, and many of them wore dark colours. It had become a tradition, and although David was aware of the undercurrent that existed between the serial mourners who turned up just for the catharsis of the occasion and the true locals who tried to go about their daily lives in the packed high street on such days, this level of tension was new to him. It was heavy, blanketing the people as they waited for the hearses, nine of them, the most amount of deaths to make up a cortege. The faces in the crowd were beyond sad. They were angry.

David stood back in the chemist's doorway and wondered how Arnie had picked it up before it had even begun. Could there have been talk in The Cornerhouse? But then, nobody went there any more. Instead, apparently, all the drunks were out on the streets at night, hanging about, breaking car windows, stealing when they got the chance. The local paper had dedicated its front page to the 'crime spree' that had hit Wootton Bassett, warning locals not to go out at night until the police had cleared up the problem.

A rougher element had descended on the town: bikers, that was the general gossip going around at David's office. But he didn't see any new faces waiting for the hearses that afternoon. They all looked familiar, set in intensity, each one wearing the same expression as the next in the row along the kerb. There were very few women and children. Men stood alone, and the sense of danger was thickening, intensifying, until it was as palpable as a storm waiting to break over the street.

The first hearse drove past.

Something terrible was about to happen. He could feel it.

The second car in the cortege was level with him when the banners went up, three of them, painted red words on ripped white sheets, waving back and forth, so the only words he could make out were WAR, FUCK, DEATH – and then the crowd rumbled, pulled back and sprang forward as one to engulf the banners and those that held them.

The hearses came to a stop as men spilled out onto the street. Some threw themselves onto the bonnets of the cars, hammering with their hands and feet. David heard breaking glass and screams, coming from further down the road. Someone stumbled into him, blocking his view, grabbing at his shirt. He pulled back into the protection of the doorway and shoved, hard, until the man fell back. Another took his place, with fists raised. David's instincts told him to duck, then aim for the gut. He connected with the white T-shirt ahead of him, felt the flesh and fat underneath give. But he was in the swell of the crowd now, moving away from the doorway. Bodies were all around him, pressing, pushing, jostling, falling into fights, the street overtaken with battles, and in the distance, police sirens, pressing closer.

Then he saw her.

She was standing by the fifth hearse, holding the door handle on the driver's side, with her baton in her other hand, held up over her head like an exclamation mark. She was trying to reach two men on the roof of the car; more were attempting to climb up from the other side. The aloneness of her was starkly visible. Her black and white uniform stood out, even though she was so small, in a sea of men. It terrified him to see her that way, as a target. He called out her name, couldn't even hear his own voice over the noise of the crowd, and started to push towards her, not taking his eyes from her in case she disappeared under the weight of the uniform.

The crush of bodies grew stronger. He felt the pressure of them, elbows digging, hands reaching, and he shoved back, not caring how he connected as long as they fell back. He heard a woman screaming and started to throw people aside with the same kind of strength that had infused him on the island. His own power amazed him. Within moments he stood at the fifth hearse, and put his body between Sam and the crowd.

She was breathing hard, her hat missing, her hair mussed, with a dusky swelling below her left eye that promised to be a beauty of a bruise. The screams had not been hers, but she was holding her left hand at a strange angle, cradling it in her right. He reached for it.

'No!' she shouted over the din, snatching it back. 'It's bad.'

Someone jostled David from behind, and he turned around and punched, randomly. He felt his fist connect, and then there was a groan of pain.

'Reinforcements,' she shouted. 'On the way.'

He looked over her head, around the scene. It looked like chaos, a kind of hell, men fighting, men crying, men trampling over each other. He realised something down the street was on fire; the smell of burning rubber was growing stronger. 'We need to go.'

'What?'

'Let's go,' he shouted.

'Where?'

He needed time to think, and a better field of vision. He swung himself up onto the bonnet of the hearse, and kicked the legs of the men on the roof until they crumpled and fell into the street. Then he pulled Sam up beside him, hauling her by her shoulders, and helped her up to the roof.

The first two hearses in the cortege had been overturned, and one was alight. The police were forming a line across the street at The Cornerhouse end, and had linked arms to start a march forward, but the men were not moving back, not obeying the shouted commands. Some of them had armed themselves with stones and bits of wood, and pulled the hoods of their jackets up over their faces. This is an organised attack, he thought, and a surge of adrenaline ripped through him. The seconds slowed to a crawl as he took in the pattern of the crowd, and the twenty or so men who had formed a group were working their way down the hearses, destroying each one in turn.

Behind him, at the other end of the street that led in the direction of the library, there was no organisation, just random destruction, men running, shouting, smashing with contorted faces, fighting each other in the madness of the moment. It was too dangerous – he couldn't see a way through. But the small alley that led to the library car park, that looked clear, although it was in shadow and so impossible to tell who might be lurking inside.

David made his decision. It was his best chance to get Sam to safety.

There was no time to explain. He picked her up, threw her over his shoulder in a fireman's lift, and jumped down from the roof. As his feet impacted on the ground, time began to move forward at an extraordinary rate, as if a fast-forward button had been pressed. He ran for the alley, weaving and dodging, hugging Sam's legs against his chest. She was so light, so easy to carry. He could have run with her for miles.

He reached the alley, edged inside, ran through the semi-darkness, and burst out into the car park. It was full, the cars in perfect order, each one parked between the white painted lines, as they should be. How ridiculous they looked, after such chaos.

There was nobody in sight.

'Can you walk?' he asked her, then realised she could hardly reply from that position, so put her down. She looked red-faced, in pain, holding her arm against her breasts. 'Sorry about that. Did I shake it about?'

'I should be back there.'

'No. You need to see a doctor.'

'Listen, I'm glad you were there, but I don't need— This isn't about wanting anything from you.'

'I know,' he said. 'It's okay.'

But it wasn't. The sensation of being watched pricked at his senses. He scanned the car park again, more carefully, looking for something out of place, anything.

The feeling of malevolence, directed solely at him, was so strong that his body reacted. His muscles clenched, his feet shifted apart to a fighting stance; it was intuitive.

'What is it?' said Sam.

'I'm not sure.' The feeling intensified. 'Get behind me.'

She moved back, and he was grateful that she had the sense not to argue. There was danger here. Someone was calculating, planning to hurt them. It came to David that perhaps photographs were being taken.

'Come out,' he called, at the gaps between the cars, the dense part of the hedges, the corner of the library building.

Nothing.

The feeling passed as quickly as it had arrived. Suddenly it was just him and Sam, alone in the car park, and as he turned to face her he realised she was no longer flushed, but pale, almost grey, and her eyes had lost their focus.

He caught her as she fainted. He swung her up so he could cradle her against his chest and started a jog away from the fighting, the noise, keeping to the back streets that led to the local surgery, letting the pall of smoke and the sound of men shouting fade into the distance.

* * *

'I'm fine,' she said, yet again, as David put a cup of sugary tea on the bedside cabinet. She was still fully dressed, lying on the bed, having refused to get into her nightdress. 'Really. You can go home now.'

It saddened him that she was so uncomfortable. He felt no such awkwardness; the familiarity of the purple duvet, the matching curtains, the string of bells along the staircase, was soothing, calming. And they had shared such an intense experience that afternoon. He had held her, saved her.

'I'll go in a bit,' he said. 'Once you're asleep.'

He didn't want to get home, sink into the armchair, and end up watching the news, with running commentary on what had gone wrong and whether the gangs had been dispersed from the high street. He only wanted to stay by Sam, his soporific, and care for her broken wrist. He couldn't help remembering an ancient custom he had once heard of – saving the life of somebody meant they belonged to you. It seemed obvious that Sam belonged to him, in a way that Marianne never had.

'I can't sleep with you here. Not after… Where's your wife, anyway? Shouldn't you tell her you're okay?'

'We've split up.' Was that the truth? Yes, he supposed it was. They had both accepted that they couldn't be together any more. Still, the words sounded wrong, and it must have shown on his face, because Sam said, 'I'm sorry, really,' before falling back into silence. 'At least let me make you some dinner,' he offered. The late afternoon sunlight was waning, hovering on the brink of collapse into another long night. Swindon hospital had taken up hours – crowded, frenetic, with ambulances arriving and subdued, beaten men slumped into the orange plastic chairs scattered through A&E.

'I'm not hungry.'

'I don't believe you.' He was ravenous; how could she not be? Didn't they feel the same things? He was certain that their thoughts and emotions were linked in some way. 'I'll make something anyway, and you can throw it away if you like.'

She shrugged, and winced.

'Is it still very painful? You can have another painkiller if you like.'

'I don't need you to tell me what I can and can't have!' She struggled to a more upright position, leaning back against the pillows. 'You are such a hypocrite, standing there, pretending to look after me, to care, when you—'

'I do care.'

'You went after Marianne! You chased her to that island.'

'You said I should.'

'I changed my mind.' She started to cry, and it burned that he couldn't help. He suspected she would never allow him to touch her again. All he could do was stand there and watch her pain.

When she finally caught her breath and subsided into sobs, he risked sitting next to her on the bed. She didn't scream at him to get out, at least.

'This is all wrong,' he said, keeping his voice low, comforting. 'I know it; you don't need to tell me. All I can say is that something has happened to me. I'm not the person that I was before I left for the island. I'm not the man you knew, but I'm also not Marianne's husband any more, not in any way that counts. I'm not anything normal. Being this new person, it's got… responsibilities. That I can't explain. But I think you're one of those responsibilities. I feel that I want to look after you.'

Marianne would have hated such a sentiment, but Sam nodded and wiped her eyes with the back of her hand. 'Okay. I can see how you feel that. I can't pretend that doesn't make me happy. So you can look after me, if you like. Just as long as you don't, don't just… As long as it doesn't just tail off into nothing, is what I'm trying to say.'

'I don't think it can. It feels really… permanent.'

She gave him her hand again, the unbroken one. It wasn't love, not in the sense that he knew it. But there was rightness in it.

'I want to hug you but I can't,' she said, so he moved around to sit behind her, squeezing between her back and the pillows so she could recline against his chest. He put his arms around her, breathed in time, and felt a deep peace penetrate him. The smell of her, her dried sweat and fear and the last gasp of whatever deodorant she had applied that morning, made him want her. He kissed her neck.

'I left home at sixteen,' she said. 'I couldn't stand it. Every day was the same as the one before, and I wanted… I wanted my life to mean something. It's not that my parents were bad people. It was me. I couldn't bear to be like them. It felt as if they were already dead. I never went back. I've always been moving towards a more exciting life. Sometimes it was so difficult, working for it, searching for it. Now it's here. With you. I feel alive for the first time. Is that a cliché?'

For the first time it occurred to him that she was still very young. 'I think we're meant to be together,' he said. He thought of Sam's clean walls, without photographs, deliberately wiped clean of memories. And then he thought of Marianne, alone on her island, and of the last promise he had made to her. 'I have things I have to do, though.'

'What things?'

'The man who attacked Marianne. I promised her I would find him and stop him. I think he was at the library car park today, watching us.'

'Why would he come back there? He's not stupid.' She slid her fingers along his wrist, and he felt himself grow hard for her. He could bury himself inside her, take away all of their bad memories from today.

'I don't know. It's become a contest. He knows who I am. He's laughing at me. Men who do these things, they have to be stopped.'

'Yes. We can stop him, together. If you need to catch this man, I'm going to help you. I need it too. I was out every night, checking that car park, waiting for him…' She shivered, and he tightened his hold on her. 'Let me help you. If he's in competition with you, then he'll want me. I can draw him out for you.'

'No! That's not—'

'I'm not scared. I told you. We belong together now.' She sighed, a deep, long sound of satisfaction, and relaxed against him. A few moments later, while he was still thinking of some way to dissuade her, he realised she had won the argument by simply falling asleep.

CHAPTER SEVENTEEN

Rebecca steps off the boat with her arms held out to the sides, as if performing a balancing act. She's wearing very high heels. They are black and glossy and utterly unsuited to the rough planks of the landing platform or the shingle of the beach; she had to know this, having been here before. But she's obviously chosen to forget it. Or maybe her need to be dressed impressively outweighed her desire to be able to walk without wobbling.

When she sees me coming towards her, she nearly falls over, but I sprint the last few feet and catch her hands, steady her, and take her bag from the amused fisherman standing on the dock.

'Thanks, Barney,' I say, and he nods, and returns to his boat, casting off once more.

'I never thought you'd be opening it up again,' says Rebecca.

'Why not?'

She shrugs. It's one of those February days with a permanent icy fog, the kind that can penetrate your clothes in seconds. I feel it through my parka. But at least Rebecca has on a proper winter coat too: long, woollen, black to match her shoes. Her hair is glorious henna red in contrast, straight out of the bottle. I wonder what shade of grey she is underneath by now.

'Come on,' I say. 'Let's walk up to the house. If your leg is fine with that.'

In response she sets off at a fast pace. Within moments she has to slow again, as she reaches the boggy fields and her high heels squelch into the mud.

'So the house is all finished, then?' she says, her breathing coming faster.

'Nearly. Turns out builders work a lot faster when you give a bonus for meeting deadlines.'

'Lucky you, with all that money. I would have thought you'd have moved to the Bahamas by now.'

'There's no place like this, I've discovered.'

'A great location to have a break from reality,' she snaps. She's so very angry with me, for some reason. But still, she walks on, and shows no sign of attempting to turn around, to signal to the fisherman to take her back.

When we reach the gravel path she stops, catches her breath, and attempts to scrape some of the mud from her heels onto tufts of wild grass. Her movements fling yet more mud up onto her coat, and I try not to smile as I wait, with my walking boots and thick socks and spattered trousers in place.

She takes one look at my expression and scowls. 'I've brought more sensible shoes in my bag, okay?'

'Well, good.'

'I just— This is armour, okay? I knew it was ridiculous, but I needed armour. Besides, isn't this a job interview? If it's a real job.'

'It's a real job,' I tell her.

She doesn't respond. The house is in view now, as close to the original as I could get it. Work is nearly done on a conical extension, rising up from the centre of the house, a kind of tower that will act as a library for the new declarations. It will be a light, airy construction, with plenty of windows to catch the sun, and shine out like a lighthouse.

'Are you sure your leg's okay?' I ask her.

'It's fine.'

'And how's Hamish?'

'I've left him.'

'Seriously?' This astounds me. 'Why?'

She ignores the question. 'Have you left David, then?'

'Not exactly. We agreed that we had to be apart.'

'How very mature you are.'

In silence, we come up to the house, enter the hallway. It has been reconstructed in the familiar black and white tiles. I walk through into the dining room, and we take off our coats and sit on either side of the table. Rebecca shakes her head at me. 'It looks exactly the same.'

'I wanted to capture the original feel of it. Lots of things are different; some of the artefacts were damaged, and I donated others to museums.'

'If I was your therapist I'd suggest to you that this is not going to help you to move on.'

'It's a good thing you're not, then.' I don't want to argue with her, but she's making it impossible to avoid. In desperation, to break through to something real, I say, 'But the job of Resident Therapist is yours, if you want it.'

'What?' She glances around the room, as if expecting to spot hidden cameras. 'Are you kidding?'

'I'm not interviewing anyone else. As I said in my letter, I'm reopening the island, and I think you're perfect for it.'

She bursts into tears, then clamps her hands over her face and takes shuddering breaths. I don't know what to do. Eventually I get up, go out to the kitchen and pour her a glass of water. When I come back to the dining room she is composed, mascara clotting around the corners of her eyes.

'Thank you,' she says. She takes the water and sips it. 'But I don't know if I can accept.' Her face quirks into despair, then straightens once more.

'Why not?'

'I believe this island should help women to establish real answers to their very real problems, and I want to be a part of that. I'm not sure what you believe. I think it has something to do with statues that come to life and suck up words. I couldn't encourage you in this fantasy. Let me be clear about this.'

Her morally superior tone of voice reminds me of how irritating she can be, but I'm determined to have her here to be my voice of reason. Nobody will work harder to restore this island to what it should be – the way that she pictures it, as a haven. Besides, she links me to the roots of this island – why I came, what I expected to find.

'I don't need you to believe what I believe. I just need you to be yourself.'

'That's easy.'

'Only you could say that, Rebecca.' I tell her of my vision of the island. How it will differ from what it was, and how we'll try to make it work.

She listens hard, nodding, frowning, then puts down the cup of water, and runs her fingers through her hair. I sense she's decided to accept my offer; it's in the way she looks around the room, this time with the fresh perspective, evaluating it as a home.

'So what happens now?' she says.

'You can start whenever you're ready.'

'I'm ready now.'

'What about your stuff?'

'All in the bag.'

It occurs to me that there's something more going on here than I had bargained for. 'Rebecca, what's going on?'

'I told you – I've left Hamish. I really don't want to go back and see him. It wasn't amicable. He became...' She bites her lip. 'Listen, I can't go into this. You'll feed it into your fantasy and make it part of your reality, and... God, this is ridiculous! I can't do this.'

'What did Hamish become?'

'I... Look, he set up a network of internet friends to monitor and report back on paedophiles. People they thought might be paedophiles. There was a man living on our street and Hamish thought he was... Well, he had been convicted of something, and Hamish got really concerned over it, and so did some others. And then he set up an online group and it just grew. It went from a few friends to thousands of them. All over the country. He said he was doing it to keep everyone safe, to keep our grandkids safe. When I pointed out we didn't have grandkids he wasn't even listening. And he always listens. We communicate. That's who we've always been, as a couple. We communicate.'

She stops talking. I don't try to break the silence that surrounds us. Eventually, she says, 'See? I can feel you thinking it.'

'I'm only concerned for you,' I tell her, but I'm a terrible liar, and she shrugs it off.

'You're right, though, it's all men. His group, all men. Doing vigilante things. Organised packs, on the streets. He said I needed to be protected, that all women and children have to be kept safe in these times. What kind of a person says things like that? That's not Hamish. But I can't fight him, I can't stay and watch him…' She shakes her head. Her grief and pain are waves that emanate from the core of her. I can feel it washing over me, dragging me down too. 'I don't know what's gone wrong with the world. It's the media, perhaps. The pressure of the news, the tabloids. It's not what you're thinking, Marianne.'

I try to focus, to not let my feelings for David get caught up in this. 'But you don't want to be out there any more, whatever it is. You want to be here. Where it's safe. I can understand that.'

She clears her throat. 'Oddly enough, I do feel safe here. Safe alone with the only certifiable loony I know. Sorry, I shouldn't use such terms, should I? Very unlike a counsellor.'

'Well, you're not alone. Inger is here too. She's very efficient. With her help we're going to be back in business in no time.'

'That's great. Listen, I didn't mean it, the loony thing. It's just the stress.'

'You did mean it. But it's okay. I actually kind of like being called a loony. It makes me feel less boring.'

Rebecca straightens her skirt with the palms of her hands. 'Marianne, no matter what you do, nobody could ever call you boring.'

The idea of this – that I am beyond the conventional in every way – appeals to me. 'Thanks.'

'It wasn't exactly a compliment.'

I hear footsteps coming down the stairs, then Inger knocks on the open door and shoots me a look that I translate as concern. Do I look in need of help? I don't feel it. 'Inger, come on in. Do you remember Rebecca?'

'We never met properly.' They shake hands, a very businesslike gesture.

'So you're on board?' says Inger. She's so very direct. I hope Rebecca will respond in kind.

'Yes, all right, consider me signed up.' Rebecca lets out a long breath. 'So where do we begin?'

I wait for them both to sit down again, so we are all gathered around the table. Inger has brought along a pen and paper, and looks ready to take notes. This has officially become a business. 'We're going to start by getting Moira back.'

'The statue,' says Rebecca.

'Yes.'

'The statue that got destroyed in the basement.'

Inger and Rebecca exchange looks. Well, let them both think I'm mad, as long as it unites them. They have to learn to work together.

'It didn't get destroyed. It's in Crete.'

Rebecca gives me her best maternal, disapproving look, as if she's just walked into the kitchen to find me smearing jam on the walls. 'What would it be doing in Crete?'

'You have to trust me on this.' Or perhaps I'm asking too much. 'No, okay, you don't even have to do that. You just have to get this place up and running while I go to the cave in Crete, find her and bring her back here where she belongs.'

'The cave in Amelia Worthington's story?' says Rebecca. 'Seriously? Why would Moira – the statue – be back there, anyway?'

'Because women go round in circles.'

Inger and Rebecca stare at me, and then we all burst out laughing.

'It's not safe to be travelling alone,' says Rebecca, finally, and the atmosphere in the room changes, thickens, into a sense of uncomfortable possibility. I really am going to Mount Ida.

'You sound like Hamish,' I tell her. 'And I'm not asking you to condone my decision. I'm asking you to run this place.

That's what you'll be good at. The two of you, together – the unstoppable administrators.'

'I don't think much of that as a super-power, do you?' she says to Inger.

Inger leans forward and takes my hand across the table. It's such an unexpected gesture that I feel my cheeks flush and tears prick my eyes. For all Rebecca's objections, it's Inger's compassion that could undo me. I could ask them to go with me, to risk walking into that cave.

And then I force myself to remember what Moira did to the last people who entered the cave in Mount Ida, and I know I have to go alone. I stand up and pull my hand free. 'Listen, it's going to be fine. Inger, can you show Rebecca to the staff accommodation? I've got to organise my flight.'

I walk out of the room before anything more can be said. Between them, they will do everything that must be done to get this place running. They won't need me at all.

CHAPTER EIGHTEEN

In the back of Sam's Mini, he crouched: cold, squashed, numb.

They had agreed on 8:30 p.m., but David didn't dare check his watch for fear that the light on the dial could possibly be spotted from outside. It was so dark, beyond what he had imagined when he pictured this moment. It made him sure that he had failed to envisage other happenings – what hadn't he planned for? How could he keep Sam safe in every circumstance? It was impossible to guarantee.

He tried to push such thoughts away, and forced his mind to return to the plan.

Sam would return from the supermarket laden with carrier bags at 8:30 p.m. She would walk through the deserted car park, and then open the boot to her Mini to load the bags. She would slam the boot and walk around to the driver's seat, and if nothing happened in that time span, she would simply get in and drive away.

But if something did happen, David was ready.

Except that his legs were slowly turning to stone in this position. He had no sensation left in his cramped thighs.

That was what he hadn't counted on – he wouldn't be able to get to her, to leap from the car in time to save her. Surely his body would never respond.

He had to trust it. His body would automatically respond to Sam's need. It would wake up, come to life, as it did whenever she walked into the room. They had been living together for three weeks now and he couldn't get enough of her, couldn't get close enough. He only felt sure of her safety when he was inside her. At all other times, from morning to night, he watched her, trying to protect her. If she was threatened, he was certain something in him would awaken. Something primitive, violent.

'I hear you're shacked up with the policewoman,' Arnie had said last night, over a pint in The Cornerhouse.

'Yes, I, um…'

'Good on you.' Arnie clapped him on the back, a strange, congratulatory gesture that belonged to a different age. 'She's a pretty little thing. Going to help you catch that bastard, is she?'

'How did you know that?'

He tapped the side of his head. 'Saw it. Geoff'll be coming along too, just as back up.'

'No, I think I'd rather handle it alone,' David said, his eyes on Mags, who was slumped over the bar, her hands in her hair, her white blouse dishevelled. Every time he saw her she looked smaller, greyer.

'Up to you. But it won't work out in your favour without Geoff.' Arnie took a sip of his pint. 'It's just how I've seen it. Tomorrow night. You in the car, her as bait. Geoff'll just happen to be walking past, like.'

And, because Arnie had seen it, David went along with it.

The world had gone crazy anyway. Crime rates were rising, the internet was filled with talk of taking matters into your own hands, forming groups, taking stands. It had become, so quickly, a world of them and us, retribution and revenge, derisions and decisions that would affect thousands. It was a pandemic of punishment; believing that one old man could see the future seemed like the least of David's worries.

He shifted his weight and rubbed his legs. Where was Geoff? It was impossible to see anything outside the car, now that the timed safety light on the library wall had switched back off. Sam had assured him that the police had moved on from their patrols in this area. Crime was everywhere – they couldn't afford to sit outside one building while gangs of teenage boys staged battles in the streets.

There was still no sign of Sam.

Maybe his enemy had been waiting in the alley instead. He could have grabbed her while David crouched there, like an idiot, could have dragged her to a quiet place where he could take his photographs and work up the courage to put his fingers where his lens had gone. The thought was enough to make David move. He stretched up, reached for the inner handle of the car.

Footsteps.

The steps, quick and light, approached the car. The safety light switched on, cast shadows around the back seat. He heard the blip of the key fob, and the locks in the Mini slid up. The boot opened. Cold air poured into the car and the rustle of plastic bags, so close to his head, made him flinch.

The boot slammed shut. He heard Sam's feet move to the driver's door, not too fast, taking her time.

'Excuse me?'

A man's voice, low, in a local accent, close to the car. 'Excuse me, have you dropped this?'

It had to be him. David felt it, knew it, as adrenaline uncurled in his stomach and spread through his veins; it was him.

'No, no, that's not mine,' said Sam.

'Oh right… Only I just found it on the ground over there… What do you think I should do with it? Should I hand it in somewhere?'

'Leave it on the rail next to the library, maybe?'

'Where's that?'

'Just up—' David could picture her turning, pointing. Then nothing. Her voice simply stopped. He waited on, expecting something to happen: the sound of a struggle, a scream, anything to galvanise him, send him into action. The silence enveloped him, bringing its own inertia. But then the enormity of the moment stung him, like an injection into the heart, and he leapt up, ignoring aching muscles and doubt, and sprang out of the car.

There was nobody there.

The ground crackled underfoot from the cold, and the air was tight in his lungs. On the bonnet of the Mini rested one red knitted glove, without an owner. No noise, no sound, no sense of proximity to anyone, anything living.

The surreality of it was so strong, he wondered if he'd fallen into a flashback from the cubes. Maybe everything was a lie, a dream. Maybe Marianne had never gone back to the island and all this was a game in his head. He could walk home, now, at this moment, and find her there, curled up in their bed, dreaming of books and beauty.

A flash of movement from the alleyway, the glint of the safety light on glass. Geoff stepped forward, his glasses illuminated into two small, round mirrors, and shook his head. David read his meaning – *They didn't come this way.*

Where, then? Through the hedge? Unlikely, without making any noise. To another car? Then Sam was still here. Nobody had pulled away. David jogged around the car park, between the rows, looking into each window, narrowing down that avenue of escape to an impossibility.

There was only one place left.

He walked up to the library door and was unsurprised to find it ajar. He pulled it open, walked into the darkness, used his memory to take him around the displays of paperbacks on circular stands to the front desk.

The door to the back office was closed and a yellow sliver of light crept from under it.

David put his hand to the handle. He took a breath, and opened the door.

The light confused him, made a jumble of the small room, and then the space began to pull into sense, and – Sam. Alive, still clothed, untouched – the relief of it, of being in time, took him over. His eyes held hers, tried to comfort her. She was sitting on the desk, her arms crossed over her stomach, her shoulders hunched. Beside her stood the man he had come to stop.

It wasn't an ugly face.

The eyes weren't too close together, the lips weren't narrowed or cruel, and the hairline wasn't receding. The nose wasn't bent. It wasn't an unremarkable face either; it was a shade beyond that, in the direction of pleasant, amiable, easy to like, with an upward curve to the jaw that suggested a permanent smile. He was the kind of man who could have had a girlfriend, if he wanted to. He could have had friends, a life, nights out down the pub.

David felt a pure white blast of hatred for him, this man who had choices, and had instead decided to hurt, to maim. It might have been possible to pity an ugly man. Instead David felt bloated, pregnant, with rage.

Sam made a sound in her throat, a whine, and he saw the knife at her thigh, level with the crotch of her jeans. It was small, straight, pointed. A paring knife, did they call it? For peeling fruit. There was a pair of handcuffs on the desk beside him.

'Don't hurt her,' he said.

'I just showed it to her in the car park and she came with me. I didn't even have to do anything. What's your name?'

'David.'

'I'm Mark.' He had no sense of urgency. It was one of those slow, relaxed voices, almost like a radio presenter on a show late at night. 'Listen, they always do as they're told. I think they like it really, I mean, deep down. I'm not just saying that to try to wriggle out of it. If they said no I would stop, that's my point. I'm not an animal, here.'

'Yes, you are,' said David.

Mark nodded. His smile widened. 'All right. Let's be honest. I knew who she was. I knew you'd be coming for me. I'm not scared of you. I'm more scared of myself. Where all this could go. I know it's not right, but I'm not going to let you just... I bet women throw themselves at you, don't they? Knight in shining armour.'

'I'm just a normal man. You could have been that too.'

'No, I couldn't. I don't want to be. Neither do you.' Mark looked around the room. David followed his gaze – the computer, the swivel chair, the display of thank you cards pinned to a cork board. *Thanks for finding that book. I'd given up all hope.* 'I took your wife here. With the camera. Just photos. I only wanted to look.'

David pointed at the handcuffs. 'Then what are they for?'

'Protection,' said Mark.

Sam gulped, such a loud sound, surprising, and Mark looked at her as if he had forgotten she existed.

'Do you want to go?' he said. 'You weren't really my type, anyway.' He let the knife drop from her thigh. She didn't move, for a moment, a long breath, then she took a step towards David, and another, crossing the room in tiny increments, making such slow progress that David felt the urge to grab her and push her through the door.

Instead he said, very gently, 'Go, I'll meet you outside. Honestly, go.' She turned her enormous eyes up to his, and then she left.

'What now?' said Mark. 'Now there's no policewoman, are you going to perform a citizen's arrest?'

David kept his attention on the knife. There had to be some kind of instinct within him that would tell him what to do.

'I think it was meant to be like this,' said Mark. 'Do you know what I mean?'

'There's no excuse.'

'How do you know? Did you choose to be here?'

'Yes,' he said, but it was impossible to believe it. Marianne had told him to be here, and Arnie had told him when to be here, and apparently this was all exactly as it was meant to be. Who was in charge? He was the vessel of other people's decisions. And maybe Mark was the same.

'Prove it,' said Mark. 'Don't do what they tell you to do. Do what you want to do. I can see you don't want to be here. Take my word for it that I'll never do it again, and you go home, and I go home, and nobody gets hurt, do they? You don't want to be responsible for this, not really. And I want to stop doing it, I swear. I can stop. I'll just stop.'

But the terrifying revelation at the heart of his words was that Mark wouldn't stop. He was right. It was beyond control, not Mark's decision to make. And that meant David could do only one thing. The inevitability of it was breathtaking. It infused him, filled him with the conviction that the moment had come, all options had been reduced to one, and there was nothing left to do but kill him.

Mark raised the knife. 'So move out of the way, okay? I'm leaving now. You can just let me go, and we'll never see each other again.'

'I can't let you do that.'

'Listen, I look at your wife's insides every night on my computer, in her mouth, up her legs. She's all soft and pink and ready. You want to go home to that, don't you?' He flicked out with the knife. It was a weak movement, without conviction. 'You're not going to make a move, are you?'

David felt nothing. He watched the movements of the knife, as Mark talked on, working himself up, trying to pry him from his position in the doorway.

'You're really going to take me on? Just walk away, mate, you don't need it. I'll cut you, I swear, I'll cut you.'

'You take photographs. This isn't New York. You're not a gang member. You don't know what the hell you're doing with that knife. You're standing in a small public library in Wootton Bassett.'

Mark flashed forward, lifted the knife to David's face, laid it against his left cheek. The coldness of the blade was astonishing; it was all David could do not to flinch. 'I suppose you're going to tell me this is an overdue library book?'

David reached up, grabbed Mark's hand as he started to put pressure onto the knife, felt a cut opening under his eye, and then twisted Mark's wrist with all his strength. The snap of the bone was audible. It was easy to keep twisting until the point of the knife touched Mark's throat.

Through the skin, through the fibrous muscle, to the larynx, slipping past the cartilage of the jaw.

Mark hissed on it, a sound like the releasing of steam, and David let go of the knife and took him by the upper arms to steer him into the swivel chair.

'It's all right,' he said. 'Let it go. It's time to let it go.' He took off his coat and wrapped it around Mark's neck, knife and all, tying the sleeves tight in a double knot. 'It's not your fault. It's the way we were made. Better to be dead.'

He realised he was speaking a deep truth, the deepest, as he patted Mark's hand and tried to soothe the pleading in his eyes. If a man had no choice but to cause pain, then it was better to be dead, undeniably. Why did Mark have to fight this, try to speak, make faces of agony and fear? David couldn't bear it any longer. He pinched shut the nose and mouth, and sang over and over, 'Go to sleep, go to sleep,' until the desperate eyes finally rolled over, and the story was done.

David pulled the material of his coat over Mark's face. He walked to the office door and clung to the frame as he called for Sam.

She came, with Geoff running after her, his face shining with excitement. 'What happened?' he said.

'I killed him. Call the police.'

'You're bleeding.' Sam touched his face, traced the path of the blood with one finger, as soft and cool as a raindrop.

'I've got a plaster,' said Geoff, and pulled a small first aid box from his coat pocket. David found himself laughing, and Sam had to tell him to stop so that she could apply the plaster underneath his eye. Once she was done, she kissed his cheek.

'Thank you,' she said.

There was no reply to that. Had he done it for her? He supposed he must have: for her, and Marianne, and for all women everywhere.

'Call the police,' he told her.

'I am the police. Let me deal with this. I'm not going to let you go to prison over that bastard, do you understand? You need rest. A good night's sleep. Geoff, give me a hand.'

Sam held one arm, and Geoff held the other, and David let them lead him from the library, through the car park, back to the passenger seat of her Mini.

'Stay here.' She kissed his lips, like Friday night wine at the end of a long week. She kissed his forehead, and he felt absolved, anointed. Her mouth, her words, her touch – it was enough to send him into sleep without guilt.

He didn't remember the drive home, or being put to bed. When he woke, it was bright outside. A cold, crisp winter sun penetrated the curtains, and Sam was beside him, naked, her mouth open, her legs splayed in sleep.

And downstairs, on the doormat, waiting for him, was a package from Skein Island.

PART FIVE

CHAPTER NINETEEN

I sit at the tiny kitchen table. The salad I prepared sits in a large glass bowl: sliced tomatoes, cubes of feta, a local type of ham. It's looking limp already. Salad is wrong in this weather, late February, and the white archways and tiled floors of the apartment are too cold to bear. I've been here for three hours and I haven't managed to take off my coat yet. It's sunset, and warmer outside – warmer than Britain, anyway. But I can't bring myself to sit out on the veranda, with the mountains rising up behind me like a threat.

Both Heathrow and Heraklion airports were a mess of cancelled flights and missing staff. So many men aren't turning up for work. They have more important things to do, more spectacular stories to be part of. Moira's power seems to be bursting out, maybe as a reaction against her years of confinement. It's changing the world.

At least the car rental agent was a woman. She checked my details and gave me the keys with a quiet efficiency, and I tried not to stare at the love bite on her neck, enormous, like a mark of ownership. She has become a man's property.

At Heathrow, before my flight was called, I sat in the departures lounge and watched people hurrying between the gates, fear on their faces. A male member of staff in a blue uniform, topped with a perfectly tied cravat, walked up and remonstrated with me about the dangers of travelling. He was so earnest, almost evangelical.

At first I didn't understand what he meant. I thought he was selling sunscreen when he told me I shouldn't be without protection. I said, 'But it's not even that hot out in Crete right now,' and he looked so confused. That was when I realised he meant I shouldn't be travelling without a man to protect me.

The apartment is in a complex, all the balconies facing the same way, overlooking a bright blue swimming pool with a dolphin represented in green mosaic at the bottom. The kitchen and the living room is one room, the fridge next to the sofa that doubles as a bed. I can see the pool through the French windows. The loungers are all stacked at the far end, the top ones in each stack covered by tarpaulin, pulled tight with ropes. The semicircular bar shows signs of use – the wooden stools are still out, and one beach umbrella is propped up against the back wall – but it is not open now. Everything seems deserted. I let myself into the apartment with the key, under the mat, just as the emailed instructions advised when I booked the place. I've yet to see another person in this complex.

The feeling of being alone is overwhelming.

How ridiculous it is to feel so scared, when, after all, this is just another island. How different is it from Skein Island? In fact, many more thousands of people live here than on Skein Island, and there are safety nets in place here, to catch you if danger pushes you over the edge.

But that is what I'm scared of. The people, the safety nets. The men who think they'll be helping me, and the men who'll want to hurt me. Moira's influence will be so strong here, and I have yet to think of what I'm going to say to her. What story can I possibly tell her that will hold her attention?

There's a knock at the door. I freeze.

'Marianne?'

David's voice, it's David's voice, and the feeling that everything is going to be okay is overwhelming. I stand up too quickly, and knock over the chair. It clatters to the tiled floor.

I run to the door and throw it open. He's there, looking tall and straight and just like a man I used to know, like stepping back in time; yes, he's still my husband. Somehow he's taken us back to the first years of our marriage when there was nothing but the delight of being his wife.

'Marianne,' says David, and it undoes me. I go to him, feel him put his arms around me, and I forget everything, everyone else. Whatever happens will happen, but I have David again, just for a few hours, and I don't know how I ever managed without him, the smell of him, the strength of him. He fortifies me. But it also terrifies me – he shouldn't be here, so close to Moira, in danger from her presence.

'No, you need to go. It's not safe—'

'I'm fine,' he says, 'I'm fine, don't worry. I've been close to her before, remember?'

Of course I remember. In the basement, he rescued me, and he touched Moira when he pulled my mother free of her. And yet he's okay. For now.

I need him to kiss me.

I lift my face to his and claim him, keep on kissing him, until he belongs to me again. At some point during the process he moves me backwards, shuts the door, shuffles me to the sofa and cradles me on his lap. He touches me, takes off my clothes, so I take off his, and we sit together, naked, not passionate so much as still and whole in the dusk, overlooking the dolphin mosaic in the deep blue pool.

We make love. He says, 'Like this?' as he strokes me, very gently, and I sit astride him, lower myself on to him, rock back and forth and take pleasure in him. The dusk turns to dark, and the room is shadowed when we disentangle ourselves and pull apart, just enough to let the world start moving again. Questions are coming, with difficult answers. But not just yet. Not yet.

He takes my hands and leads me to the kitchen, then pours himself some water from the bottle next to the sink. The salad looks even worse off than before.

'Were you going to eat that?' he says.

'It was all I bought at the minimart.'

'Is it wrong to go for pizza instead?'

'I could eat pizza.' Like a normal holiday. The thought of it makes me smile. It's perfection.

'It's freezing in here,' he says. He puts down the glass and pulls me back into his arms.

'Terrible.'

'It's not even that cold outside.'

'I know.'

'Arnie's here.'

'What?' I pull back, look into David's face. There is a cut just under one eye, drawing attention to the lines of his cheekbones. I see guilt in his gaze, and determination.

'Rebecca wrote and told me what you've been planning. She asked me to come and talk to you. Reason with you not to do this alone. She and Inger are worried about you. So I came; I had to come and find you, and Arnie said he had to come too.'

'Arnie was worried about me too?' The idea of it is incongruous with the mental image I have of my father in The Cornerhouse, flirting with the barmaid, drinking until it's easy to slump in the corner and dream of a different life.

David caresses the back of my neck. We are still naked, and it's wrong for this conversation. How quickly it's become serious. And the big questions are here already, knocking on the door. I move away from him, back to my clothes, and start to dress.

'Arnie sees the future.'

Of course. All men are heroes, villains, sages or sidekicks. Arnie is a wise man, even though I've been trying to make him the villain in my personal story. 'So what did he see?'

'He saw us all in the cave. You, me, him and Geoff.'

'Who the hell is Geoff?'

'He helped me out.'

'He's your sidekick.' So David the Hero has a team. But who have they been playing against? As David puts on his jeans and shirt I think about the cut under his eye, and suddenly I see that he has diverged from me, led his own story into new and disturbing directions. 'Did Arnie and Geoff help you find the man who attacked me? Is that it?'

David nods.

'And did you…'

'I've dealt with him.'

Shouldn't I feel freed by this information? Instead I'm horrified at what has happened, what I set in motion. 'How? What… What did you…?'

He moves to the open window, turns his back to me, and says, 'He asked if you could forgive him, at the end. He said he was sorry.'

'He was sorry?'

'The police took him away. For a different crime. Another attack. No need for you to testify. It's done with. You asked me to deal with it, and I did.'

I go to him, press myself against his back, and feel the tension in his shoulders, his legs. 'Thank you.'

'Does that help?'

'Does it?' I do the only thing I can. I lie. 'Yes, that helps. Like you say, it's done with. You dealt with it.'

There never will be a time when it will be done with. No matter what happens to my attacker, no matter what happens to me. It will be inside my head forever, and I will circle it, like a moth around a bulb, forever getting too close to it, forever getting scorched by that memory. Sometimes I think it would be better to be dead, but I go on, just the same.

Yet more cowardice on my part. I don't deserve David. I'm beginning to think that I never did.

He turns, and hugs me so tight, as if forgiving the untruths we have just told each other. 'Arnie and Geoff are sharing an apartment on the other side of the complex. Let's go and get them and plan our next move over pizza.'

'There is no next move. I'm going to a cave tomorrow, up in the mountains. On my own. You're going home. It's the only way I can do this.'

'We'll see,' he says, in a tone I recognise, and I realise this will have to be a negotiation. When a hero walks into a story, he doesn't do as he's told.

*　*　*

An Irish bar that claims to serve the best pint of Guinness on Crete is still open, one in a row of seafront eateries that have shut for the season, and it serves two types of pizza: margherita or Irish sausage. Only Geoff plumped for the sausage option. The waiter brought out discs of undercooked dough with scattered blobs of cheese and tomato on the surface. The Irish sausage pizza is huge and floppy, with a peculiarly yellow cheese, upon which the diced sausage floats. Geoff cuts off strips of pizza, folds them up, and pops them into his mouth as if sampling a delicacy. It's ridiculous to still care about food at a time like this, but I find I do. I can't help it. That's part of being human, perhaps: caring about what you smell, taste, see and hear even when you might be dead tomorrow. Because you might be dead tomorrow.

We are sitting outside, between two space heaters that are doing a fine job of keeping the night's chill away, around a rough, circular wooden table positioned for a view over the pebbly beach and the rippling sea. It makes a shushing sound, only audible when there's a pause between pop songs coming from the interior of the empty bar. So far we have concentrated on eating, but I have to take control of the situation and turn their attention back to what I've come here to do. Without their interference.

'Here's what we know,' I say, hoping I sound like a general addressing the troops in a key moment of a hard-fought war. 'The Ideon Andron is a cave on Mount Ida, only ten minutes' drive away. It's a tourist attraction now, so it's fairly easy to get to.' I think of the video footage I watched on YouTube. Holidaymakers stood around the large mouth of the cave in summer heat, waving at the camera, sunglasses reflecting back, and then the scene panned away over to the sea while a Demis Roussos song swelled up to monstrous proportions. 'There are four chambers, and the... person I'm looking for is in the last one. She's very dangerous to men, but she won't hurt me. So I'll go in alone, retrieve the statue that belongs back on Skein Island, and then call for you to come and take it away, okay?'

'I thought we were hunting a monster,' says Geoff, mournfully, like a child being told the trip to Disneyland is off. I remember him from the library. He would come in every month or so and take out an adventure novel – Wilbur Smith or Clive Cussler – and often he'd bring them back late and have to pay a fine. All I really know about him is that he's a slow reader. Now I find I like him and pity him in equal measure.

'Who told you that?' I ask him.

He points at David. 'I told them what I knew,' he says.

'A goddess,' says Arnie. 'Fate.' It's the first time he's spoken since his pizza arrived. It lies untouched before him, as does his beer. Pale and with a permanent frown, he looks familiarly hungover. I wonder if he drank too much on the plane.

'They've played the cubes too.' David shrugs.

Of course. They've all had their own visions of Moira, caused by the water containing her essence. No wonder Geoff looks enthusiastic about going to meet her. He probably thinks he's going to find some fantasy female with flowing hair and bouncy breasts – a Greek pin-up girl. 'She will kill you if you get too close. Or you'll kill each other.'

'Don't worry about us,' says David. 'We'll take you to the cave, we'll wait outside. When you shout for us, we'll come in. We get it.'

But I don't believe him. I don't feel in control of them. They have their own agenda; I can read it on their faces.

'We all need to be there,' says Arnie. 'This won't work unless we're there. David, go and order me a – an ouzo, is it? Whatever they drink around here.'

'You're sure?'

Arnie nods. As soon as David has left the table, he looks at Geoff. 'Push off for a minute, lad, all right?' Geoff gets up, uncomplaining, and slopes off in the direction of the sea.

I'm alone with my father for the first time in months. 'Right,' he says. 'It's like this. This is David's fight, not yours. It's not a woman's place to take on Fate. You know that.'

'No, I don't.'

'The only way this is going to work is if you let David take her on. He touched her, on the island, didn't he? And somehow he survived. It's made him too powerful. Like in the big stories of old. Like Ulysses, and Theseus, and all that.'

'Even those heroes couldn't beat Fate.'

'But you think you can?' He slumps back in his chair, and puts one hand on his forehead. 'Don't argue with me, Marianne. I've seen it.'

And that, in his eyes, should be the end of the argument. He's a wise man. Born that way. He has a natural advantage over me, over all women.

He is utterly full of shit and he will never see it. How he loves the high ground, doing what he thinks is best, thinking it's the only way. Forging letters from my mother and destroying the real letters, deciding I should never know the truth, making such decisions in the name of being a father. And yet failing to be a father in the way that mattered – by listening to me.

But he will listen to me now.

I pick up my beer and throw it in his face.

He is astonished. The beer drips from his grizzled hair, his eyebrows, his nose and chin. He opens his mouth and shuts it.

I hand him a napkin. 'Didn't see that coming, did you?'

He mops at his face.

'So it turns out you don't see everything after all. You don't see me. You never did. That's because I am not under Fate's control. I'm not a hero or a villain. I don't have to be David's little helper, and I will never be able to predict the future. That's because the future isn't already written for me. Only men are controlled by Moira, not women. Now do you understand why I can win this fight? I'm not under her control. I'm not under anyone's control. Not even yours.'

He doesn't reply. He crumples up the napkin and drops it on the table.

'I'm sorry that my mother left us and chose a different life. But that was her choice. Not yours. And you have always been too much of a fucking idiot to understand it.'

I stand up and walk off, down to the beach, to where Geoff is picking up pebbles and attempting to skim them across the waves. He's rubbish at it. I watch him for a while, feeling Arnie's gaze on my back, making my shoulder-blades prickle.

'Not enough wrist,' I tell him, and pick up a stone to demonstrate. It skims three, four, times, before losing all energy and sinking to the bottom. My father taught me how to skim stones when I was very little. We used to go to Camber Sands for holidays, and I'd amaze the other kids with my skimming ability.

I turn around and look up, to the bar. Arnie has gone. He's probably inside, complaining to David about me, telling him they should leave me behind in the morning.

Over my dead body.

Geoff tries to emulate my skimming style and fails dismally. 'I never could do this,' he says.

'Practice.'

'That's what everyone says, but I've been practising all my life at everything and I'm still rubbish. Do you know what it's like to not be good at anything? I bet you don't.'

'David said you were a big help to him.'

He looks pleased with this. 'Yeah, I did a good job, clearing that whole mess up. Sam said—' He claps a hand over his mouth.

'It's all right. I know who Sam is.'

I know enough, anyway. More than I want to know. She's in David's life when I am not, and I have no right to hate her for that. But I do anyway.

The sea moves quietly, drawing closer to my feet, then pulling back: an eternal pattern. Behind us, the pop music from the bar changes to a slower song. Geoff sings along, words about not wanting to fall asleep, not wanting to miss a thing.

Suddenly it seems important to find out more about him. 'Don't you listen to music at home sometimes?' I ask him.

'Not really. I watch telly. Do you like *EastEnders*?'

'No, not my kind of thing. Do you live alone?'

'With my parents.'

'They must be getting on. I hope you don't mind me asking – how old are you?' He looks on the wrong side of middle age but his behaviour is so young, even immature. It's difficult to get the measure of him.

'Look,' says Geoff. 'It's not really a big deal, is it? I don't mind talking about stuff if you like, but I get the feeling you should concentrate on what we came here to do, right? Who cares if my favourite colour is yellow? I'm here to help David. He's the important one.'

There is nothing I can say to that.

I wish there was something else in his life. I wish he wasn't just a sidekick, had not been born that way. He is prepared to die for my husband, and he will get nothing in return.

I want to give him a memory that is not about David. So I reach out to him, and take his hands. I pull him into a rhythm, a step to the left, a step to the right, and we dance out the song while he sings along.

He knows every word.

* * *

'This is it.'

The mouth of the cave yawns wide.

A bird overhead makes a curious sound, like a laugh, loud and mechanical. I look up into the clouds, but can't see it.

It's been a long morning. The men didn't leave without me. When I awoke, David was waiting with coffee and a croissant, of all things, claiming to have found them in the minimart down the road. He watched me eat, and told me to wear practical clothes. I picked out trousers and a jumper, utilitarian, and he nodded. Then we went to find Geoff and Arnie.

We shared a car to get here: David driving, Arnie in the passenger seat, looking even worse than before, even though the only beer he swallowed last night was by accident when I threw it over him, Geoff in the back seat with me. The ring road around the island was clear, easy to negotiate, but when David turned off to take the mountain road it became pebbly, potholed. About a mile back we started to encounter debris on the road: rocks, branches. In some cases David had to stop the car and Geoff helped him to move these obstacles aside.

We passed a taverna, shut up, the wooden tables overturned to form a barricade against the front door. I thought I couldn't feel any more scared, but the tables, in a haphazard, frantic pile, terrified me. It spoke of a future where everything is overturned, abandoned.

When we arrived at our destination, I found myself climbing from the car and into David's arms. I've not been able to let go of him since. I hold his hand, so tight, as we approach the mouth, and stare into the darkness. There's a set of steps, gouged out of the stone, worn by so many tourists' feet, and an orange rope set into the wall by metal rings, making handholds. It looks so normal. I must be wrong. Moira must be somewhere else, far away, in a place I would never think of looking.

'It's here,' says David. He lets go of my hand.

I look up into his face and see a faraway fascination, eyes glazed, lips loose.

'What is it?'

'The colours. Don't you see them?'

Geoff comes up to join us. 'It's beautiful,' he says. 'Like a rainbow. A trail. Leading inside.'

A shout cuts through the silence of the mountain. I spin round. Arnie is on his knees, his back to us, bent forward at the waist, his hands over his face. I run to him. There is blood on his fingers; he is clawing at his eyes, gouging. I take his hands and try to force them down but he's strong, so strong. I can't stop him from putting his fingernails into the corners of his eyes and ripping, ripping. David and Geoff grab him, wrestle him, until they have him still, lying on his back on the ground. He stops struggling and starts whispering. I put my ear to his lips, and hear, 'Not any more, not see any more, no colours, no colours.'

David says to me, 'Can you hold him while I get the first aid kit?'

I put my hands on Arnie's chest and David slips off the backpack he's wearing, then crouches over it, searching through the pockets. I can't look at Arnie's face, his ruined eyes. I stare at his hands, lying placidly on the ground. They are slick with his blood.

David unzips a small green case and unwraps a sterile gauze pad, then snips lengths of surgical tape to hold it in place over Arnie's eye socket. He repeats the action for the other socket. I want to scream at him, tell him to run for help, find a hospital – shouldn't we all be in the car, breaking speed limits, looking for doctors? But he snips the gauze, methodically, and Geoff watches the procedure with interest.

White tape knitting the remains of his face together, the gauze already staining pink, Arnie lies still, unmoving. I stand up. The broken rocks of the mountains form asymmetrical grey and brown patterns to the sea, which stretches onwards, like the promise of a calmness to come. But not now. Something is building. I can feel it.

'The colours,' whispers Arnie, and then he wails, like a dog hit by a car, a noise of such pain and fear that I can't bear it. I step back; I want to be away from him, my own father, and I would rather that I died than have to hear that sound. He gets to his feet. I take his arms and he shakes me off, then starts to walk, fast, up the path that leads to the higher peaks of the mountains; he doesn't need eyes, I don't know how he's doing it, but he's climbing higher, leaving the path, dropping to his hands and moving like an animal over the rocks and stones, at speed.

'Dad!' I shout after him. He doesn't look back. I run to David, pull at his arms. 'Go after him!'

'No. That's his choice.'

'He's not… He's damaged himself, he needs…'

David and Geoff turn back to the mouth of the cave. I can

hear Arnie's wails, getting further away, and I never wanted things to be like this, never; this is why I came here by myself. This is not what I wanted. I have to keep them safe. I have to go in alone. I pull myself up straight, try to take control.

'Get Arnie. Drive him to hospital. Come back for me later.'

David grabs my wrist. 'No,' he says. 'You and Geoff stay here.'

'No, that's not—'

'This is right. I know it. Arnie said it.'

'No.' I try to break free, but his grip is so strong. 'David. Please.'

He kisses me on the forehead, and I hate him for it. The hate, the wash of it over me, unravels my decisions, my certainty, and I feel my face contorting, my tears spilling.

'Geoff, this is your job. Keep her safe. Keep her out of the cave.'

Geoff nods, very seriously.

'I love you,' David tells me, but I can tell he's already thinking of the colours, the wonderful colours that Moira brings to the world, and he is going to find her and stay with her, because he won't be able to stop her. And I am a puddle on the floor, I am all tears and no spine, just a woman, a typical weak woman, unable to do anything but wait and despair in equal measure.

He lets me go, and takes off his backpack once more, digging around inside it to produce a small silver flask. He unscrews the lid.

'Do you know what this is?'

'I...'

'Rebecca and Inger sent it to me. It came from your basement.'

There was nothing left from the basement, not after the collapse. I think through what remained: a few pieces of paper, random pages from declarations and one barrel of water. Moira's water. Her essence, contained in the liquid. Used in tiny amounts to give men a taste of her power.

David is about to drink it.

'No,' I tell him, 'I don't know what that will do to you.'

He strokes my face, and in that gesture I realise I no longer know him. Even before he drinks, before he faces the monster, he has become a stranger, a protagonist in some terrible tale in which I was never going to be important. He is going on without me, just as it should be. As Moira wants it.

He puts the flask to his lips and drinks. His throat moves, the swallowing motion, so calm, so controlled. He drinks it all, then takes a torch from his backpack, and walks away from me.

I watch him go into the cave. My failure skewers me, drops me to my knees, and Geoff stands over me as I mourn.

CHAPTER TWENTY

The first three caves were easy to negotiate. Not only were the paths clearly set out for the tourists, but the rainbow led him onwards. As long as he stayed in its stream, he felt the rightness of his route.

The third cave was smaller, and at the point that the path ended, the orange rope tied up on the final metal ring to form a double knot, the rainbow took over completely, pulling him towards the darkest area where it disappeared abruptly. David followed, found a hole in the stone walls that became a tunnel, where the rainbow pattern stretched onwards, slow-motion, like an undulating ribbon caught in the currents of the sea. He flicked on the torch, and the rainbow disappeared. Instead there was only the length of the narrowing tunnel, regular and smooth, leading downwards to what looked like a dead end – a fall of rocks and earth. He dropped the torch and wriggled his way into the tunnel, trying not to think of how he might not be able to turn around in such a small space.

The hard, packed surface at the end of the tunnel was as deliberate as a wall. Could the monster have placed it there?

David put his palms to the rocks and pushed, and it did not give. He punched it, short jabs of his fist, as there was no space to bend back his elbow for a larger blow. After five attempts he felt the skin on his knuckles split, and the pain of it lanced through him, fierce and prophetic. It awoke the liquid in his stomach, and he felt it expand, grow warm, uncurl through his veins, snakes of intent, of meaning. They took him over, slid out through his fingertips like the tendrils of plants and slid between the cracks in the rock surface, so that the stones trembled, shuddered, collapsed into water, breaking like bubbles. The tendrils receded and the water filled up the tunnel. The light of the torch fizzled and died, and it was easy to see the rainbow once more, to swim along its wake.

The tunnel widened and David changed from dog-paddle to breaststroke, kicking out his feet. The trail tilted upwards, and he angled his body to follow, feeling the beginning of pain in his lungs, the constriction of his throat, the demand for oxygen, shouting for it, screaming, and the involuntary breath that followed, allowing the water to enter him, sink into his chest, icy stones.

It didn't hurt any more. He swam on in perfect silence, encased in water.

The rainbow grew lighter, turned to white, and he broke through to the surface of a small, calm pool, reached out with his hands and clutched at hard rock once more, a flat surface onto which he pulled himself, and stood upright. He felt no need to cough or clear his lungs. His clothes were not wet. It wasn't only that he wasn't in pain. He had moved beyond such considerations to something new; nerve-endings and neurological signals had become controllable. He was impervious. The white path of light called him onwards, and he walked forward, without hesitation, through shades of darkness, until the cave walls opened out into a holy cathedral of space, as tall and steepled as the mountain, reaching up in an orderly worship of stalactites. It was the ordained place: a home, a birth, a tomb. The space where a hero could slay a monster.

All his life, he had been waiting for the moment when he became the man he was born to be. He had lived in the promise of it, standing upright, being a defender, a protector. This was his perfect moment. All other memories would pale in comparison to it: his wedding day, the death of Mark, the saving of Sam, had all been trial runs for this.

He felt it grow near.

His body assumed a fighting stance, hands in bunched fists, feet apart.

It homed in on him, and it was a woman, so familiar, as soft as Sam, as sharp as Marianne. It was the perfect woman, a goddess. He had met her before, in the back room of The Cornerhouse, where she had enveloped him, penetrated him, slain him. This time he had to be the conqueror.

She cleaved to him, moulding to him in a rush of sex scent and promises that turned the cave crimson as blood, and she offered him her submission, the sinking of their bodies together, into each other. He felt the danger of it, the secret victory that lay within her offer.

But he wanted it, this death at the behest of his flowing damsel – to be swarmed, surrounded, kept within forever. She was close enough to touch, floating in front of him, soft pink gauze wrapped around her, legs and smile spread wide, her eyes shut, her hands reaching for the zip of his trousers. He should have known all along, they all should have known that there could be no fighting this, no way to win, to control it, he would kill for it, make the world deserving of it, be the man it could marry, change himself, change the earth, the stones, the water. Her hands found him, guided him inside her, and he watched her face, wanting her eyes to open, to be submerged, suspended in their stare—

'David!'

His name, sudden, rebounding inside the cavern, brought him back to himself. Geoff had emerged from the tunnel, his eyes wide, fixed on the monster. David had no idea what he was seeing, but it transfixed the man, in a place beyond fear or desire. And Marianne was crawling through, slithering out of the tunnel. What could she see? There was no truth in this place, no way to trust his senses. David felt a compulsion, so strong, to reach up and tear out his eyes, then rip off his ears, his tongue, but he refused to obey, found the strength to keep his arms down by his sides.

Geoff shrieked, and the cave reverberated with his pain. He ran towards Moira, his arms outstretched. David didn't know whether he meant to love her or kill her, but either way, it made no difference. She reached into his chest and took his heart in her hands, a simple gesture, like plucking a flower, and squeezed it between her palms as he shuddered, his body convulsing, his head flopping. Then he dropped to the ground.

She tilted her head as she surveyed her conquest, then looked up.

She wanted him to join her.

David felt it, the strength of it, like the playful command of a lover when the game evolves from foreplay into capitulation. She wanted his eyes on her, she wanted to eat him up with her gaze.

He met it, and understood.

She loved to weave stories, stories of men and their great deeds. And, like every child who delights in fairy tales, she wanted to some day be part of the story: a princess, a damsel, a prize. But her loneliness could not be pierced. It was inviolate. Every man who drew close to her went mad under her gaze, misunderstood what he was meant to be, his part in the pattern. It left her desolate, empty. After thousands of years of hearing stories, she wanted to have a voice of her own, but it was an impossibility, and she was awash with her impotent rage. So many men would make more stories, new stories. She would make the world anew as a dark and dangerous place. Every man would have a part to play in it.

Unless he satisfied her. Unless he gave her a story, and saved the world.

He moved towards her, and she held out her arms to him. The power of the liquid coursed through him; he could match her, he could be her equal – a new god. This cave would be the birthplace of a new Zeus. He stripped off his clothes and, naked, penetrated her; she wrapped her legs and arms around him and undulated, her cold flesh against his, attempting to smother him in her love, but he kissed her, hard, forced his tongue into her empty mouth and demanded her obeisance.

'No,' said a voice, such a small voice, and then there was a blinding pain behind his left ear that overcame everything and left him falling, falling, into a deep, soft bed of darkness that carried him away into oblivion.

CHAPTER TWENTY-ONE

I drop the torch and kneel beside David's body. I manage to turn him over, and put my ear to his chest. He still breathes, in and out, still living, still mine.

Moira is so close, so angry. I feel her reach out to me, to tear me apart for taking away her sport, but I know now what I must say to stop her. The words begin to leave my mouth, and she freezes, can't help herself, has to listen as I close my eyes and tell her:

Once there was a goddess called Moira. She was so beautiful, so perfect, that every man wanted her, but she was Fate itself, and she had no role to play in the patterns of men. She could not change that fact, even though there was nothing more she desired than to be in her own story. After so many years of making myths and legends out of ordinary men, she realised that she would always be separate. Her loneliness drove her deep into a cave, and she hid there, trying to no longer care about the heroes, villains, sages and sidekicks she was creating. She could feel them out there, acting out the patterns that sprang out of her even though she wanted it otherwise. She was so very sad that no man could overcome the skein she wove unwillingly.

Then, one day, a band of men found her hiding place, and brought with them a woman who intrigued her. Women had never been of interest before. They had been only the props and prizes in her stories: Penelope who had waited for Odysseus, Helen who had launched a thousand ships. But this woman forced herself into the skein. She shouted at Moira, and made her listen. She told a fresh story – of how it feels to be a woman in a world run by men. She spoke of love and hope and happiness, not giving it to men, but taking it from them. And Moira realised that maybe the world had changed after all. She wanted to see it again, to learn about women who take. She hoped that one day she could learn to take too.

And so she worked a little ancient magic and transformed herself to stone, and the woman took her out into the world. Moira was all excitement throughout the long sea voyage to her new home, but once she arrived she found herself locked in a small, dark place, not unlike the cave that had once been her home. She felt sadness descend upon her again, and it only got worse as the woman started to read to her. She read stories that made no sense, stories told by women of men who did no heroic deeds, acted in boredom rather than villainy, lived in the present with no interest in the future. Where had all the good stories gone? Moira did not know, and she was so tired, and so sad, that she could not find the energy to break free.

Until one day she sensed the presence of a hero. He came to the island and drew near to her. She could read his intention – to save his woman. It was written through him. The eloquence of his thread sang to her, brought her back to life, and she ripped free from her stone disguise and became a goddess once more. She flew into the sky, and brought her influence to bear on the clouds, the rain, the soil, the sea, the land – she impregnated them with her desire for new stories, better stories, and once more men started to become heroes and villains, sages and sidekicks.

The world erupted into a chaos, an agony of rebirth, as men fought and women ran, powerless to stop them.

Moira felt sorry for them. She had come to know them so well, these foolish women, but now they suffered more and they did not deserve it. All they wanted was what she wanted – to be masters of their own stories. They couldn't see that men cannot share the power of the story. They do not know how to, and they cannot be taught. And so Moira ran back to her cave and wept for women everywhere, including herself amongst their number for the first time.

But then the hero returned. He came to the cave and took Moira in his arms, and offered to tame her. He wanted to be the master of her. She could become part of his skein. She could be his Marian, his Penelope, his Andromeda.

She had a terrible decision to make.

Should she trust her hero? Or should she return to the world as a statue, where a quiet tower awaited her, with a view over a peaceful sea, and with many women's stories to listen to?

I stop speaking and open my eyes.

Moira stands in front of me, so still. Her face is old, and tired, and her body sags, her breasts low, her legs sturdy. The wrinkles around her eyes and mouth are long lines of experience, and her expression holds such sadness, along with deep, troubled acceptance, as if she has forced herself to look squarely at the world and found it wanting, yet unchangeable.

She is stone.

CHAPTER TWENTY-TWO

It takes all the crew of the ferry to place the crate in the completed tower, but the men who touch it seem unbothered by it.

So many strings had to be pulled to get her here, but now she is, and once we are alone David prises back the boards to reveal her – Moira, my monster, a statue once more. Except this time, as I look at her, I see no inkling of intelligence, no sorrows in a changing face. It is a sculpture of an aging woman, heavy breasts, waist thickened, eyes half-open and capable hands set on hips, as if to say: *So that's the way it is.*

'We did it,' David says.

'No,' I tell him. 'I did it.'

I am not willing to play this game. He's not a hero any more; I have made that clear. When he came round, he wanted to believe that he had saved me, saved the world, and just couldn't remember it. But I keep refusing to feed his fantasy, and I'm certain that he hates me for it. It's breaking my heart, a little more every day, as he realises I won't ask him to keep me safe. Not ever again.

'What will happen now?'

That's a question I can't answer. This is what I thought I wanted – a level playing field. But now I have it, the length and breadth of it, stretching away from me in all directions, it is terrifying. No protectors any more for us women. It's nobody's duty to keep us safe.

He steps back, and moves to the row of windows in my tower, overlooking the lay of the island: the swimming pool, the reception building, the rows of bungalows. It is a miniature town from up here, toy buildings and felt carpet fields. Spring is coming, and the sun shines upon it with the fervour of a blessing. I will spend a lot of time up here, enjoying it, what it gives to me. It means something important to own such a place.

'I'm reopening it as a centre,' I tell him. 'A place for a week out, to learn about yourself, to reflect. To make friends. Write a declaration. But not only for women. For anyone who needs time away from being what they think they're meant to be.' I will read these new declarations aloud to Moira, and she will appreciate stories of all kinds, about many things. There are so many stories in the world.

'If it's a place for new stories then I don't belong here. My story is done, isn't it?' He turns back to me, and in his face I see something horrible, that wounds me more than I ever thought it could; I see relief. He is glad to have an excuse not to stay.

'You'll go back to Bassett?'

'That's where I belong.'

'Do you think Arnie will be there?'

David hesitates, then shakes his head. 'I don't think he's coming back.'

I have to agree. Is Arnie dead, like poor Geoff, whom I persuaded into the cave in order to save David? I don't know. I didn't think losing Arnie would be any great loss, but it is, it is. I am fatherless for the first time. All of my men are being stripped from me, and it is a horrible feeling.

Arnie cannot watch over me, and I have emasculated David.

He is free of the need to protect me.

Suddenly I realise what he will do. 'You'll go back to Sam.'

He doesn't reply.

I don't want to be alone, like Moira. For the first time I understand how much she must hate being alone.

'Sam needs me. I can't explain it.'

I look into Moira's face once more. It is unchanged.

So that's the way it is.

'I'll stay tonight, if that's okay. Have you got space for me?'

'Yes, of course.' I can't imagine touching him ever again. 'In one of the guest bungalows. Reception will set you up with whatever you need.' I want him to get out, to get out, out, out. I want to hit him, cry, rage, break open the statue and make Moira turn him back into my hero.

He frowns, crosses to the door, and descends from my tower. Time passes in slow increments and realisations. I am alone.

I am loveless. I have only myself to blame. And, right at the moment when I thought the danger had passed, I need to find new reserves of strength. I must get through this abandonment, and so must all other women, all over the world.

There's a knock at the door. Rebecca and Inger enter, come to stand beside me, and look at Moira with expressions of fear and fascination.

'We're sorry,' says Inger. 'About going behind your back. But we knew you couldn't do it alone.'

'And we were right, weren't we?' Rebecca chimes in. She does so love to be right.

Inger looks very young today. Her skin shines; her lips are full and pink.

Rebecca looks much older. She has stopped applying henna to her hair, and only the bottom third of her curls are red. The rest is a dirty grey, and it makes the yellowing skin around her mouth and neck so much more obvious.

I put my arms around them, one on each side, and I think that we are like sisters in this endeavour: Inger the brave, Marianne the manipulative, Rebecca the cynic. We share a vision of a future, and we will work towards it.

'So how do we do it?' says Inger. 'Do we accept everyone at this island, and hope they'll all get along somehow? How can we show people everywhere that the world has changed? That they can tell new kinds of stories?'

How many stories are there that we can tell? When I think about my own past, couldn't I be the hero, the victim, the sidekick, the sage, even the villain, all at the same time? Is it really up to me to decide which part of my history defines me?

I look into the eyes of the statue, then at the faces of my sisters, and I tell them the truth.

I have absolutely no idea.

EPILOGUE

David pulled up outside her house, and found her sitting on the doorstep, in the sunlight, enjoying the first warm day of the year. She held knitting needles in her hands. A ball of blue wool bobbed between her feet.

He got out of the car, and walked over to her. She didn't get up. Instead she stopped knitting, smiled up at him and said, 'I've been waiting for you.'

He sat beside her on the doorstep and said, 'I'm here now.' Sam nodded.

There was no need to speak, to explain. He watched her knit, the deftness of her fingers, the twists and turns of the wool. From inside the house floated music, orchestral, swelling strings.

'What are you making?'

'A scarf. For you.'

'But spring's coming.'

'I know, but it's the only thing I can knit.' Sam held it up. It was already long, and fat, haphazard, messy, with stitches dropped. 'Do you like it?'

'I love it,' he said.

She made a small sound of satisfaction, and carried on knitting.

THE COLD
SMOKE
DECLARATION

'This smoke is disgusting.'

I'm washed in cold morning air as Dave sits up, taking the duvet with him, but I try to cling to sleep regardless. I won't be beaten that easily. 'Ignore him,' I mumble.

'I'm going home.'

'He's not, he doesn't...' But Dave is up and putting on yesterday's clothes at speed. He's gone in no time at all.

At least I have the duvet again.

There's a dry chuckle beside my ear.

My house-ghost is laughing at his destruction of yet another of my relationships. No matter what preparatory work I put in, my boyfriends never last the night. The problem isn't the night itself but the dawn, when their eyelids flutter open and they breathe in that chewy smoke. The smell of an old man luxuriating in his cigar habit.

'Screw you,' I tell the ghost, and settle back down to sleep.

* * *

Min, I can't go on like this. Do something.

'Do what?' I tell the back of the receipt for croissants – bought specially for a romantic lie-in this morning – on which Dave has written his ultimatum. He's gone from understanding, even indulgent, to accusatory. Apparently I'm to blame. When I first told him a ghost visits me early every morning, he laughed. The reality of sharing space, either with the ghost or with me, turned out to be different from whatever he was picturing.

I sit down at the kitchen table and fold the receipt many times until it's as small as I can make it, and then flick it in the direction of the bin. I pick up a pen and grab an old envelope from the mail pile. I start to write what I can't say.

Dave –

A different woman might mind that you're leaving me to face this ongoing issue alone, but the truth is I'm not alone. Not since the ghost came into my life. He found me in my first flat. Or perhaps I should say I found him. I'd been living in a hall of residence for my first year at university, and then all the people I'd asked to share a house with me in the second year decided they'd rather share between themselves, due to a misunderstanding over who owned certain things in the fridge, and they moved into the house I'd found without me. I was alone, and low on choices. I ended up in the only place still available at short notice at a decent rent, and that was the flat above the fish and chip shop.

Nobody wanted to live there because of the smell. It was pervasive and greasy at night, after a day's frying, and in the early morning I'd wake to a deep, woody fug hanging over the bed, blue against the light through the thin curtains. I didn't identify that smell as cigar smoke for the first year that I lived there. I didn't think the laugh I kept hearing could be a laugh. A ghost? Surely not. That would be scary and would necessitate action on my part. I would have to find another place to live, or reason with an unknown entity. The experience would have to be chalked up as frightening and not... soothing. Yes. It was soothing to breathe in that smoke and feel the presence of amused old eyes upon me when I woke, but only if it was not real and not exactly in my head either. Not scary. Not pathological. Not examined.

I lived there for two years. When I left the smoke and the presence came with me, and I was glad.

I look over what I've written and realise that these aren't words for Dave at all. They are true statements I've made for myself. I don't want to stop, and I also don't want to go on. Writing down true things sounds dangerously like creating signposts in a wilderness. Once a place has been pointed out, sooner or later somebody will end up travelling to it.

* * *

A few months ago Susan, a work colleague, went to Skein Island. We all laughed at her. She smiled patiently at the jokes about getting in touch with her feelings and wearing a pair of dungarees; what kind of people were we? We were a pack looking for the lowest member to pick on. It wasn't new behaviour. We do it most days, using cruelty to avert boredom, and she left for the island to the sound of our derisive comments.

When she returned she seemed the same at first, but it dawned on us all at one point or another that something had changed. We stopped making jokes at her expense. One morning I found myself alone with her in the ladies' toilets on the fifth floor, and we looked at each other's reflections in the mirror above the row of sinks.

'What was it like?' I asked her. I got the feeling from her instant response that she had been replying to that question a lot. Perhaps we'd all been sidling up to her one at a time, picking our moments.

'It was unique,' she said.

She stepped back from the sink and moved to the drier, and I found myself saying over the din of hot air, 'No, really. I really want to know.'

She finished drying her hands and walked to the door. Then she said, without looking back at me, 'No distractions. Nobody else I knew, or who thought they knew me. When there was nothing else there to keep me from seeing it, I turned out to not be what I thought I was. There was… more of me.'

A few days later Susan gave in her notice. I haven't seen her since.

And now I'm standing in front of the mirror in the ladies' toilets on the fifth floor. Far too often recently I've been daydreaming about where Susan is now, and those dreams are ridiculous and romantic. She's parasailing or dancing the Argentine tango. She's eating oysters or driving a Ferrari, and she's doing all of these things with some faceless lover.

If that lover doesn't have a face, how can I be so certain that they're beautiful?

There are things that none of us are seeing. There are so many things that we're not seeing.

* * *

The queue for the number 37 is longer than usual, and I find myself thinking of the unfamiliar faces, none of them beautiful, as interlopers. What's so interesting about my route home today? Don't these people have other places to be?

A man who looks about my age – maybe out of education for a few years but no wiser about what being an adult actually means – is handing out leaflets. He works his way down the queue and when he reaches me I take a leaflet automatically to avoid a conversation. Perhaps it'll contain wisdom that I need. Wisdom hidden as an advertisement. I'd like to believe in serendipity, and I'm already starting to believe in the importance of words on paper.

BOGOF!
Balls and tees special at
JIMBO'S GOLF ACCESSORIES EMPORIUM

If there's wisdom in there I can't see it.

The usual double-decker arrives and I manage to get a seat on the top deck. An older woman takes the seat next to mine and we sit with our knees touching because it can't be helped. She puts her large patent leather handbag on her lap and hunches over it, opening and closing the silver clasp.

I pull myself into that inner space I've perfected specifically for journeys on public transport. The town centre slowly rolls past, punctuated by the stops and starts of arrivals and departures. I have a long way to go yet.

'Here,' says the woman sitting next to me. She's holding out a pen.

'Pardon?'

She points at my hands. I'm still holding the leaflet, but I've folded it once, down the centre, to reveal its clean white reverse. It looks like it's waiting to be written on.

'Did you need this?' she says. Then she looks past me, out of the window, and jumps up to push the stop button on the vertical bar. She leaves the pen – a cheap biro – on the seat, and walks away. I watch her descend the stairs and emerge on the pavement. The bus jerks, and moves on.

So there are signs, when it comes to writing. I'm not strong enough to resist them.

My ghost is an old man.

He's not a kind old grandfather type. He's annoyed and bitter and he sees the funny side of being stuck in those emotions forever when he thought they would switch off. The cigar habit probably killed him – that rasping edge to the laugh gives it away – so now he smokes them ironically, no longer needing the nicotine but wanting to make a point of not giving up because it keeps him human, even in death.

I bet he got offered the chance to go to the afterlife. I bet there was a long tunnel, white and swirling, and he felt the pull of it at the moment of surrendering his corporeal form. It opened up above the armchair in which he was slumped (in a cheap-end-of-the-market nursing home, with the skeleton of a half-formed jigsaw puzzle on a small wobbly table beside him) and he looked up at the afterlife to see relatives waving at him, beckoning him in. Then he thought: No thanks very much, I'll hang about at the fish and chip shop and scare generations of bloody students instead.

Who knows how long he'd been doing exactly that before I came along? Perhaps I was the first one who didn't shiver or scream at the whiff of tobacco and the throaty laugh. I'd imagine my lack of interest in his tricks piqued his interest. It touched him in a way he hadn't been touched in a long time, metaphorically speaking, because he obviously hadn't been touched at all. I stayed with him and he got to know me, and when I moved out he decided to follow. He thought: I'll stick with you, girl. You're all right.

We're happy together. Sort of. He hates my boyfriends

*because not one of them has been worthy of me yet. He chases
them away and he will continue to do so until Mr Right comes
along and then he'll disappear up to heaven, job done, and
this is turning into a ridiculous fairy tale and I have no idea
who my ghost is or what he wants or even what I'm writing
about and now I'm at the bottom of this piece of*

I look up. The road is unfamiliar. I've gone past my stop
and run out of paper. We pass a road sign: Uneven Road
Surface Ahead.

I'm sick of signs.

* * *

When you visit Skein Island you write a declaration. It is
the story of your life. You give up your declaration to be
stored in the library along with the stories of the thousands
of other women who have visited. This isn't about your
story being read, or appreciated, or turned into a thrilling
adventure for all the family. It's how it has to be enough to
know your story exists because that's all there is.

Susan wrote her declaration, then came back to this town
to discover she had been set free from it. She could move on
and create a new story. There was more to her.

I sit at my kitchen table, before my open laptop that
displays Skein Island's official website, and I make a phone
call to their administrative office before I can change my
mind.

The woman on the other end of the line is polite but regretful. No, they can't accommodate me just because I've discovered the burning need to write a declaration right now. No, I can't get a place without filling in an application form, and no, it won't make any difference if I just turn up at the dock to see if anyone else drops out at the last minute. Sorry.

So I pour myself a glass of wine and fill out the online application, and all the writing I've been doing makes it easier to reach into myself and find some strange new twist of truth in the Other Information That May Influence Your Application box:

> *The ghost of an old man visits my bedroom at dawn each day. He sits on the edge of the bed and smokes a vile cigar. He chuckles to himself. I want to go to a place where he can't reach me because I have no idea who am I without him, and I'm scared that I no longer want to find out.*
>
> *Everyone knows men aren't allowed on Skein Island. Can the same be said of ghosts? Will my ghost obey your rules?*

* * *

An open-plan kitchen and living room. A sofa and an armchair, a microwave and a fridge. Behind a thin partition wall I find a bedroom with two single beds positioned as far away from each other as possible, which isn't far. There's the same amount of space as I'd have in my flat. Do I feel at home?

But it's the view outside the window that matters. A ragged expanse of green grass and weeds, wild and tufted, leads my eyes to a cliff edge, and the blue sea beyond. Late summer on an island. It's the feeling of being held in position as the giant world turns and the tide sweeps in and out according to its own rules.

I waited four months for this, and got lucky with a cancellation. I'm not sure whether it's serendipity or not. I'm still attempting to believe in that concept.

I choose the bed nearest the window and put my case on it. I find my thick socks within and slide them over the socks I'm already wearing. The floorboards are cold, and there's a strong draft at ankle-level; the main door has a thick gap at the bottom through which I can see daylight. This place is not well-built, it seems. It's a flimsy shelter with its makeshift walls and breeze-admitting gaps. How is it meant to keep out a ghost?

The light at the bottom of the door is blocked. Then the door swings back with a creak.

For a moment I expect my ghost, made flesh.

'You all right?'

No. No, it's a woman. Of course it's a woman.

'There's a draft,' I say. 'Hi. I'm Min.'

'I suppose we're sharing this cabin. I'm Katie. Is this my bed, then?'

'I've put my case on this one,' I say. 'I hope that's okay.'

'It's fine. Why wouldn't it be fine?' She shakes her head and frowns as she shrugs off her small rucksack and places it on the other bed. I don't know whether she's annoyed or not. Her dark hair is cut very short, threaded with white, and she's dressed entirely in red of varying shades of stridency. I'd guess she's at least twenty years older than me but wearing it very well. She looks complete, comfortable, finished. I still feel like a work in progress.

'A single bed,' she muses. 'I haven't slept in one of those for a long time. I've got a king-size all to myself at home. I'm difficult to live with at the best of times so I should probably apologise up front. I'm sorry you got me as your companion for the week, Min.'

'Why are you so difficult to live with?' I ask.

'I can see right through everyone's bullshit,' she says, and gives me a hard stare. I feel my innards shrinking away from her.

'I'm just messing with you,' she says. 'Sorry. I'm not good with people. It's also probably why I became an estate agent. Dicking people around on the topic of the most expensive purchase they'll ever make appealed to me. Again, just messing.' She sits on her bed and removes her leather boots, pushing down the long zips from her knees to her ankles so they slide from her feet to land on the floor. She's wearing scarlet socks, too. 'What do you do?'

'I'm in administration.'

'Well.' She looks out of the window, then says, 'Someone has to be. I thought all the cabins were for four people? How come we've ended up in a two-person outfit? There must be something special about us. What do you think it is?'

At what point do you tell an acquaintance that you're followed around by a ghost? I start to speak but she holds up a finger and says, 'No, no, I'll find out for myself.'

'All right. It's your funeral.'

I have no idea why those particular words came to mind. Those are obviously not the right words for this situation; I can tell that from the way she's choosing to ignore them.

'I'm not good with people,' she says. 'I came here to learn if I wanted to be. Good with them. If I'm missing something.'

'What do you think you're missing?'

'I already suspect the answer to that question is nothing.' She hums as she unpacks.

She probably thinks I'm an idiot. But that's okay because I think she's an overconfident bully who's attempting to verbally dominate me. At least we have one thing in common: We'll both find out what's going on for ourselves. We are women together for a whole week.

I've got a feeling it's going to pass slowly.

* * *

What makes a boy?

When I first began to understand that I was not a boy, I began to look around me and categorise others as I was being categorised in turn. I couldn't have been more than six years old; I remember many things feeling new to me, including school. I hadn't settled into familiarity with the routine or the others of my age who now surrounded me on a daily basis. There were so many of us, all in orbit around the larger bodies of teachers. I understood I was a kid, but not that I was a girl. That came later. I don't really understand it now, except if I define it as *not a boy*.

I don't believe girls exist, really, except as a disguise. And I'm still not certain that boys grow into men. Perhaps a man is a disguise too. An acceptance of certain rules. No different to firing a gun in the playground and demanding that the other fella lies down dead.

Having had these thoughts during a long and sleepless night, I'm in no way surprised when my ghost turns up with the first creeping rays of dawn. He sits on the end of my bed, and I wonder why I thought the rules of Skein Island might ever apply to him. If he wasn't really a man when he was a man, then why would he be one as a spirit?

I wish I could talk to him.

I feel the pressure of him, by my legs. He's not large. He's creating only the smallest of dents in the mattress. He shifts his weight every now and again, and I can imagine him muttering to himself – *bloody sciatic nerve, won't leave me in peace even for a nice sit-down* – but if he is talking I can't hear it. I thought the countryside was meant to be quiet but the birds outside the thin window are rhythmically raucous. I've never heard these throaty calls before; I think it must be the sound of seagulls en masse. I lie there and listen.

My ghost gets up and breathes out his smoke, long and freely, into the room. I think he likes the extra space to fill.

I watch the smoke stream forth from an empty space, then form a thin fog above my bed. A pause. Then he does the same over Katie's bed, and he laughs.

She coughs. She's awake.

We both lie there, being awake. Being breathed over.

'Oh God,' she says.

'He's just a ghost. An old man's ghost,' I tell her. 'It's really not a big deal. He visits me at dawn every day. He doesn't mean any harm.'

He chuckles again, and is gone. The light of day is brighter, strengthening, but it cannot chase away his smoke. It's still chewy.

I get up and pad over to the tiny bathroom. I close the door gently, then have a wee and brush my teeth. The toothpaste never quite takes all of the taste of cigars away. It has a habit of sitting right at the back of my throat.

When I emerge Katie is still in bed. 'Come over here,' she says. I sit beside her. She looks younger. Her eyes are very wide and her lips are pale. I keep watching them as she speaks; I find it difficult to follow what she's saying, in a jumbled rush.

'...understand how that could be because it's been years and why would he be with you? Unless you've got some sort of other connection to him?'

'What?' The seagulls are raucous and it's so early. I don't want her to feel in control of this. Why is she talking about a connection? 'It's a spirit. A ghost. I know that's a bit of a shock—'

'It's my grandfather,' she says.

'No, it's not your grandfather—'

'I knew him straight away. It's him. It's him. How do you know him? Tell me why he's here. Is he here to speak to me? Has he told you about me? Is that why you came? You asked the staff to put us together? Did you—'

'I think it's time for breakfast,' I tell her. I get up and walk to the kitchen.

'Min,' she calls as I hunt out a bowl for cereal, and switch on the kettle. 'Min.'

Let her wait.

Let her fail to take him as her own.

* * *

We have a morning of activities ahead of us. Yoga and poetry and self-defence. Katie finds a space beside me for all of these classes. She seems weakened, in a way I can't define. She overbalances while attempting Crescent Moon pose and puts out her hand, urgently, to me; I grasp it, and hold her as she rights herself.

During a group conversation about overcoming personal issues one of our number reveals that she has a degenerative disease. She doesn't tell us what the disease is, and nobody asks. I notice nothing but a slight tremor in her voice as she talks. It could just as easily be down to nerves, if she's not used to public speaking.

'I wonder what bits of me will last the longest,' she says,

to our circle. 'Not physically, so much, but mentally. No, not even that. Not my faculties but my personality. How it feels to be me. The way I pick at the sleeves of my jumpers until they start to unravel, and the way I hate the smell of salad cream, even at a distance. What if one day soon I lose the ability to smell salad cream and be repulsed by it? I won't be me any more at that point.'

'Your entire personality hinges on salad cream?' says Katie, waspishly, perhaps even maliciously, and it triggers a reaction from the group that feels passionate and righteous. There's a general condemnation of saying hurtful things for the sake of humour, and I find I want to say something too. Something loud. Shouting would suit me now, but what would I shout about? The only thing that comes to mind is an explanation of how hating salad cream might turn out to be the only element of a person that remains in their afterlife, and wouldn't that be worse? The woman with the degenerative disease is frightened to lose herself entirely but I suspect she'd prefer that to becoming a vengeful spirit who roams around restaurants slapping sachets of salad cream out of the hands of unsuspecting diners.

They're all shouting about the same thing, which is the need to listen to each other, and it takes them a while to realise it. I sit in my own circle of silence, and observe. The moderator restores order and the session goes on. People list what they would most hate to lose about themselves and when it comes to my turn I say, 'My sense of humour.' Let me remain as a long mouthless laugh that hangs in a room.

I can see the appeal of that destiny, now.

Next it's Katie's turn. She says, 'My personality.'

'You can't lose that,' says someone. 'Nobody can ever take that away.'

'How naïve of you,' says Katie, triggering another intense conversation. She doesn't speak in the group session again.

*   *   *

She only wants to talk about the ghost, and all I want is to refuse her. Whenever she tries to raise the issue I put another task between us and the conversation. A swim. A shower. Dinner. And now, at the end of the day with the meal all eaten, I demand to spend half an hour on my declaration.

Katie sits across from me at the kitchen table and puts down her own words. She writes fast, without pause. She has a lot to say.

I don't try to pick up where I left off. I don't think this whole thing will find any order, chronologically or otherwise.

I feel so badly for that woman with the wasting disease. I'm learning from her. She taught me something. But who wants to be there just to be an inspiration? We went around the group and said our names and I registered hers for a second at most, then forgot it. Her pain is nothing more than an impetus for me to have my own thoughts. She's a ghost too, I suppose. We're all ghosts to each other. We breathe out smoke, and others take it in. But we're no more than the smoke.

I must be more.

Those are all the words that will come to me. I put down my pen and wait for Katie to stop writing. She levels a calm stare at me, and I meet it.

'All right,' I say. 'Tell me about your grandfather.'

She reads it straight off the page in front of her and I try to take it in and hold it.

The Declaration of Katharine Johnston

I'm forty-seven years old and I have never been close to anyone if I can help it. I mean that in both the emotional and the physical sense, although I've had times when I've been unable to keep my barriers in place. I feel disappointment in myself when these rare events occur. I can't explain why, except to say closeness appals me. It feels like a way of avoiding certain realities. We're born alone, we die alone; that kind of thing. I hate the things people do to evade this inevitability, like taking a scenic diversion to a place that you already know is a shithole.

I think my attitude to life is probably very similar to my grandfather's way of seeing the world. Let me give you an example:

My grandfather got married for a bet. It wasn't even a bet he made.

He couldn't have cared less about the idea of human companionship as a necessity for a fulfilled life. Nothing mattered to him but being outdoors, alone, miles from anyone.

When he was young he would go walking for months, across the breadth of Yorkshire. He would eat what he could find, beg or steal. He would only return when his shoes had worn through.

At least, that's what my father told me. My father, the social being and needy romantic.

On one of these occasions of return my great uncle, one year younger than his brother, told my grandfather over the dinner table of a conversation he'd had during a night out at the pub in the village. A bet had been mooted that my grandfather would never get married – but who would be stupid enough to take such a bet? Everyone knew he would never tie the knot. He'd never even so much as looked at a girl. Eventually my great uncle had reluctantly taken the bet, out of a sense of familial duty. After relating this story he had, apparently, shrugged and said, 'That's good money wasted, unless you're willing to pay me back for it.'

That had been enough.

My grandfather set his sights on a girl. The girl who became my grandmother, who was always 'the girl' to him, if he spoke of her at all. She left him, and my father, soon after my father started school. There wasn't even a picture of her for me to examine as I wanted to. I was keen to see what the face of a traitor looked like; that was how I thought of her, for years, until I understood life better.

My father told me that story of the marriage as a gamble often, trotting out the familiar sentences to a little girl who was too young to make sense of it. He told it as if it were a parable, and wisdom could be unlocked if only the listener heard with better ears. For a while I blamed myself for failing to find an answer within it.

My father is an idiot. He loves people and their many problems. He can't walk through the market square of our home town in less than an entire morning because so many people want to stop and chat, even now. I can remember having to hold his hand throughout, pinned in his grasp, shamed by his inane conversations. I shifted my weight from one foot to the other as he chatted. I was wearing yellow wellington boots. This must be one of my earliest memories.

I know my mother went out to work for the local solicitors' office while my father stayed home with me – an unusual choice in the seventies, perhaps born from his time spent alone while he was growing up. He wanted to keep me company every minute. But occasionally he would grab a day of work for a removals firm or on a building site, and then my grandfather would turn up on the doorstep.

There was always a sense of reluctance to leave me in his care; I felt that from very early on. I used to think my father was needlessly worried that the old man wouldn't really notice if I lived or died, which I took as a reflection on his own upbringing. Now I suspect he was more concerned about my grandfather encouraging the sociopath in me to emerge, by giving it a proper role model.

We had one proper conversation about the bet early in my teenage years.

'Katie,' my father said to me, 'think of it this way. He likes to pretend he's an island, but he still made me and raised me. Not

well, perhaps, and with long absences, but he did. He wants people to think he doesn't have feelings, and that's his choice. It's not a choice I would make, but he lives with it.'

'Has he never loved anyone?' I asked, meaning: Why doesn't he love me? It's a difficult thing for a young person to understand.

'He made a baby and lost a wife, and both of those events were his own fault. But he comes here to look after you, every once in a while. That has to mean something.'

I don't know if my father genuinely believed that. I'm not so certain that love can be measured in distance travelled, or tasks performed.

I'm not the way I am because of my grandfather, although I wouldn't deny that he proved to me that living without having to hold fast to another human being was possible. I stress that it was humanity alone that didn't appeal to him; he loved the beauty of all other living things and knew everything about them. The only time I saw him smile was when he took me out of the house, into the wild.

That only happened once. My parents decided to take a summer holiday to France and I didn't want to go. In fact, I remember I was angling to be left alone in the house. A week without having to say a word to anybody – the school summer break had started – appealed to me deeply after my father's endless neediness. But it wasn't to be. My grandfather turned up on the doorstep on the morning of their departure, and was admitted. They all stood in the kitchen together, and I watched from the doorway.

'She'll be fine,' he said to my parents.

My mother said, 'I'll hold you to that, Michael,' in a warning tone. I think my grandfather was a little afraid of her. But as soon as I'd been kissed goodbye, and my parents had driven away, he looked me up and down and pronounced me old enough to do some proper walking.

'Where are we going?' I asked him.

'Outside.'

He had a strong sense of where to go, veering through side-streets that led out of town and stomping down back roads that bore signposts to the names of villages I didn't know. Or he would simply set off across the fields, flattening crops with his stride. When the last rays of the sunset faded we were walking uphill with not a word spoken to each other in hours. We stopped in the lea of a dry stone wall, on thin grass, and I watched the sheep huddling together by the gate as he shook out two sleeping bags from his old rucksack, followed by a thermos flask of coffee and a tin of beans.

'Get comfy,' he said.

We shared the beans. I was ravenous.

This might seem strange, but I was not a girl, and he was not a man. We were not people. I have never felt so light, so free of expectation, and that was terrifying. If I wasn't to be treated like a woman-in-training, then what was I?

I don't remember falling asleep. I do remember waking, in the light of the dawn, and never having felt so cold in my life. I lay there, in its grip, and smelled burning. Nothing made sense. The smell was pungent, deep, rich. My grandfather *laughed, and I turned my stiff neck towards him. He was leaning back against the wall, smoking one of his cigars. He puffed out a cloud in my direction, then took the cigar from his lips and smiled. It was not a smile for me. I don't think he knew I was awake.*

I imagined that was his routine. A cigar at dawn, and a private joke at the world's expense. At all busy, boring people, and their day to come.

* * *

'That's it,' says Katie. 'So far, anyway.'

'When did he die?'

'A while back. Lung problems. Emphysema.'

'What year, though?' I ask. I want to place it in my own timeline.

She thinks it through, her head tilted. 'I think around 1997? I remember visiting him in the hospital. He'd been found in a barn by a farmer.'

'Was that in Bristol?' My student life, the fish and chip shop.

'Bristol – no. No. I don't think he ever went south of Manchester.'

'Then why would I have found him in Bristol? Why would he have followed me to Skein Island?'

She has no answer for that.

'It can't be him,' I say. 'My ghost likes people. He likes me.'

'It is him.'

'What makes you so sure?'

'The laugh.'

A person can be expected to know a laugh beyond reasonable doubt.

'He hated everyone,' she says. 'Why would he hang around? What did he find that's worth staying for?'

It's still light outside, although it's getting late. Even a short journey makes a difference to the perception of the beginning and the end of the day.

'It's too much of a coincidence,' I say. 'Think about it.'

'I am!'

'It's ridiculous.'

'Unless he already knew we'd meet at some point. Unless it's all pre-ordained. Written.' She says it thoughtfully. I can tell she likes the idea.

I don't. Because it means I'm not the star of my own life. I'm the warm-up act for some tale of grandfather and granddaughter reunited, and my ghost is not my ghost at all. He's used me as a method of transport to reach an entirely different destination, and I realise in a rush that I don't want him to leave me, not like this. Not for her.

'If this is all about you, wouldn't he just turn up at your house?' I ask. 'Why waste all this time, hanging around with me, waking me up every morning?'

'Who knows?' she says. 'There are more things on heaven and Earth...'

We are not friends. We're not going to be friends. It's not a surprise. She has already been clear that she doesn't make friends. It's only a certainty, now, from my point of view.

'Not good enough,' I say. 'We need answers.'

She considers this.

'Come with me,' she says. 'Bring your duvet.'

* * *

I've never been camping before and I'm not sure this really qualifies. Duvets under the stars, wearing all the clothes I brought with me to keep out the cold that permeates all British nights, regardless of the season. Katie's grandfather was used to this.

'What's this going to prove?' I ask her.

'I'll know it when it comes to me.' She's lying close beside me, within touching distance. She picked the spot for us to sleep, after we walked the length of the island, tramping around until she found a place that worked for her. I wonder if she chose it according to her memory of that night; we are in the shadow of a stone wall, and there are sheep in the field beyond. It's as if she was describing this place all along, in her declaration.

At least a tent would create the illusion of safety, and a little heat. Mingled breath, and the warmth that living bodies give out. Instead there's only my heightened awareness of the dark, and what it can hide, and the stars overhead don't seem to light a thing.

'Do you go camping a lot?'

'This is my second time,' she says, dryly.

'What...' It strikes me as an insolent question, but I'm

going to ask it anyway. 'What was it about your grandfather that makes you want to emulate some areas of his life but not others? You don't go camping, you don't smoke cigars. But you do refuse to get into relationships. Or would you only get into one for a bet?'

'I'm not emulating him,' she says. 'It was only that we understood each other. I realised because of him that it was okay to not like people.'

'Because you liked him.'

'Yes,' she says, as if that wasn't a contradiction.

'I don't understand that.'

I'm putting off attempting to sleep by having this ridiculous conversation, I know it. I don't want to wake up early tomorrow and find out her truth.

'Are you in a relationship?' she asks me, from where she lies.

'Yeah.' I try to sound convincing, but my initial pause was too long. 'It's complicated.'

'Of course it is.' I hear smugness in her voice. 'If it was going well you wouldn't be here, on this island, would you? Taking advantage of the one visit policy. Using your Get Out of Jail Free card, at least for a week.'

Is that what I'm doing? 'It's just a sticky patch.'

'Have you been in lots of relationships?'

'The usual amount.'

'And they all hit sticky patches, and you keep wading through them. See, that. That, I don't understand.'

I turn over and face away from her.

'Good night,' she says, softly, and a little while later she has the temerity to softly snore.

*　*　*

I wake up to clean air.

The sky is a dark, deep blue above me, and I am the coldest I have ever been. I force myself to sit up, gathering the duvet around me, and notice how the sky is changing colour on the horizon. As I watch pale streaks form and collate and turn to glorious orange. It's dawn.

He's not here.

I want to call out to him, but it would be a presumption to use the name Katie knows him by. And even if he had that name once, it surely wouldn't fit him now.

This is what loneliness feels like.

Katie stretches and mutters.

My eyes water and sting. My cheeks are raw.

A chuckle.

I place it. It came from behind me, on the stone wall. He's sitting on the wall. I swivel and see the cigar smoke, rising up and dissipating to blow out to sea, away from where we lie.

'Is it you?' Katie whispers.

Nothing happens.

'It's you,' she says.

He's here, with me. With us. There can't be any explanations. How could he tell us about his choices? He's nothing more than a feeling, a scent, a sound.

'Why are you here?' she asks. 'Tell me. Tell me.'

The sun rises just that little bit further, just enough to clarify, solidify, to a new day.

'You can't tell me, can you? You don't want to.' She sounds reconciled to her own words, as if she's hit upon an answer of her own, somehow.

He's gone.

Katie holds out her hand to me and I take it. We are frozen together. She thinks she's found him, and I think I've lost him, and we're good and strong in this moment for different reasons that don't really matter.

* * *

The week passes.

Katie and I take classes, and swim, and talk to each other. We talk about her grandfather and my ghost, and the ways they were the same and they were different. We can find no answers between us.

We also talk to many women about their lives, lives that come across as strange and normal at the same time. It's only a glimpse of what makes us all work. I find I want more.

We take half an hour after dinner every night to work on our declarations.

The last thing I write is:

I wonder what he would have said to me if he could have talked. I think it would have been something like – Min, girl, you're concentrating on the wrong stuff. It doesn't matter who I am. What matters is that you needed me without knowing it, and now you have to do better than that. You have to want something. What do you want?

This voice I give to him is nothing like the voice he would have had when he was alive, I'm sure.

Sometimes I think about asking Katie to tell me how her declaration ends, but I never do, and she doesn't offer to read it to me.

Every day I wake up at dawn and every day I breathe in, and listen. I don't move. All my concentration is on the smell and the sound of the air around me. He's not there. He's not there.

I miss him.

I'm ready to go home.

* * *

We stand on the dock and watch the boat coming in. It takes its time. The women talk and laugh quietly. We don't join in but it's good to be on the periphery, as the silent but accepted members. They don't know much about us, but what they know is enough.

'We don't have to keep in touch,' I tell her.

'Good, because I don't do that stuff,' she says.

'No, really?' I make my shocked face.

'I'm just reminding you.'

'That's very handy, because I nearly forgot your personality, there, for a second.'

'Glad we've got that settled.'

'Think of me when you dick around with people trying to purchase houses.'

'Yeah, spare me a thought when you have conversations with boring people as part of your administrative job.'

'You make it sound soul-destroying,' I say.

'It is.'

'I don't think so.' I'm not certain how I feel about it. I don't feel that my life and my job should be escaped, not right now. Not before I know what I should leave it all behind for. I have a feeling that maybe I could make a difference there. Alter the crueller behaviours of the pack by leading from the front. Is that realistic?

The boat draws closer.

'I wonder if he's going to stay here,' I say. 'On the island. Breaking the rules and smoking over the visitors. Would that suit him?'

'Not in the least. Not unless he's changed.'

'Of course he's changed!'

'Yes, of course he's changed,' she echoes. 'I didn't ever really know him, you know.'

'No. Me neither.'

'Let me have your mobile number,' she says.

'Okay.' I find a scrap of paper and a pen in my bag, and write it out for her.

'Thanks.'

'It's fine,' I say.

'I don't need it. I might want it, though. One day.'

'I don't even know what that means.'

'Yeah. That's going around,' she says.

* * *

Is it okay to know people, just a little, and only want them when you want them? To take the parts you like and leave the rest, on your own terms?

I don't have an answer for that.

Katie is right again, though. Not having an answer is going around.

My time on Skein Island has given me a taste for the outdoors, but I prefer it in smaller doses. I visit Jimbo's Golf Accessories Emporium and kit myself out, then sign up for lessons at the golf course. It's a good walk through a maintained landscape, and if I get cold I can give up and return to the clubhouse for a drink.

I'm standing at the bar, chatting about the water hazard on the ninth hole with some of my new friends, when I feel a tap on my shoulder. My first thought is for my ghost and my second thought is for Katie. But no, it's not either of those options. It's Dave.

'Hi,' he says. 'I didn't know you played golf.'

'I've just taken it up.'

'I heard you went to Skein Island.'

'I did. And no, I didn't wear dungarees and get in touch

with my inner goddess or whatever.' I've heard all the jokes in these past few weeks, and none of them even begin to bother me. I'm getting tougher.

'I wasn't going to say that. I just wanted to say – I'm sorry. That it didn't work out between us. It was the cigar smoke. I hate cigar smoke.'

'The ghost's gone,' I tell him.

He rolls his eyes at me. 'You're not on about that again, are you?'

'What?' It takes me a moment to realise what he means. 'You don't believe in the ghost?'

'If you don't like the smoke, stop smoking. Smoking in bed is disgusting and dangerous.'

'I don't smoke!'

'And stop making stuff up. This ghost guy – you created him to push me away... You realise that, don't you? He was only there to make me jealous. I told you, you need to do something about it. I wish you the best in solving your problems. I really do.'

The things we tell ourselves to make certain we're front and centre in our own stories. 'Goodbye, Dave,' I say. I turn my back on him. I hear him sigh, and then walk away.

* * *

I lie very still, early the next morning, in the first light of dawn, and I think of what my ghost would have said to me about the whole thing. *Min, girl, that wasn't the right man for you. He fooled his own memory to make you out to be the bad guy. He decided not to believe in me, even though I'm right here. Plain as the smoke drifting past your nose.*

Except you're not here any more, are you? There's no more smoke.

I pick up my phone and take it with me under the duvet. In the warm darkness, I find there's a text message from Katie.

> All right?

I wonder what it cost her to write that, and whether she'll hate herself for it later.

I text back, and we start a conversation. I tell her about Dave and she calls him deluded, which makes me feel much better.

> Forget him. Irrelevant. Bloody people. I still hate them all.

I text back:

> I hate them all too. Do you want to meet up? I was thinking about trying parasailing, or taking tango lessons.

There's a long pause. Just at the point where I'm about to put the phone down and return to sleep, she texts:

But I'm miles away.

I'm not sure who she is and I have no clue who I am, but I know us just enough to be sure that we'll find something that brings us together, real or imaginary. It doesn't matter which.

I text back:

I'll come to you.

If there's more to us both, we'll find it.

AUTHOR'S NOTE

Skein Island is set in a world that's not quite the same as our own. Although the story contains real towns and places it also has quite a few imaginative liberties taken with those places. Apologies to anyone who knows the locations and gets confused by the geographical alterations. It's also worth mentioning that the book was written more than a few years ago, and some elements, such as the repatriation days that used to take place at Wootton Bassett, and certain technological developments, have changed in reality. I decided to leave them as they are in this revised version.

The novelette that accompanies *Skein Island* was a recent revisit to the island, to look afresh at some of the themes from an older (and probably not wiser) point of view. I hope it works as a complement to the original story.

Big thanks to Neil Ayres, John Griffiths, Tim Stretton, George Sandison, Gary Budden, Max Edwards, Adam Lowe, Victoria Hooper, Francesca Kemp, and everyone at UKAuthors and Titan Books. And thanks to Libby's Café for the coffee and teacakes.

This book wouldn't exist without the support of the people who give me daily injections of confidence. Nick, Elsa, Mum, Dad, Harley and Barney, and the best big brother in the world – Jim Ovey, my hero – thank you.